Praise for Meg Donohue

"Even if my daughter hadn't recently rescued a dog, our first, I would have fallen in love with Meg Donohue's *Dog Crazy*. On these pages you will find love, healing, forgiveness, and pure unbridled joy of the human and canine kind."

—Adriana Trigiani, *New York Times* bestselling author of *The Shoemaker's Wife*

"Wonderful! Anyone who has ever loved and lost a dog will find wisdom and comfort in this sweet, smart story."

—Allie Larkin, author of *Stay*

"Donohue has written a delightful tale with heart-wrenching emotions (both high and low), entertaining high jinks and a well-deserved happy ending for the many vivid characters you'll grow to love. Add to that Donohue's zippy prose, and you've got an entertaining, can't-put-down page-turner you'll want to share."

—*RT Book Reviews* (top pick)

"Deliciously engaging. Donohue writes with charm and grace. What could be better than friendship and cupcakes?"

—Rebecca Rasmussen, author of *The Bird Sisters*

"Beautifully written and quietly wise, Meg Donohue's *How to Eat a Cupcake* is an achingly honest portrayal of the many layers of friendship—a story so vividly told, you can (almost) taste the buttercream."

—Sarah Jio, author of *The Violets of March* and *The Bungalow*

"*How to Eat a Cupcake* is a sparkling, witty story about an unlikely, yet redemptive, friendship. Donohue's voice is lovely, intelligent, and alluring. Grab one of these for your best friend and read it together—preferably with a plate of Meyer lemon cupcakes nearby."

—Katie Crouch, bestselling author of *Girls in Trucks* and *Men and Dogs*

"A heartwarming and unpredictable tale of friendship, family, and frosting."

—Zoe Fishman, author of *Balancing Acts*

"An irresistible blend of sweet and tart, this book is truly a treat to be savored."

—Beth Kendrick, author of *The Bake-Off* and *Second Time Around*

"*All the Summer Girls* is a beautifully wrought story about the tender yet resilient bonds of friendship and the damage of kept secrets. Meg Donohue writes with keen insight, prodding readers to re-examine their own past choices, while gracefully examining themes of family, friendship, and forgiveness."

—Karen White, *New York Times* bestselling author

"Beach Book Extraordinaire! *All the Summer Girls* delivered me back to my college summers and the sweet spot between indulging youthful desires and becoming an adult. Donohue's three protagonists are irresistibly sympathetic as they try to unbury their true selves from the ruinous secrets of their shared past."

—Elin Hilderbrand

"*All the Summer Girls* is an honest and engaging look at the complicated and powerful bonds of female friendship. Donohue takes us on a weekend reunion full of secrets, resentment, and regret—in other words, once you start this book, you won't be able to put it down!"

—Jennifer Close, bestselling author of *Girls in White Dresses*

"A fast-paced novel about the enduring friendship of three young women who spent their summers in Avalon on the Jersey shore before dispersing across the country. . . . A good beach read."

—*Kirkus Reviews*

"*All the Summer Girls* celebrates the healing power of friendship for three very different young women with a shared past and different roles in the same guilty secret. Meg Donohue paints a compassionate portrait of what it means to be adrift—in love, and in one's own sense of self—with engaging heroines both flawed and utterly real."

—Nichole Bernier, author of *The Unfinished Work of Elizabeth D.*

"Meg Donohue's *All the Summer Girls* is an intimate, heartfelt, beautiful exploration of friendship, family, and the ties that bind and the secrets that destroy us. Read it first, pass it to your girlfriend later. She'll be grateful."

—*New York Times* bestselling author Allison Winn Scotch

"Donohue captures the beauty and frustration of reconnecting with old friends—they know you so well, and they don't know you at all. Perfect for a staycation for readers who like the beachy drama of Elin Hilderbrand and Susan Wiggs."

—*Booklist*

EVERY WILD HEART

Also by Meg Donohue

Dog Crazy

All the Summer Girls

How to Eat a Cupcake

EVERY WILD HEART

A Novel

MEG DONOHUE

wm

WILLIAM MORROW
An Imprint of HarperCollins*Publishers*

This is a work of fiction. Names, characters, places, and incidents are products of the author's imagination or are used fictitiously and are not to be construed as real. Any resemblance to actual events, locales, organizations, or persons, living or dead, is entirely coincidental.

HarperCollins books may be purchased for educational, business, or sales promotional use. For information, please email the Special Markets Department at SPsales@harpercollins.com.

FIRST EDITION

Designed by Diahann Sturge

Library of Congress Cataloging-in-Publication Data has been applied for.

ISBN 978-0-06-242983-4
ISBN 978-0-06-265958-3 (library hardcover edition)

17 18 19 20 21 RRD 10 9 8 7 6 5 4 3 2 1

For my mother and for my daughters

Love is a banquet on which we feed.
—Patti Smith and Bruce Springsteen, "Because the Night"

We know what we are now, but not what we may become.
—William Shakespeare, *Hamlet*

EVERY WILD HEART

Chapter 1

The first threat didn't rattle me. It was Monday, after all, and Monday was always the wildest show of the week, the phone lines jammed with callers who had been forced to put a cork in their unwieldy, increasingly combustible feelings for me all weekend long and were now set to explode. The show's tone mellowed considerably as the week went on, but Mondays? Unpredictable, messy, raw.

They were my favorite.

"You're on air with Gail Gideon," I said on that particular Monday, leaning into the microphone. "Tell me everything, starting with your name."

On the other end of the line there was a woman crying, her hurried flood of speech so garbled that it sounded more like water rushing through a storm drain than words.

"Deep breath, Caller," I said. "I can't help you if I can't understand you." A note of annoyance escaped into my voice, but that was fine. I wasn't my listeners' "Mommy." They didn't call me to be coddled, and if they did, they quickly realized their mistake.

Through the glass partition, the engineering booth was now a beehive, disturbed. Simone, my producer, met my gaze and muttered something with bite to her assistant, Ann, who responded with a noticeable cringe. Ann was in charge of screening callers. Emotional callers made for a great show; incoherent ones did not. Whoever this was on the line, she was Ann's mistake. Claire, my engineer, tried to pick up the slack by moving her hands over the audio board, apparently in search of a magical dial that could isolate the voice within the caller's sobs.

And there it was! Claire had done it; Ann was saved. The caller's voice—still soggy, and hiccuping now, too—slipped through my headphones:

"Is it really you, G.G.?"

For most of my life only my family and friends had called me G.G., but when the press latched onto the nickname nine years ago, my listeners had quickly followed suit. Of all the many strange things that came along with being a public figure, this had proven among the hardest to grow accustomed to: strangers calling me by the nickname that my parents had given me forty years earlier. It was hard not to think of my father when this happened. I knew better than to wonder if he was listening; he had once told me that my show was not his "cup of tea."

"Yes, I'm right here," I said. "What's your name?"

Abruptly, the caller's wet breathing quieted.

"You ruined *everything*, G.G.," she hissed. I suddenly had the distinct impression that her anguish had been an act, her ticket to getting on air. Now, her voice honed to a glinting dagger and inside of me something leapt to life, sharpening in response. "And in return I'm going to *ruin your fucking life*—"

I cut the call. There was a seven-second delay but even without it I knew that Claire—who claimed to have the fastest fingers in radio—would have managed to mute the word "fucking." Claire had a fair amount of experience with this sort of censorship. For every one hundred generous, grateful listeners there was one crazy woman—or man; they were often men—who hated me with an intensity that I knew could not possibly, at its core, have anything to do with me. I was just an attractive target—a successful single woman with a lot of opinions about the power of women and a live radio show that welcomed call-ins. Radio, like the internet, offered a cloak of anonymity that suited harassers perfectly; add to that the dark hours of night during which I was on air, and *The Gail Gideon Show* had proven itself catnip for crazies.

Simone and I usually let those sorts of calls roll for as long as we could, well aware that Martin Jansen, Talk960's program director, loved angry listeners. Whenever Martin heard that we'd received a threatening phone call, he'd do this overexcited blinking thing, like he was having trouble seeing around all of the advertising money that was piling up in front of him. "Enraged is engaged!" he liked to say. To Martin, those types of calls were simply proof that the millions of women who tuned in to my show didn't think of me as a disembodied voice on the radio; I was someone familiar enough to hate. "You're not just *the* Gail Gideon," he'd tell me. "You're *their* Gail Gideon."

He was right about one thing: those calls were great entertainment. Often, I'd spar with the caller, never losing the upper hand, and later my listeners would phone in (and email, and Tweet, and post to Facebook) to voice their support. The fervor of those callers didn't scare me. In fact, I'd say I thrived on it. I enjoyed showing off my strength, flexing my muscles. More and more lately, I looked forward to those kinds of calls, their unpredictability, their infusion of color. But if a caller resorted to threats, I cut the call. My house, my rules. My audience had grown to expect nothing less.

From the engineering booth, Simone locked eyes with me. There was a deep crease between her brows. *Jenny?* she mouthed.

I shook my head. Jenny Long had been one of my more troubling fans, but I hadn't heard from her or seen her since I'd served her with a restraining order more than a year earlier. Besides, even during the stretch of time that she had camped outside of Hawke Media, it had always seemed that Jenny was dabbling in stalking out of desperation, not anger. This caller, on the other hand, was obviously pissed.

I leaned into the microphone and let out a whistle. Then I laughed. I *laughed*.

"Caller," I began. "Oh, dear, rabid caller . . . under other circumstances, I think we might have been friends! All of the passion in your voice! The *fire*!" I let out a low, admiring whistle. "I *salute* your anger, Caller. Really, I do. Never let it go."

"Anger." I repeated the word slowly, turning it into a growl. Journalists always described the rasp in my voice as distinctive, my signature, but when I noticed it all I could think of were the hours that I'd spent inside my headphones as a kid, belting out terrible accompaniment to Patti Smith, Siouxsie Sioux, and Chrissie Hynde. Those musicians, along with so many others, had dared me to be the person that I believed I was instead of the person that my parents kept insisting I become. Those women were my tribe and their music saved me, gifting me with visions of a rock 'n' roll life. If you'd told that teenage girl that, instead, she'd have the number three talk-radio program for women in the country (number one if you didn't count religious radio, thank you very much), she would not have believed you. Then again, Teenage Me

wouldn't have believed that someday she'd fall in love with and marry a man who liked to play golf. Or that in her twenties she'd host *Love Songs After Dark*, a radio show that aired a stream of music so sappy that she showered each night when she returned home in an attempt to wash off the residual sugar. And Teenage Me definitely would not have believed that when her golf-loving husband left her five years after the birth of their daughter, her ensuing on-air rant would go viral thanks to a newly installed webcam and a charming little website called YouTube. That she'd wake up the next morning not only as a newly single mother, but also as the country's latest controversial overnight celebrity . . . and with an offer to capitalize on said celebrity by leaving music-format radio in her dust and branching into talk. Talk, talk, talk.

"Anger gets a bad rap," I said into the mic, "but it's one of my favorite emotions. Nothing motivates like anger. Anger is an engine. It moves people. It *changes* people. It propels people down new paths, away from the paths that they are too angry to stay on for one second longer.

"So when *you* feel anger building, here's what I say: Don't push it down. Don't ignore it. Don't cover up your anger by being *quiet* and *accommodating* and *polite*. But *do* control your anger. Make it work for you. Harness all that energy and ride it toward a goal that's worthy of you and your awesome fire."

The monitor in front of me was an ever-expanding list of the calls that poured in as I spoke. I already knew these callers' stories—the bones of them at least. The women who called *The Gail Gideon Show* were mired in one of the many stages of heartbreak. The ones who called in tears were generally in the early stages. The ones with clear voices were soldiering on and calling in with stories of triumph, of heartache overcome. That's what *The Gail Gideon Show* was about, after all: finding love again after the darkness of heartbreak. Not love with a man—or another woman, for that matter—but with yourself. The show was a rallying cry for the single woman, a bad-ass-platform-boot kick to the stigma of singledom. It's never too late to reinvent yourself, I told my heartbroken listeners. It's never too late to become the person you want to be, with or without a life partner. Happiness is an equal-opportunity state of being, available without regard to relationship status. My listeners took my advice to heart. My producer, Simone, liked to say that we were building an army, but then she'd always had something of a militant bent. It was one of the reasons why, despite thinking of Simone as an equal partner in the success of the show, I did the talking.

In the engineering booth, Ann was on the phone. Simone was answering calls now, too. Claire was watching me, nodding, one competent hand adjusting her glasses while the other hovered over the audio board. Everyone looked pumped. We were on hour one of a three-hour show.

"We've all been angry," I said, thinking back to how angry I'd been when Tyler bailed on our marriage. I could laugh about it now, but the truth was that the prick of my anger, my hurt, still needled me all those years later. "You all know *I've* been angry. I wouldn't be where I am today if I hadn't been so angry. Anger changed my life for the better. It helped me become the woman I was meant to be.

"But that's enough from me. You all know *my* story backwards and forwards. I want to know what's making *you* angry. Let's come up with a plan for harnessing that energy and riding it toward your goals."

The air in the studio was electric. We were all warmed up now and ready to rock. I pressed one of the waiting phone lines, the threat of the last caller so easily tossed aside, already a fading memory. New call, new adventure. I leaned toward the mic.

"You're on air with Gail Gideon. Tell me everything, starting with your name."

A STORM HAD moved in over the city while I was in the studio. Rain in September was an unusual sight in San Francisco. Lightning was rarer still. I watched, startled, from my office as a sudden flash brightened the nighttime sky above the buildings across the street. I usually loved storms, but now I thought of my daughter Nic, home alone. I turned my back to the window and quickly gathered my things.

I'd texted Roy before getting in the elevator, and he was waiting for me with an umbrella when I stepped into the downstairs lobby of the Hawke Media Building. Of all the perks of having one of the most listened-to radio programs in the country, my driver, Roy, was my favorite. He knew the streets of San Francisco so well it was like he'd planned the city himself, and after nine years together, I'd say he knew me nearly as well. He kept the car temperature set at sixty-five degrees because he knew I always ran hot. He also knew that I liked chatting on the drive from my house to the studio in the afternoon, and listening to music on the way home after work. We shared a love of spicy food, the peculiar energy of San Francisco at night, and, most of all, my daughter, for whom Roy cared like a doting grandfather.

"How was Nic?" I asked, slipping into the backseat of the car. It was always my first question. In the afternoon, after picking me up at home in Bernal Heights and dropping me off downtown at the Hawke Media Building, Roy collected Nic from her high school in Hillsborough, a suburb south of the city, and drove her to Corcoran Stables in Pacifica. The barn overlooked the distant ocean and abutted a large park veined by trails. There, Nic spent a couple of hours riding and caring for her horse, Tru. Afterward, Roy drove her home and then returned to the station to wait for me.

"She seemed . . ." Roy hesitated, searching for the right word. He was forever walking the line between making me happy and telling me the truth. "Tired."

I nodded. The backseat of the car still held the lingering scents of the barn, smells that I'd developed an affection for long ago. I breathed them in and thought of Nic. I'd taken lessons at Corcoran Stables, too, as a girl, and though I hadn't ridden in twenty-five years, I could remember the feel of swinging my leg around the back of a horse and settling into the saddle like I'd done it just that morning. Moving a horse from a canter to a gallop. Dropping my weight into my heels and holding myself off his back as he thundered around the ring. Riding was empowering; it had been my great hope that Nic believed that, too.

She'd been a late talker, and when her first sentences eventually emerged they'd brought with them a stutter. At home, Nic was bright and affectionate, hardly seeming to notice when her tongue tripped over her words. At school, though, anxiety hounded her. On her first day of kindergarten, she held herself apart from the other children and barely spoke. (Late at night I worried—as it felt almost my duty, as her mother, to worry—that my big personality and comfort in the spotlight had done her some damage. Had I given her room to shine?) Her timidity worsened when her father, Tyler, moved out a few months into the school year. It was then that I decided to enroll Nic in riding lessons. She had always loved animals; I hoped the sport might instill confidence and, more importantly, bring her joy.

During her first lesson, she'd started off standing three feet away from the half-awake palomino pony to which she'd been assigned, and nearly jumped out of her skin when the pony blew a gentle burst of air from his nostrils. But when Denny Corcoran, the owner of the barn, handed her a hoof pick and taught her how to ask the horse to lift his leg, Nic's apprehension melted away. She leaned into the pony with her little body, he picked up his hoof, and she cradled it in one hand while clearing the dirt and pebbles with the pick in her other hand. The look on her face as she moved on to the second hoof was proud and serious. In the ring, before riding the pony, she stood on her tiptoes and whispered in his ear, and something about the act, her instinctual partnership with the animal, made my eyes fill with tears.

From that day on, Nic was deeply in love with riding. Or, if not with riding, then with horses—she'd always seemed more drawn to the placid, poetic, communing-with-the-natural-world aspect of horsemanship than the physical act of riding. This was a shame, in a way, because Nic was a fantastic rider. Whenever I worried about Nic, I reminded myself of the strength that emanated from her when she was around horses. If music had been my lifeline in childhood, riding was Nic's. She was a natural. Denny Corcoran had said as much himself. He'd even once used the word "exceptional" to describe Nic's ability, which I remembered specifically because it was the exact word that came to my mind whenever I thought of my daughter.

Exceptional.

"Tell *her*," I'd practically begged Denny at the time. "Tell her she should compete." But Denny had just given me a look that I couldn't read. He'd been a kid when I rode at Corcoran, a few years younger than me. Now his parents were retired and he owned the place.

"She'll figure it out herself," he said. Then he shrugged. "Or she won't."

A font of wisdom, that Denny.

We were halfway home from the studio, driving more slowly than usual due to the rain that hit the windshield as though tossed from buckets, when my cell phone rang. It was my agent.

"Hey, Shayne," I said, picking up.

"Who was that asshole who called in tonight? I'd like to wring her neck."

"You listened. I'm touched."

"Listened? Of course I listened. I listen every night. Well, not every night. I'm taking a stab at having a life. But you know I'm your number one fan, Geej. And speaking of numbers . . ."

I had to laugh. Shayne was always calling about numbers. Even when she wasn't calling about numbers, she was calling about numbers.

"I spoke with Lev Curtain tonight," she said. There was a pregnant pause. "Lev Curtain at ZoneTV."

"Who is it? When?" Talk show appearances usually came through my publicist, but every once in a while a big one came through Shayne first.

"G.G.," Shayne said. Her typically dry tone couldn't mask her glee. "That's what they want to call your show. *G.G.* Coming this summer on ZoneTV."

A tremor of excitement moved through my body. "Wait . . . *what*?"

Roy glanced at me in the rearview mirror and then pegged his eyes back to the road. He was an avid and terribly obvious eavesdropper, a fact that somehow made him all the more endearing to me.

"I told you! I've always told you!" Shayne said. "You may have a voice for radio, but you have a face for television. It's finally happening! You have one of the highest-rated shows for women in the country. You've written a bestselling self-help book. Television is your next frontier. It's what we've been talking about for years and now we finally have the right offer."

"Which is what, exactly?"

"Starts with a five," Shayne said. She sounded like she was having trouble refraining from bursting into song.

"And ends with?"

"A million! Five million dollars. And that's just the *starting* offer."

"Holy shit," I breathed.

"Specifically, *ZoneTV* would like you to . . ." There was a moment of muffled sound as Shayne searched for something, and then she began to read, "'. . . share the no-nonsense, tough-love wisdom and humor and heart of Gail Gideon's beloved, lightning-rod radio show with a wider television audience.' Geej, this would be like your radio show *on steroids*." She hesitated. "They're thinking the show's tagline could be 'Fall in love with the single you!'"

I felt myself grimace. Roy veered the car onto the freeway exit at Cesar Chavez and then made a quick turn down Alabama Street. I'd driven this route so many times that I could have closed my eyes and still known exactly where we were.

"We can work on the tagline. Nothing's set in stone," Shayne said, reading my silence. "They want a six-week trial this summer with syndication following in the fall."

"This summer! Where?"

"The Hollywood lot," Shayne answered. "We can finally get you girls out of the fog and into the sun."

"Nic just started high school—"

"The schools here are great. They're the *best.* She'll love it. It will be just like San Francisco except much, much better. Moving is the easy part."

But moving *wasn't* easy for a girl like Nic. It took her ages to find her footing in new situations. Though she had shed her stutter years earlier, she continued to be extremely self-conscious and uncomfortable at school. It was nearly a month into her freshman year and still each morning as we neared the Kirke School she grew quiet, her cheerful smile weakening mile by mile. Inevitably, by the time I pulled the car into the school's entrance, her lips were pressed into a tight, quivering line. And yet, I knew that by the end of the school year, Kirke would seem familiar to Nic and she would take her version of comfort in that. Could I deny her that promise of familiarity when I knew how much it meant to her? Could I ask her to start all over again as a sophomore at a new school in a new city?

"We'll find a barn for her horse," added Shayne.

Shit. Nic loved Corcoran Stables. I was pretty sure she loved it more than our house, that she'd probably sleep there if she could. It was at Corcoran Stables that Nic truly blossomed.

And then of course there was Tyler, my ex-husband. Nic spent every other weekend with him and his not-so-new wife and their two sons in Marin, a short drive from our house in the city.

"I have to say I expected a little more excitement, G.G.!" Shayne said. "Your contract with Hawke Media is coming up for renewal, so this is perfect timing."

"What about Simone?" I asked. "She got a good offer, too, right?"

There was a second of silence. My stomach dropped.

"The deal is just for you."

"No," I said firmly. I glanced up at Roy just in time to see his eyes slide back to the road ahead. "Simone is my producer." She had also, after nine years of working together, become my closest friend.

"She's your producer on your radio show. We're talking about your *television* show." Shayne was quiet for a moment. "Simone is radio. That's where she thrives. You made her a ton of money and now she gets to keep on doing what she does best. You don't need to worry about Simone."

At that moment, I noticed my reflection in the car window and was startled by how worried I looked, and how small. I found it nearly impossible to remember that I was short; it always surprised me when people described me as petite. I straightened in the seat and cleared my throat.

"Simone," I said into the phone, "is nonnegotiable."

"Okay, Geej. I hear you," Shayne said smoothly. "I'll see what I can do. But if we get her on board, are you in?"

I could tell that Shayne was truly baffled by my hesitation; when she sent a new opportunity my way, I usually grabbed it by the lapels and kissed it. But as intrigued as I was by the idea of shaking up my career and embarking on a new adventure, my decision would upend my daughter's life. I couldn't make it hastily.

"Give me time to think about it," I said.

Shayne sighed, her mood deflating; the call had not gone as she'd planned.

After we said goodbye, the quiet in the car grew thick, the tires whispering over the wet streets. I rubbed at my temples again. In my reflection, the worry moved back in, deepening the lines that had appeared around my mouth and eyes a few years earlier, surprising me. Teenage Me would never have believed that someday she'd be forty.

Age awesomely, I mouthed to my reflection, a command.

The car shuddered over a couple of little potholes.

Roy glanced at me in the rearview mirror, his face like a stone. "It's not my fault," he said. "It's the asphalt." I'd heard this joke about four hundred times, but Roy broke into such a hopeful grin that I could not help but laugh.

The car rolled to a stop in front of our house, which wasn't much more than a bungalow, really. I could afford something larger now, and in a fancier neighborhood, but Tyler and I had bought this little house in Bernal Heights way back when, before we were even married, when we had to stretch to afford it and we stayed up at night worrying about how we'd pay the mortgage. It surprised people, that little house. Famous people weren't supposed to live like this—I'd received the memo and had decided to ignore it. Nic and I didn't need any more space. Besides, that house held good memories for both of us. It was hard to imagine living anywhere else.

I was disappointed to see that Nic's bedroom light was off. In fact, all of the lights that should have been visible from the street were dark, including the outside light that I asked Nic to always leave on. The house looked empty, vulnerable, and dreary in the rain, and I hated knowing that my daughter was inside, alone.

A few weeks earlier, when Nic had entered her freshman year of high school, I'd finally agreed that she was old enough to not need a sitter on the nights—Monday through Friday—that I went to the studio. I still wasn't entirely convinced that this was a good idea, but Nic—quiet, diligent Nic, who was probably the least demanding teenager in history; a hell of a lot better, anyway, than I'd been at her age—had, for once, put her foot down. In a calm voice, her words enunciated, she'd told me she was old enough to spend her weeknights at home unsupervised. I'd hoped for years that she would find her voice and stick up for herself, so even though it didn't feel right to say yes, it felt more wrong to say no.

Now, looking up at the little house being battered by rain, I was struck by a feeling of alarm that I knew would remain, prickling just under my skin, until I saw my daughter.

"Thanks, Roy," I said. I hopped out of the car before he could grab his umbrella and shepherd me to the door.

"Goodnight!" he called. I felt his eyes on my back as I took the steps two at a time. I knew he would wait there, watching, until I'd shut the front door behind me.

Inside, the house was cool and dark and still. I hurried up the staircase and flicked on the hall light. My bedroom was at the back of the house; Nic's was at the front. I opened her door slowly, quietly, not wanting to wake her, but when the hall light fell onto her bed I saw only a blank white slash of pillow, the duvet tucked underneath it in the careful way that Nic always left her bed in the morning.

"Hey, Mom."

I spun around. "Nic! You scared me half to death! Why aren't you in bed?"

"Couldn't sleep. I was reading in the den." When she held up a copy of *Hamlet*, her narrow wrist poked out from her flannel pajamas. She was outgrowing her clothes faster than I could replace them. I put my hand above my heart and felt it racing, still. For fourteen years now, I'd carried with me a fear that something bad would happen to my daughter. I loved her too much; it tempted fate.

She pulled back the covers of her bed and climbed in. There was a distant look in her green eyes. I'd seen this new expression of hers a few times recently. Each time I had the unsettling sense that her thoughts were focused intensely elsewhere; it seemed less like she was daydreaming than planning.

"What are you thinking about?" I asked. I'd already put a mental pin in Shayne's news about the television show offer, deciding that I would discuss it with Nic on the weekend when the conversation wouldn't feel rushed.

"Nothing. School, I guess." From her pillow, she looked up at me. A wayward strand of her hair snaked a dark line across her throat. I couldn't resist reaching down and brushing it away. She didn't flinch.

"Do I have to go?" she asked.

"To bed or to school?"

"School."

"Well, I suppose I could homeschool you. We could start with seventies New Wave and be on nineties grunge by the end of the semester. I've always wanted to read an essay on Debbie Harry's influence on Shirley Manson."

My daughter rolled onto her side. "Mom."

"What else am I qualified to teach? From an educational standpoint, I think you're in better hands with the teachers at Kirke. But it's up to you."

Nic released a stoic sigh. "Oh, fine." She scrunched her body further under the covers so that only her face was visible above the white blanket. She reached out and touched my knee, exposed by a large hole in my jeans. "It might be time to retire those."

I feigned horror. "Never."

"Cut them into shorts then?"

I looked down at the jeans. They were my favorite pair, more than a decade old, and worn to more concerts than I could count. My wardrobe was another thing I'd chosen not to upgrade after fame plumped up my bank account. I'd even worn a rotation of my favorite band T-shirts on my book tour a few years earlier, and had taken great delight in the baffled expressions of the bookstore managers who greeted me at each stop. The usual look of self-help speakers, I learned, entailed blazers and pumps and hair straighteners, none of which I owned or had any intention of purchasing.

I bent to kiss Nic's forehead. "Some things magically become more perfect over time."

She smiled, but as I shut the door behind me I saw her eyes blinking against the dark room.

I waited for a few moments in the hall, listening. For what? I suppose Nic's request to stay home alone while I was at work still sat uneasily with me. I was surprised to realize that I felt a twinge of suspicion regarding her motives. We're all changing all the time. I, of all people, *knew* this: I'd practically staked my career on it. Nic was a freshman in high school now. She was growing up and she was changing, and I probably should have been happy about that, even if it meant that I might not know the new Nic as well as I knew the old Nic—even if it meant she might have secrets that I'd never learn.

Chapter 2

Nic's day began in disappointment, the lush landscape of her dream wrenched aside like a curtain, leaving her blinking against the dull light of morning. Her heart pounded as though she were still riding a galloping horse through a field, electrified with a version of joy, or triumph, or maybe power, that she had never experienced in real life. The bedroom took shape around her, the alarm clock on her nightstand minutes away from ringing. As the silky threads of her dream slipped away, Nic remembered who she was, and who she was not.

Her gaze roamed from the ceiling to the beautiful yellow dress in her closet, a birthday gift from her mother.

"The color made me think of you," her mother had said when Nic opened the box. Truly, the dress was more gold than yellow, the rich, warm color of the sun in a child's imagination. Nic had lifted the dress from the box and awkwardly held it to her torso. She'd felt as though she were embracing a stranger. It was a simple shirtdress . . . but that *color.* Regret flickered over her mother's face—Nic saw it there, but she felt it, too, a ripple in the air between them.

"Let's return it," her mother had said quickly. The large hammered metal cuff near the top of her ear appeared and disappeared as her wild auburn hair moved. "We'll go together and you can pick out something else."

But Nic shook her head. She loved her mother with an intensity that she was never entirely sure was normal and she felt bad that her mother felt bad. Besides, the cotton was very soft and she was surprised to find herself clinging to it.

The dress had hung in her closet ever since, a ribbon of light among her gray and brown shirts. That dress hung in her closet, not beckoning or taunting exactly, but just sort of breathing. Well, maybe taunting a little, too.

A girl who wore a yellow dress to school didn't sit in the back of the classroom. A girl in a yellow dress didn't have a heartbeat that thudded in her ears every time a teacher called on her. That girl didn't worry about her skin turning the color of an angry burn, or her mouth flooding with saliva at the very moment she was expected to speak, or her words piling up behind an unending stutter. A girl in a yellow dress didn't move along the edges of halls, silent as a shadow, shackled by fears that she could not even name. She linked arms with her best friends and tossed her head back when she laughed. She was confident and brave and cool.

Nic stepped out of her pajamas and pulled on the dress. She stood in front of the mirror and fastened its buttons. She tied the soft belt around her waist. She combed her dark hair around her shoulders and put on lip gloss. She threw her head back and laughed.

Does everyone think they're going to start high school and become someone else? That it's a chance to start over with a clean slate? To change? Nic had convinced herself it was possible, even giving herself a little pep talk on the subject as she'd approached the front doors of the Kirke School on her first day three weeks earlier. And then she'd walked through the formidable foyer of the school—once a railroad tycoon's chateau-style mansion, black-and-white marble floors and all—and instantly felt an overwhelming desire to just . . . *disappear.* That's when she realized that she'd known the truth all along, even through all of her fantasizing over the summer about the new life she'd have when she started at Kirke. She would always be exactly who she'd always been, except now she was in high school.

And yet. For weeks, Nic had a sense of something swelling and then retreating inside of her. She felt it now, building, as she stood in her bedroom. In her ears that feeling became the sound of her own voice daring her to wear the dress to school.

She touched the yellow collar, light against her neck. She felt wrapped in her mother's love, the beautiful sunshine color that had made her mother think of her.

"Nice dress, Nic!" her new classmates would say. Imagining the attention made her cheeks burn—more rash than blush. She had to turn away from her reflection in the mirror. The voice in her mind fell to deafening silence.

She wore jeans and a gray T-shirt to school.

And so of course *that* was the day that Lucas Holt started at Kirke. Nic could have been the girl in the yellow dress to Lucas, but instead she was just . . . herself. No, not even herself, because really, somewhere inside, she was someone else entirely. She just couldn't seem to let the person she was on the inside, out.

Nic knew Lucas was new that day because Kirke wasn't very big. She was sure that she would have noticed him if he'd been going there since the school year had begun, even if he was a senior. Nic could have sworn the entire cafeteria got quiet when he walked in. He knew what to do with the attention, too. He didn't turn red or drop his eyes (or dart out of the room—as Nic might have done in his place). He had the kind of self-possession that allowed him to be still. He stood there by the cafeteria doors, looking around the large room. She didn't have the sense that he was looking for someone in particular; he was taking in the scene. There was a light within him, a glow that seemed to function like a magnet.

His eyes connected with Nic's. She was sure that they did. He looked right at her and his eyes flickered with something that felt to Nic like acknowledgment. Time stopped. That feeling swelled in her again, became her voice in her ear telling her, *goading* her, to stand and wave to the boy, invite him to her table.

Do it.

She didn't. She couldn't. She sat, flooded with shame as the moment passed and Lucas's eyes flicked away, moving along as if he hadn't even seen her at all. Maybe he hadn't. Maybe she'd made the whole thing up. Her T-shirt was the same nothing color as the dust bunnies under her bed. She practically blended into the cafeteria's walls.

In the end, Lucas headed for the table reserved for the coolest and most beautiful of Kirke, a collection of seniors that, it seemed to Nic, held in common nothing more than a sense of confidence that each wielded like a superpower. Among them: Jasmine Cane, captain of the swim team and all-around Kirke golden girl; Emory Torres, star of the drama department; Simon Pinelli, a triple-threat of quarterback, school president, and industrious pot smoker; and Hunter Nolan, who with his cherubic blond curls and relentless menacing of the underclassmen had already earned himself the nickname Angel Bully in the privacy of Nic's thoughts. These were the unique few that thrived in the thin air of Kirke; they bloomed colorful and bright, unabashed by their own beauty and talent.

Not one of these seniors or the small crew that surrounded them waved Lucas to their table; he just walked up and sat down and they accepted him. It was as if everyone knew their table was where he belonged, like he'd telepathically revealed a password that made the doors of that world open and then shut behind him.

Nic sometimes found herself staring at people, trying to determine how they were so comfortable in their own skin, imagining how it would feel to be them. She didn't *intend* to stare, but it was hard for her to stop herself. When she was caught—and she was often caught—her embarrassment made her feel combustible, as though at any second she might explode. Sometimes she wished for this explosion. But it never came. Instead the heat inside of her, that spinning orb of humiliation, steadily grew.

Nic forced herself to look down at her turkey-and-cheese sandwich. She thought about what might have happened if she'd been wearing the yellow dress.

"Um, hotness," said her friend Lila Dorian. They had the table to themselves.

Nic bit into her sandwich.

"That's Lucas Holt," Lila told her. "He just moved to town with his mom." Nic didn't question how Lila had acquired this information; her friend always seemed to know everything about everyone.

"I feel like we had a moment there," Lila said. "Like our eyes *connected*." She spoke in a dreamy sort of way, as though she were just thinking out loud. Nic had recently become aware that she had this effect on people—she guessed she said so little herself that people thought speaking to her was the same as speaking to themselves.

How humiliating that Lila and Nic both had the same silly fantasy running through their heads! Maybe, Nic thought, there wasn't a dorky girl on earth who didn't envision a whole new perfect life that would unfurl before her like a red carpet if only a boy like Lucas Holt took notice of her.

Nic knew how her mother would react to this sort of rescue fantasy: she would groan, pretend to gouge out her own eyeballs with her thumbs, drop down to the floor and do a few big death shudders and then, finally, she'd stick out her tongue and go completely still like she was dead. Gail Gideon was, quite literally, *famous* for raging against the idea of a woman needing a man to make her life better; she'd made it her life's mission to enlighten women who'd been brainwashed by what she called the Cinderella Complex. And here was her own daughter, hoping the popular new boy would save her from her—"self-imposed!" Nic's mother would undoubtedly shout—exile as a wallflower.

Jasmine Cane had switched seats with Simon Pinelli so that she sat on one side of Lucas and Emory Torres sat on the other. Both girls had their heads cocked toward him.

"The Lurk is going to have a field day with that situation," Lila said thoughtfully, eying the threesome.

Nic felt her stomach twist. *TheKirkeLurk7* was an Instagram account that posted photographs of Kirke students accompanied by snarky commentary. No one knew who controlled the account—each time the school managed to shut it down, a new one popped up in its place. According to Lila, this had been going on for years, with different students taking the helm at different points in time.

Nic didn't have an Instagram account. She wasn't on Facebook or Snapchat or Twitter either. She had a cell phone, but her mother, worried that her radio show pulled "the crazies from their cobwebs," had asked Nic not to have an online presence. Her mother had never been big on rules, so Nic took this one seriously. In truth, her mother's request was something of a relief to Nic, who was pretty sure that she had enough social anxiety without adding online friending and unfriending and liking and commenting to her life. She didn't even like when Lila insisted on sharing her own phone so that Nic could see the updates to *TheKirkeLurk7*'s Instagram feed. Nic kept expecting to see her own face appear on the screen along with whatever damning judgment came by way of the comments below. So far, thankfully, she had not found herself on the Lurk's radar, but the name alone was enough to set her on edge.

"Om shalom," said Lila, shrugging. She was still watching the table of seniors.

Lila's father, who owned a chain of yoga studios, had told her to create a mantra that she could repeat in moments of stress. Somehow Lila had landed on the words "om shalom." Over the weeks that Nic had known her, the mantra had evolved from something Lila whispered when their math teacher announced a pop quiz to something she declared loudly in a bored tone at random intervals, the way another of their classmates might say *"whatever."*

"Om shalom," Nic said, agreeing. It had been years since she'd truly stuttered, but still, every single time that she spoke clearly, easily, she felt relieved. She worried that this feeling would never go away, that she would forever carry inside of her the stuttering child she'd once been.

Lila began ferociously stabbing at the kale, farro, and chia seed salad that her dad had packed. She took an enormous bite and chewed quickly, one dangling ribbon of kale twitching at the corner of her mouth. Lila was tiny with keen brown eyes and sharp features; her steady diet of seeds and greens did nothing to alleviate her overall squirrel air. She vibrated with a unique mix of anxiety and optimism, aware of—but not particularly discouraged by—her low rank on the school's totem pole. Nic admired Lila for this, and was grateful for her friendship.

"Anyway," Lila said, chewing, "I can't believe Mr. Hylan wants us to write ten pages on one speech from *Hamlet*. Ten pages on one speech? That's *torture*!" Lila would rather have written ten one-page essays on ten different plays; her mind was always spiraling from one subject to another.

Nic, though, didn't mind the writing part of the assignment. She was almost looking forward to it. But Mr. Hylan also wanted them to memorize and recite an assigned Shakespeare monologue in front of the whole class, and just thinking about this made Nic's sandwich congeal into a lump in her throat. Maybe she'd pretend to be sick that day. There was no use to that, though; she could already tell Mr. Hylan was the type to make her give the presentation on the first day she returned to school. He'd probably be the first teacher at Kirke to call her mom in for a conference. Or maybe that distinction would fall to her world history teacher—three weeks into the school year, Nic still hadn't said more than a word or two in class. And in Spanish, where Mrs. Taylor ruthlessly insisted on participation, Nic was so nervous that she sounded like she was choking each time she answered a question.

She took stock of the remaining hours in the school day. Three more classes: biology, P.E., algebra. And then: freedom. Roy, her mother's driver, would take her to the barn where she would ride her horse, Tru. Time moved slowly at school, but at the barn, the hours dissolved. A sense of calm hung in the air at Corcoran Stables and when Nic breathed it in, the humiliations of the day receded.

She took a drink of water, letting her eyes roam back to the table where Lucas sat. He was talking with Emory Torres now, and something he said made her toss back her head and laugh just as Nic had done in the mirror that morning. Nic watched Lucas's shoulders lower, his posture loosening as he grew ever more comfortable. She suspected she was more attuned than most people to the small movements of the body that hinted at the shifts of emotion and intention below the surface. Maybe she'd honed the skill during the hours she spent with Tru each day, immersed in nonverbal communication, the body language of animals.

Now Emory moved slightly toward Lucas. At first Nic thought it was the terrible cafeteria lights that made the girl's hair glow, but then she realized that Emory's black bun was veined with yellow streaks, the same yellow-gold color that had made her mother think of her. The desire to be free, to escape, overwhelmed Nic. The hours between lunch and seeing Tru stretched unbearably long. She listened to Lila spin breathlessly from one subject to another, and she watched Emory's beautiful hair glow, and she ate her sandwich, and she felt herself becoming smaller, and smaller, and smaller until it made complete sense that no one but little Lila Dorian could see her.

From Nic's tiny perch, the cafeteria was an orchestra warming up before a dark opera, a churning sea of color, a terrible Wonderland. If only, like Alice, she might find a piece of cake bearing the promise of change (to grow large or to shrink so small that she disappeared entirely; each alternative held an appeal). The voice in her ear would tell her to lift this cake to her lips and swallow it whole, and this time Nic was quite sure that she would listen.

Chapter 3

After Tyler moved out, I used my first paycheck from *The Gail Gideon Show* to hire a carpenter to build floor-to-ceiling shelves in the living room for my music collection. Once the shelves and the wall behind them were painted a matte black, the compact discs almost seemed to float. Yes, my wall of music was composed of *compact discs*, proving that, though the music I loved most was created in the seventies, the bulk of my music purchases were made in the nineties. I bought music digitally now, of course, but when I really loved an album, I also bought the CD. Every album on that wall meant something to me, and I wanted to be able to hold each one in my hand from time to time. The carpenter who did the work had peered down at me from two feet away and suggested he include a rolling ladder so that I could reach the CDs on the highest shelves. Nic had loved riding that ladder back and forth across the wall of music when she was little.

The morning after Shayne called to tell me about the offer from ZoneTV, I stood in the living room and trailed my fingers along a shelf of CDs. I'd just returned from dropping off Nic at school—in the afternoon, we placed ourselves in Roy's capable hands, but in the morning I liked to drive Nic myself. The house was quiet now, that wall of CDs like a bank of memories that silently beckoned me. Even those shelves, created without Tyler's input or assistance, made me think of him. They were tied to our chronology, the history of us. What would it be like to live somewhere else, somewhere that did not make me think of Tyler every day?

I tried to untangle my true feelings about the ZoneTV offer from my worries for my daughter. A television show would be the biggest change I'd faced in years. That thought might scare some people—my daughter included—but change had always excited me. Even on the night Tyler left me and I talked on and on during my show, leaning into the studio microphone, not realizing that every movement I made was being streamed onto the web, there was no fear in my message. Rage, yes. Indignation, shock, confusion—yes. Sadness, oh yes. But I wasn't afraid. In fact, I think even in those moments when I was babbling about being a phoenix that would rise from the ashes of my marriage stronger and more inspired than ever to embrace a life of happiness, I shook as much from exhilaration as I did from anger. But the idea of pushing myself had always attracted me; I'd always wanted the truth and also the dare.

Once upon a time, Tyler had loved that about me.

I pulled the Velvet Underground's eponymous album from its shelf and let it spin. Lou Reed's voice filled the room. I sat on the couch and drank coffee and listened to "Pale Blue Eyes." It was the song I had not been able to resist singing to Tyler on the night we met. I'd always thought that album was a bit too sweet, but within moments of meeting Tyler, I felt differently.

I never thought that I'd be a wife, much less enjoy it. For a long time I teased Tyler that he'd tricked me into falling in love with him. We were juniors at Reed College on the night I first saw him, and it was Halloween. Tyler had dressed as Jim Morrison, a look he could pull off because he was tall and lanky and, at the time, wore his dark hair to his shoulders. I'd forgotten it was a costume party and arrived in the same clothes I'd been wearing for days—baby-doll dress, Doc Martens. With my smudged eyeliner and bedhead (I'd just awakened from a nap), Tyler later told me he'd thought I was in costume as Courtney Love.

When someone bumped into me, I bumped into Tyler, spilling my drink. Tyler took off his whiskey-soaked shirt and tucked it into his pants so that it hung against his thigh like a painter's rag. Four long, beaded necklaces swung against his chest.

I hooked my finger into one of his necklaces, looked up into his pale blue eyes, and did my best Lou Reed impression.

He smiled.

We didn't leave each other's side all night.

By the time I realized that he was soft-spoken and preppy, raised in Maryland on football games and hot chocolate, I was halfway in love. My college crew was a ragtag group of musicians and artists; no one understood my attraction to Tyler, who attended every one of his classes and spent his free time playing Frisbee golf. What could I say? He struck me as authentic. I'd never met someone so sure of himself, so true to himself. I was surprised by how his goodness moved me. He tried, for my sake, to understand punk rock. He delighted in finding ways to make me smile. He often succeeded.

I'd been an angry child. Back in the Bay Area, my parents were deeply invested in what I called "country club life." They visibly recoiled from my black clothes and loud music. My father claimed to love art, but his definition of the word was narrow; even art was an exclusive club in his mind and he rolled his eyes at the musicians that I admired. I dreamed of being a performer—of finding some way to express myself and someday inspiring people in the way that I'd been moved, comforted, and energized by the singers I loved. My father the art lover never once encouraged or supported me on that path. I suspected he was afraid of what I would say. I felt misunderstood, unloved—or loved, but conditionally, which to me was no love at all. It seemed to me that my parents strived for a life that was superficially beautiful: a gilded, empty box. Their aspirations horrified me as much as mine horrified them. I wanted to be free of their rules and shallow expectations. Most of all, perhaps, I wanted to prove them wrong.

I had my own radio show on the Reed College station from ten at night until one in the morning. I could play, and say, anything I wanted. I played all of my favorites, those awesomely raging and rocking women from the sixties and seventies and eighties and nineties, and I would jump around the studio, singing along. In between tracks, I'd read a few lines from songs that I'd written. Sometimes I'd talk about how music made me feel. On the radio, I was an open book and people seemed to connect with me, with what I was doing. I developed a small, loyal group of listeners, some of whom would call in to the show from time to time. I wouldn't say that I gave those callers advice; we'd just talk, and sometimes argue, about music. I'm sure I'd cringe to hear those shows now, but I'm still proud of my much younger self for doing them. It took guts to put myself out there, to share with strangers the music that mattered to me, to share the person that I was becoming.

I loved being alone in the studio in the dark of night, but I was surprised to find that I also loved returning to my off-campus apartment and finding Tyler asleep in my bed. I'd strip down to my underwear and curl my small body against his long one. In the morning, he'd wake me with a cup of coffee that he'd bought at a café; he'd already been in the library for hours.

Tyler was not at all like me, but he loved me. His love went a long way to healing me, to helping me know that I could be loved and be myself at the same time. I had not always known what to do with my energy—if I wasn't talking, I was singing, and if I wasn't singing, I was listening to music, each song pulsing through me like a life-saving blood transfusion. I felt propelled—maybe even tormented, at times—by a need to do something meaningful with my life. I took a breath when I was with Tyler. We were young. I was happier with him than I'd ever been without him.

After graduation, he cut his hair and got a job at a management-consulting firm in San Francisco. Thanks to the cult following I'd developed at Reed, I landed a lowly gig behind the scenes of a Bay Area adult-contemporary radio station owned by Hawke Media. When Tyler asked me to marry him, I answered yes, surprising myself. I didn't think we needed to be married to have the kind of life that I wanted to have, but he felt differently. Saying yes was my gift to him; his happiness was important to me. A couple of years later the music-programming director offered me the host position for a new show that they wanted to call *Love Songs After Dark*. That show would be the death of our marriage, but ironically if it hadn't been for Tyler, I don't think I would have accepted the job in the first place. Before I met him, it would have been impossible to fathom spending one night listening to saccharine ballads, let alone five nights every week. The show was so different from anything I'd envisioned for myself. It wasn't that marriage declawed me, exactly, but I did feel like a tamer version of myself. I even hummed along to those cheesy songs I spun from seven to midnight each weeknight; it was when I burst into tears while listening to Michael Bolton's "All for Love" one night in the studio that I guessed that I was pregnant. I'd pressed my hands to my stomach and promised my child that I would—that I already did—accept him or her wholly. No mother would ever love a child more. I felt an overwhelming sense of loss for the relationship that I would never have with my parents, but I also felt full of gratitude, and resolve, for all that I could and would give to my own child.

If marriage changed me, parenthood changed Tyler. His previously mild inclination for a conventional life flared when Nic was born. When he returned home from work each night, I was on air at the studio. We could not spend the evening discussing our days over plates of spaghetti, or refilling each other's wineglasses, or unwinding together with books in front of a fire. And I wasn't there to tuck Nic into bed at night Monday through Friday—if this upset anyone, I thought it should have been me or Nic, but it was Tyler who tossed and turned and grumbled when I returned home late at night about how Nic's babyhood was being short-changed. Over the next few years, he became increasingly agitated that my job kept me from being present for a family dinner on weeknights. Though we both wanted to have more children, Tyler insisted that it did not make sense to consider having another baby until my work schedule changed.

It was only in retrospect that I realized Tyler had given me an ultimatum.

At the time, I could not believe that he really wanted me to quit my job. Our daughter had a wonderful life—she spent her days with me; her nights with her father. On the weekends, we were all together. Our situation wasn't conventional, and perhaps it wasn't ideal, but who cared? Not me. I thought we were making our own way; I thought we were happy. I loved my husband, and I thought we would find a way through these challenges and, in the process, grow our family. I thought we would always be together. I felt betrayed when he asked me to find another radio job with better hours, as though this were an easy task, as though it were not rare enough that I hosted my own show before the age of thirty. It felt to me that what he was really asking was that I give up a life of music—a career that I loved—so that we could share a meal. Had I asked him to quit his job so that he could join Nic and me for lunch each day? I had not.

So I refused.

Still, I was blindsided when Tyler left. Maybe those sappy love songs from work had entered my bloodstream; I was too busy being happy to notice that my husband wasn't just annoyed—he had fallen out of love with me.

THE DOORBELL RANG. Simone was on the doorstep. I took one of the takeout cups of coffee that she held out to me and led the way back to the living room. "Thanks for coming over," I said, turning down the volume on the stereo as she settled into the couch.

"The kids are at school, Damien is at work, and I don't have to be at the studio until two today . . . what else do I have to do? It sounded like you really needed to talk." Simone fixed me with one of her looks—droll with a soft edge of concern. Her big, brown eyes were unwavering; I felt as though she could read my thoughts. "Isn't this the album that 'Pale Blue Eyes' is on?"

I shrugged. "Busted." I didn't like to talk about Tyler. Most people assumed that this was because I hated him, but Simone had long ago guessed the truth, and she knew that I played the Velvet Underground when I was thinking of him.

She stood now and walked around the couch to the wall of

music. "Let's get you back to your happy place," she said, running a finger over a row of CDs. In a moment, Patti Smith replaced the Velvet Underground. Simone settled down beside me again. The leather patches on her corduroy pants caught the overhead light. "What do we call this thing you're doing, G.G.? *Pining?*"

"It's been nine years," I said. "At this point, I prefer to think of it as 'reminiscing.' "

"Bullshit."

I smiled and took a slug of coffee. "Believe it or not, I didn't ask you to come over so we could talk about Tyler." I told her about the offer from ZoneTV. "Obviously, I wouldn't do it without you."

Her eyebrows were halfway up her forehead. "A TV show? What do I know about TV?"

"About as much as I do. We'd learn together. What could be more fun than winging it in front of a live studio audience?" I was joking, but as I spoke I realized how excited I really was. After nine years of encouraging women to embrace change, I ached to try something new myself.

Simone ran her hand over her head. I could practically see her thoughts forming behind her eyes. She wore her dark hair shorn close to her scalp; it made her eyes look that much more expressive. Forget Tyler's eyes; *those* were the kind of eyes about which songs should be written. Love songs ruled the music charts, but it was friends who were so often more deserving of the praise.

"Well, it would certainly be new territory for us," she said.

I swallowed. "A new city, too: Los Angeles."

"L.A.? Oh, G.G., I don't know about moving my whole family—"

"It's a lot," I said. "I know. I can hardly even bring myself to think about how Nic would handle the news. I can't imagine putting her through such a big change."

"She'll be okay," Simone said gently. She knew Nic well, so her words meant something to me. "If you're together, she'll be okay." Simone looked away then, her gaze landing on the couch, the coffee table, the collection of framed concert posters that Tyler and I had bought over our years together.

"And a move could be really good for you. Bust you free of old habits." Then, as though I didn't already get her point, she leaned toward me and said, "It would finally put some distance between you and Mr. Pale Blue Eyes."

"And *we* could reach a much larger audience," I said, trying to get the conversation back on track. "Think of how big our army would be." This should have appealed to Simone as much as it did to me, but the way she was chewing her lip had me worried. The fact was that Simone *loved* radio. I knew this. As a kid, she'd spent hours listening to public radio with her grandmother, and I could tell that each time she walked into a sound booth a part of her felt as though she were stepping behind the scenes of her happiest memory.

"It would be huge," Simone agreed. "We could help a lot of people. You don't need to convince me of that. It's a big opportunity for both of us. You'd become an even bigger star."

I could not pretend that this didn't thrill me. When I was sixteen, my father discovered that I had secretly gotten a large tattoo—a tangled web of thorny black roses that clung to my shoulder and crept up my neck. "If you keep going down this path, you'll never get anywhere," he said. He meant that I would never get anywhere in *his* world, a clique of society in which sameness was currency. And even though I'd hated my parents' world and wanted no part of it, the great disappointment in his voice had stung. It seemed to me that he was saying that I could not be a girl with a tattoo and his daughter at the same time. His words had felt like a goodbye—a goodbye to the daughter he'd wanted and could have loved.

Now, after every meeting with my accountant, I fought the urge to send my parents a copy of my bank statement. My radio show and my book, *Number One Single*, had made me a lot of money. A television show would make me even more.

And *more* was something for which I would always be ravenous—more experiences, more challenges, more reach, more success, more *life*.

Lost for a moment in these thoughts, it took me a beat to realize that the house phone line was ringing. No one ever called our landline. *Except Nic's school.* Kirke had the number in case of emergencies. I sprang up from the couch and raced toward the kitchen.

"Yes?" I said, yanking the phone from its cradle.

There were stifled noises on the other end of the line.

"Hello?" I said. "Who is this?"

The caller's breathing was oddly loud. Whoever it was wanted me to know that he or she was right there, listening. I immediately remembered the wet breathing and threats of the woman who had called in to my show the night before.

"Who is this?" I demanded. The breathing continued. I hung up. Then I walked to the front door and slid the deadbolt into place.

"Who was that?" Simone asked when I stepped back into the living room.

"Wrong number," I said, and hoped that I was right.

Chapter 4

Tuesday was Community Spirit Day at Kirke and this meant that at two o'clock Nic dragged herself down the school's main hall to Dr. Clay's Freshman Connection class. Dr. Clay, the school psychologist, had reportedly created the class five years earlier in the wake of three Kirke freshman suicides. Dr. Clay believed that increased academic pressure had pitted kid against kid, destroying the school's sense of community. The best weapon to fight isolation? *Connection.* Nic and her freshmen classmates spent an hour each week engaged in bonding games, team-building exercises, and what Dr. Clay called "Character Education Experiences." Dr. Clay's insistence on moving the desks into a circle made Nic pine for her other classes in which she could at least discreetly stow herself in the back row.

Nic hated to be the first or the last student to walk into any classroom; each alternative brought with it a level of attention that she felt desperate to avoid. She usually arrived a minute or two early for class and then lingered in the hall, pretending to tie her shoe or lose herself in a book until she'd seen at least a handful of students enter the room. But on that particular day she was dreading Freshman Connection so much that she miscalculated and walked *too* slowly. The hall outside of room 114 was empty when she arrived. She glanced at the hall clock and saw that she was three minutes late. Her stomach flipped. She'd have given anything to fast-forward through the next hour until the moment when Roy picked her up and drove her to the barn.

Instead, Nic took a deep breath and pushed open the classroom door. There was a hiccup in the buzz of chatter as all eyes in the room swung toward her. She hurried, cheeks flaming, to the one remaining empty chair—next to Dr. Clay, of course. As she sat down, Lila shot her a sympathetic look from across the room.

"There you are, Nic!" Dr. Clay said in her tirelessly upbeat voice. Black reading glasses were perched on top of her head, half-lost in the tangle of her curls. "I had a feeling you wouldn't miss today's class," she said. This sounded ominous, and when Dr. Clay winked, Nic's panic spiked. "That right, everyone, it's finally Buddy Day!"

Buddy Day. Nic had completely forgotten. Freshmen were to be matched with seniors for even more bonding games, team-building exercises, and CEE (Character Education Experiences). Freshmen would share their feelings and their senior buddies would comfort them by admitting that they, too, had once felt overwhelmed by the social and academic pressures of high school. No one was alone in the struggle! Connections would be made, pressures relieved, suicides prevented. Also, everyone would make a new friend!

"Now I know you are all dying"—Dr. Clay hesitated, coloring, and cleared her throat—"*very excited* to find out who your senior buddy is, but I thought I'd make things *extra* fun this year by adding a trust exercise right into the buddy reveal!" She stood and began walking around the inner circle formed by the desks, handing each student a bandanna as she passed. "I want each of you to blindfold yourself. I'm going to check to make sure you can't see anything. No cheating! Once you're all blindfolded, I'll let the seniors into the room and connect each one with his or her buddy. It's a beautiful day, and you all know I'm a big fan of bonding outside the classroom environment, so I've asked your buddies to guide you from the classroom to the soccer field. It might still be a bit wet from last night's storm, but the sun is out, and I suspect you will all find a way to make it work."

Pressure built in Nic's eardrums as the room swelled with excitement. She watched her classmates tie bandannas around their eyes. Something in her stomach felt as though it were curdling. By the time she brought herself to lift her own bandanna to her eyes, she almost welcomed its promise of darkness.

"I'm facilitating this trust exercise," Dr. Clay said, "because I want you to learn that when you feel alone, and maybe even a little scared, there will always be a member of the Kirke School community who will step up to guide you. There are no strangers here. We are not on our own. You can all depend on one another. And it's okay to feel vulnerable. Vulnerability is a beautiful thing! Let's celebrate it today! Right now!"

Despite the sunshine and rainbows and utter lack of rasp and grit in Dr. Clay's voice, the spirit of this talk reminded Nic of her mother. She could tell that Dr. Clay, like Nic's mother, felt driven to do something big with her life, to leave a mark on people. Even as a young girl, Nic had sensed this hunger, this desire to be extraordinary, in her mother. It had never faded or faltered. She wondered if living with that everlasting need was exciting or simply exhausting.

"Nic." Nic flinched at the sound of her teacher's voice. Dr. Clay could not have been more than a few inches from her desk. "How many fingers am I holding up?"

"I don't know. I can't see anything," she answered. Her voice came out surprisingly strong. It was easier, not seeing anyone. Knowing no one saw her, no one could catch her staring or blushing. Nic felt a funny surge of affection for Dr. Clay.

Dr. Clay's footsteps retreated. The door hinges creaked. Cool air from the hall brushed Nic's cheeks. She heard the footsteps of the seniors entering the room. A fresh surge of whispers and giggling surrounded her.

"Okay, I'm letting in the seniors now. Seniors, I want you to stand next to your freshman buddy. No peeking, freshmen! I'm putting A LOT OF TRUST in my seniors and I know they're going to guide you CAREFULLY out to the soccer field."

Nic wasn't aware that her fingers were wrapped around the sides of her desk until she felt someone tap her wrist. She pulled her hand into her chest with a start, then flushed with fresh embarrassment. *Easy*, she told herself. The voice in her head was the same one she'd use with a horse who had spooked, mistaking a twig for a snake.

"Sorry," a voice said. A *boy's* voice. An *amused* boy's voice. "Didn't mean to scare you."

The warmth that Nic had felt briefly for Dr. Clay disappeared. How was she supposed to feel comfortable with a senior *boy*? It would have been difficult enough to feel at ease in front of a seventeen-year-old girl. It was suddenly very hard to believe that Dr. Clay had ever been in high school. Nic wondered if she could excuse herself to use the bathroom and hide there until—

"Okay, seniors," said Dr. Clay, interrupting her thoughts. "Hands on freshmen elbows for guidance, please. Let's keep the physical contact RESPECTFUL."

When her buddy spoke again, his voice was near her ear. "This way."

They walked together in the direction of the door. Nic kept her hands out in front of her. The senior kept a steady grip on her elbow, steering her through the rush of moving students. In the hall, she could feel space opening around them. Their footsteps echoed through the school's marble foyer and then they were outside, the sun's warmth pouring down onto her shoulders and making the edges of the dark bandanna glow.

"We're at the top of the front steps now," the senior said. "There are four stairs. Ready for the first one?"

Nic nodded. She would need to speak sooner or later, and she knew that her silence was probably getting weird, but she was afraid her voice would come out in a nervous croak.

"Okay," he said. "Second step."

She took the steps slowly; the thought of tripping and falling, blindfolded, right in front of the school and this boy and all of the other seniors helping their buddies down the stairs had her nearly paralyzed. If it wouldn't have been even more embarrassing to drop to her knees, she might have taken the steps crawling.

At the bottom of the short flight of stairs there was a circular drive that would fill with cars at the end of the school day. By now, Roy had surely deposited her mother at the radio station and was on his way to Kirke. Nic released a deep, involuntary breath.

The senior led her along the driveway, and then veered off it. The pavement below her shoes turned to grass.

"If we walk a little further, there's a tree on the edge of the soccer field that we can sit under." Nic nodded, and they continued walking. "Okay, we're here. Ready to sit?"

As Nic lowered herself to the ground, she felt some part of the boy's body graze her knee. She might have sat down too quickly;

sparks appeared behind her eyelids. A cold seep of moisture rose from the dirt below the dry grass. The seat of her pants would be wet when she stood, but it was too late; the damage was already done. Her only hope was that all of the other kids on the field would be in the exact same predicament. But what if everyone else was kneeling? Wet knees were infinitely preferable to looking like you'd wet your pants.

"Sh-should I take off my blindfold?" she asked. Her voice came out exactly as she'd feared, croaky and nervous and, to her horror, with a hint of her old stutter.

"Sure," he said. Then his voice lowered and he said in a pretend sexy voice, "Or you could leave it on." His laughter sounded strained. Was it possible that he was nervous, too?

The anxious flip-flopping feeling in Nic's stomach slowed. "Maybe I will," she said. There was no stutter in her voice now, no extra saliva soaking her words. *Where did that come from?* She pulled off the bandanna and blinked into the bright sun. Lucas Holt sat in front of her. *Lucas Holt.* He had a dramatic face, thick swipes of eyebrows, and an intense gaze. When he smiled, she saw that his teeth were perfect. She felt the urge to lean forward and lick them.

"Hi," he said. "I'm Lucas."

His thatch of dark hair and his dark eyes and eyelashes made Nic think of wood blackened by fire. She realized she was staring. With effort, she pulled her gaze from Lucas's face and saw that he had led her to a far corner of the soccer field. The other freshman-senior pairs sat closer to the school, and Nic was relieved to see that everyone was sitting on their butts, just like her. Dr. Clay seemed to be admiring a bed of orange flowers near the edge of the field; her shoes dangled from her hand. Nic turned back to Lucas, leaning away from him at the moment her eyes met his.

His physical beauty felt like an impossible barrier; it insisted on a measure of distance between them.

"I'm . . ." she said finally. She couldn't seem to finish the thought. Nic thought her own face very plain, her paleness an outward marker of her inner timidity. "I'm, um . . ."

Lucas watched her, the smile falling slowly, so slowly, from his face. "You're Nicola," he said, finishing her sentence for her. "Nicola Clement. I know."

He pulled a crumpled piece of paper from his pocket, smoothed it on his knee, and handed it to her. At the top were typed the words "Your Freshman Buddy is": and below that Dr. Clay had written Nic's name. Her school photograph was stapled to the bottom. Their school photos had been taken on the fourth day of school. Nic's was epically bad. Her eyes were half-closed and something about the lighting made her skin, even her lips, look paler than they usually did. She looked like a vampire who hadn't tasted blood in days.

"Nice picture," Lucas said.

"It's horrible."

He shrugged and shoved the folded paper back into his pocket. He had an agitated energy; Nic found it hard to look away. There was something about his face that she didn't understand and she longed to study him, to feel his skin, the shape of the bones below. He was so much more of a *guy* than the boys in her class.

"You're definitely more lifelike in person," Lucas responded finally. His eyes hinted at a smile.

It was an opening, and Nic desperately wanted to respond in some witty way that would impress him. Something that would compress the impossibly huge three-year age gap between them. Her mind took the opportunity to go completely blank. Trying to come up with a clever comment felt like blindly slapping the walls of a pitch-black room looking for the light switch that she knew must be there somewhere. She dug her fingers into the grass and began to rip it up.

"Soooo," Lucas said, filling the silence. The tone of his voice had changed. Nic knew that he was beginning to realize the kind of girl that she was, and soon there would be no going back. It was easy to go from cool to uncool in someone's estimation—the slide down was oil-slick. Nic had never been cool, but she saw the fear hiding in the eyes of the kids who balanced on the outer ring of the popular circle; one wrong step and they were out. The move in the other direction—from uncool to cool—was a rare feat. You had to be prepared to claw your way up. If Nic clung to silence for another moment it would all be over: any chance she had of being someone Lucas Holt thought was worth knowing, any chance she had of making some of those dreams she'd had over the summer become a reality.

"I think as your *senior buddy*," Lucas said, his words dripping with sarcasm, "I'm supposed to give you some advice or impart some wisdom or something. But I'm new here." He'd picked up Nic's grass-pulling tic, but he did it more violently than she did. He looked at the grass in his hands, his eyes glazed over as though he didn't really see it. He was doing that thing, she realized, that thing where people talked to her as though they were talking to themselves. She was disappearing before his eyes, fading into the background. He could say anything to her and it wouldn't matter, because she didn't matter.

"It's my second day at Kirke," he continued. "You probably have more advice for me than I do for you at this point. Like what food to avoid in the cafeteria. Or where to catch a smoke without getting caught." When he glanced up at her and smiled, there was a hint of something cruel in his eyes that crushed her.

He knew she wasn't a smoker—she was an awkward freshman in an oversized T-shirt. "Or where everyone hangs out after school."

He was pulling out grass in clumps now, roots and all, a moat of dark earth growing between them. As Nic stared at the dark line, a silver bug emerged from the soil, its back a gleaming shield.

From across the field, the voices of her classmates formed a collective murmur.

Talk to him. The command rose inside of her.

"Meatball sub," she said. The words were wet with the saliva that had pooled in her mouth during her long minutes of silence.

Lucas looked at her. His long fingers went still, hidden in the grass.

As a kid, Nic had eventually figured out that the only way to *not* stutter was to envision her words as a train bursting out of a tunnel, each word a train car that was linked to another, barreling out into the bright light of day. So that's what she did: she swallowed a wad of saliva, cleared her throat, and pushed out a train of words.

"You asked what to avoid in the cafeteria, so I'm telling you: the meatball sub. They put some weird spice in it that makes your mouth feel kind of furry the rest of the day. The spice makes the sub smell good under those heat lamps on the buffet so you'll be tempted, but I promise you'll regret it later. You have to, like, gargle with bleach to get the stink out of your mouth. You shouldn't really do that. Gargle with bleach. I think you could die, and then Dr. Clay would really be pissed. I'd probably have to do a *month* of Community Spirit. It would be better for both of us if you just avoided the meatball sub.

"On a related breath-and-death note," she continued, "I don't smoke. I've never tried it. I avoid things that hasten death." Once she'd started talking, she couldn't stop. She didn't feel like Lucas was looking at her; she felt like he was *watching* her. The intensity in his eyes made her cheeks burn. "Seems like a pretty natural instinct, doesn't it? Not wanting to hasten death? Well, I saw a therapist once who said I took it too far. She said if you build up walls of fear, you're creating your own prison."

Why was she telling him this? She couldn't seem to stop. She didn't even take a breath. There was a twinge in the back of her throat that she always felt right before she started crying, but she wasn't crying yet. She was just talking.

"I don't really know where everyone goes after school," she said. "No one has ever invited me anywhere. But I doubt there's any real mystery to it. Everyone's parents are too freaked out about their kids getting into a good college to let them have much free time. Sports practice, academic clubs, the afterschool theater or arts programs. I'm sure there's a group that still finds time to sneak away and smoke pot somewhere, but I wouldn't really know. I go to Corcoran Stables to ride my horse. It's the best part of my day. I wish I could skip the whole school part and go straight to the barn. Taking care of a horse is hard work. I like that. It feels like I'm doing something real. When I'm riding, everything else in my life goes away and I just think about what I'm doing in that moment. Also, I like being on my own. And I love horses, mine particularly. His name is Tru."

Lucas was silent, watching her. Nic felt sure that he was imagining retelling this story to Emory Torres or Jasmine Cane. Things wound down quickly after that. If her words were a train, fuel was running in short supply now and she was chugging to a broken-down stop. The sun that had felt so comforting minutes earlier now felt cruelly hot. Beads of sweat wet her brow.

"I know, I know," she said. Her voice was thin. She knew she was speaking too slowly, giving the stutter a foothold. "A girl who loves horses. How predic . . . dic . . . *dic* . . ."

Nic had once watched a cartoon in which a character's sweater caught on something sharp and unraveled in a matter of seconds, leaving the character clutching her naked cartoon body, mortified, cheeks aflame. *Ha ha*, Nic had thought bitterly even then, even before she knew exactly how that felt. *How funny.*

She made a final, exasperated, horrified effort to spit the word "predictable" out in its entirety. She hadn't stuttered like this in years, but still she should have remembered, should have known better, should have realized that she was too worked up for anything good to come of continuing to try.

". . . dic . . ." she said, and again, ". . . dic . . ."

Finally, she clamped her hand over her mouth. Lucas was on the verge of saying something and she needed to get away before he said it. In his expression was a lightness, a near smile, a twinkle that made Nic think he was on the brink of telling a joke, and if that joke turned out to be at her expense, as she could only imagine it would be given her freakish monologue and stuttering, she didn't know if she could survive it.

On instinct, she scrambled to her feet and ran.

She headed down the path that hugged the side of the school and then she ducked behind a row of hedges. There, she crouched low and wrapped her arms around her knees, crying as quietly as she could. Why had she said all of that to Lucas? She hadn't even told *Lila* how she'd seen a therapist; what had made her tell Lucas Holt? What had she been thinking? She'd never done anything so impulsive, so downright *strange* in her entire life. Lucas would tell Emory or Jasmine or, *oh God*, Angel Bully. Angel Bully would tell everyone else and the story would spread through the entire school. "Some freshman, some girl named Nic, went crazy, stuttering and yelling 'DICK' at Lucas Holt!" Nic was sure that the story was somehow out there already, sprouting to life and quickly mutating in the toxic breeding ground of Kirke's gossip farm. Maybe, she thought, a fresh sob shuddering through her chest, the Lurk had been somewhere on the soccer field, watching. Already, her greatest humiliation might be available for viewing on Instagram.

Eventually, Nic pressed her face to her knees and squeezed her eyes shut. Roy would be there soon, she told herself again and again. It was almost over.

THE DIRT DRIVEWAY leading up the hill to Corcoran Stables was pocked with holes that made Roy lean forward in his seat and grumble. If you watched for it, you could see the moss that hung from the surrounding oak trees swing in the breeze. Around the final bend of the driveway, the pretty stucco stable glistened in the sun. Nic felt the painful knot in her chest loosen ever so slightly. In the paddock, a few horses—Cricket and Thunder and Hey Ho Joe—lifted their heads from the grass, mouths still working, as the car slowed to a stop. The ocean, huge and flat, glimmered in the distance beyond the paddocks and sloping hills of yellow wildflowers and ice plants.

Inside, Tru waited for her with his head hanging into the aisle. The look in his gentle eye made Nic's heart swell. A couple of hard blinks held the threat of fresh tears at bay. Below her palm, the white star marking Tru's forehead was warm. A lot of horse markings looked like vague smudges, fuzzy around their edges, but not Tru's. His star stood out, a crisp, milk-white jewel atop his dark brown forehead. She pulled an apple from her backpack, held it out to her horse, and felt his soft muzzle graze her palm as he bit into it. The crunch of his chewing was loud in the stone aisle and immediately the horses in the neighboring stalls swung their heads up, ears perked.

One of them, a chestnut mare named Georgia Peach, eyed Nic through the bars on the stall door across the aisle, her dark eyes flashing dangerously. Peach was new to Corcoran Stables, but Nic had already overheard one of the barn hands refer to her as a nasty piece of work. Denny had bought her at an auction; despite her temper and bad stable manners, she was a big warmblood and he thought she had potential. He did this a few times each year, brought troubled horses back to the barn and then sold them to new riders once he'd worked out their kinks and deemed them safe. No one seemed to know much about Peach other than the obvious: she was malnourished and had been neglected to the point of abuse or abused outright. Probably both. The veterinarian guessed she was five years old.

So far, Denny had only lunged Peach, clipping the lunge line to her halter and sending her out to move around him in a circle. Nic had watched the new horse writhe around him on the lunge line, rearing and bucking, her powerful muscles twitching in the sunlight. Peach's head was regal but her eyes were white-rimmed and mean, resistant to Denny's low, steady voice and reassuring body language. Usually when Denny worked on the ground with a horse, it looked like a dance to Nic. This seemed more like a battle. A few of the barn hands were watching, too, and they all, Nic included, gasped when Peach charged Denny. He'd stepped out of her way just in time and Peach had stopped and spun to face him, nostrils flaring, ready to do it all again.

She had bars on her stall because she tried to bite anyone who walked by. She'd recently kicked the farrier who was fitting her for new shoes clear into the wall of the wash stall, breaking the man's leg. "What woman doesn't want new shoes?" Denny had said. Nic had looked down and smiled, knowing this type of women-love-shoes joke would have driven her mom crazy.

Now Peach eyed Nic from behind the bars, her ears menacingly flattened.

"Well, you're in a delightful mood," Nic said. She immediately felt bad for her sharp tone. It wasn't Peach's fault that Nic had humiliated herself in front of Lucas Holt that afternoon, that he was probably sharing the details of her humiliation with every senior at Kirke at that very moment. Part of Nic wished that she could be like Peach—snapping her teeth and kicking anyone who came close. No one could say Peach was invisible. You wouldn't risk ignoring a horse like Peach. You wouldn't laugh at her.

From three feet away, Nic tossed an apple between the bars of Peach's stall. The horse started, huffing air from her nostrils, then lowered her head to the ground. As Nic walked to the tack room, she heard the horse take a loud bite of the apple.

The tack room was just a small, windowless room, but Nic felt better there than she did almost anywhere else. The rows of covered saddles, the bridles gleaming like thick ropes of licorice along the wall. The line of hulking tack boxes in dark shades of navy and purple. The musky scent of leather and Murphy oil soap and hay and dust and sweat and manure. Her painful rush of thoughts slowed as she went about her usual tasks: removing her saddle cover, pulling the handled wood tote of grooming brushes from her tack box, lacing up her paddock boots. Nic had never been in love, but she wondered if it felt like this, this feeling of belonging.

Nic's mom's best friend, Simone, had a five-year-old daughter named Rachel who was really into her dollhouse. Sometimes when Nic and her mom went to their house, Rachel would show Nic all of her dollhouse furniture, piece by piece. Rachel had a tiny hot-pink velour cloth—Nic thought it might have been a Barbie skirt—that she ran over each piece before she put it back in the exact place from which she'd taken it. Something about the way she'd hold up a miniature chair or table on her little palm for Nic to admire—the look of pride and love on her face—made Nic feel happy for her. And a little sad, too. She could tell that Simone was worried that Rachel had OCD or something (Nic's mom tried to make Simone feel better by joking that she was sure Rachel was just a run-of-the-mill junior fetishist), but Nic totally understood that stuff with the dollhouse. It was a form of meditation, really. Like Lila's crazy "om shalom" chant. You say certain words, or you dust your tiny dollhouse lamp, or you scrub the day's grime from the spine of your saddle, and in those moments nothing else matters. Your head clears. The world falls away.

She took down her chaps from where she'd draped them over her bridle the day before and zipped them over the jeans she'd worn to school. The chaps had been made to her measurements about a year earlier, so they fit perfectly if you didn't count the two-inch gap between where they ended and her paddock boots began. "I can't believe you're getting taller," her mom had said after she noticed the chaps one Saturday morning while watching Nic ride. "How is that even possible?" She'd looked up at Nic, incredulous. Nic knew it was weird for her that her daughter was now taller than her. Nic knew it was weird for her because she talked about how it was weird for her all of the time. Those were the kind of conversations that made Nic suspect that her mom preferred to think of her as a baby born from immaculate conception rather than as the child of her father, who, for the record, was six feet two inches tall.

She pulled her hair into a low ponytail and put on her helmet, letting the chinstrap dangle unsnapped. She carried her saddle and bridle and grooming box out to the cross ties and then headed back to Tru's stall, the heels of her paddock boots echoing against the stone floor. It was a beautiful barn. Nic didn't go to church, but it reminded her of one. The long, arched aisle, the hushed sound of horses breathing, moving through the straw that softened their stall floors, pulling mouthfuls from flakes of hay. All of those animals were a gentle choir, and their breathing and chewing and shifting was the most beautiful hymn that Nic knew. The sounds and smells filled her, warmed her. The quiet of the barn made her take deep breaths and feel her own strong heart beat within her body.

Nic carried Tru's halter into his stall. The halter was made of dark leather and had a brass nameplate on the cheek strap with Tru's name in cursive—*Yours Truly*. Nic's mom had wrapped the halter and a photograph of Tru in a box for Nic's twelfth birthday. Nic had known about Tru—she'd been trying out horses for months—but the halter was a surprise. Denny must have told her mom what kind to buy; she didn't know that much about horses even though she'd ridden for a time as a kid. "That was before I discovered boys," her mom would say, a little too ruefully, Nic thought, because if she hadn't discovered boys Nic never would have been born. Again, her mom seemed to like to forget that part of the story.

Even before Nic had ridden Tru, she'd fallen in love with his name. It was a sweet, solid name. Not too flashy. *Yours Truly. Truly. True. Tru.*

Nic thought a lot about names. Her mom's name, Gail, was perfect for her—she was herself a strong wind, a gale force that stirred up everything in her path. She had a gale of laughter, too, a big raspy waterfall of sound that she'd never think to apologize for even though in movie theaters it made Nic want to slide out of her seat and become one with the floor. And Gail Gideon—well, you're *supposed* to become famous with a name like that, which was exactly what she'd done. Nic's last name was Clement. It was her dad's last name, which probably bothered her mom, but Nic knew that she comforted herself with the thought that there was no connection between her fame and her daughter's name. She thought it kept Nic safe from . . . something. Nic didn't really know what.

It seemed to Nic that names were nothing and everything. They didn't matter at all—a rose by any other name, and all that—and yet they defined you. It was what people wanted to know when they met you—they asked about your name ages, *years*, before they ever asked about your hopes and fears, the things that really made you *you*. If they ever asked those questions at all.

Sometimes she wondered if she was the Nicola Clement her mother had envisioned when she'd settled on that name. Who had her mother wanted her to become?

"Nic," said Denny.

He was outside the stall door. Nic stood next to Tru, her fingers resting on the clasp of his halter. Tru breathed patiently. Nic had no idea how long they'd been standing in the stall like that.

She swallowed. "Hi," she said.

"A couple of big trees came down in the storm last night, and the trails are still slick from the rain. Better to just stick to the ring today. Everywhere else is a mess."

Nic considered this. She felt a tremor of something she could not place, but it was not fear. "Okay," she said, and felt the tremor again.

Denny looked at her and did not walk away. He had gray hair but his eyelashes, she'd noticed, were dark around his blue eyes. A lot of the girls at the barn had crushes on Denny. Nic had been riding at Corcoran Stables for so long that she could only think of him as some sort of grizzled, grumpy uncle. *"Denny,"* one of those girls had once whispered to another. "More like *Clooney*." Nic had been right in Tru's stall, just a few feet from the girls in the aisle, but they whispered to each other like she wasn't there.

"Well, have a good ride," said Denny eventually. He yanked on the stall door handle and it rumbled along its track, opening.

"Thanks."

He watched while she led Tru into the aisle and clipped the cross ties to the rings on either side of the halter. It seemed to Nic that there was something more he wanted to say, but after a few moments he turned and walked away, his huge old black Newfoundland padding along at his heels. The dog was named Bear. Sometimes Bear wandered into the tack room while Nic was cleaning her tack and Nic would kneel and wrap her arms around his thick neck, ignoring how the hay that was always stuck in his fur scratched her skin.

Nic picked up her rubber currycomb and began to groom Tru, working the comb in a circular motion from his neck to his haunches, pulling loose bits of undercoat and dust to the top of his dark brown coat. She finished Tru's other side and then used a hard brush in quick, flicking movements to remove the curving patterns of dirt left by the currycomb. By the time she brushed out his forelock and mane and tail, Nic had worked up a welcome sweat.

She was pretty sure Denny felt sorry for her. It was something about the way he always stopped to talk to her. He never stopped to talk to the other girls—the ones who giggled and gossiped in the aisle, hogging the cross ties—unless it was to growl at them to move along already.

Possibly Denny was just confused by her—or curious. He must have looked at Nic and wondered how it was possible that she was the daughter of the famous Gail Gideon. Nic was sure her mom had had a ton of barn friends back when she rode at Corcoran. Denny probably used to tell *her* to move along already . . . although, no, Nic realized, he was a teenager then, too, of course. Maybe he hadn't become so grumpy yet.

She ran a soft brush over Tru until his coat gleamed. When she brushed his face, he lowered his head and nudged her softly. You couldn't hide your feelings from horses; they were sensitive animals, adept at reading others. Nic and Tru had entire conversations without saying a word.

She leaned her shoulder into his leg and he lifted it, allowing her to scrape the caked-in dirt and pebbles from the grooves of his hoof. She couldn't remember learning how to do any of this stuff. It was like something she'd always known, like she'd been born with a hoof pick in her hand.

What was that Shakespeare quote that Mr. Hylan had recited in English class the other day? "Joy's soul lies in the doing." Nic had loved the line so much that she'd scribbled it into her notebook. If Nic's joy had a soul, a flame of light at the center of all that made her happy, it could be found burning bright and true and strong when she was immersed in the hard work—the grooming, the cleaning, the riding, the *doing*—at Corcoran Stables. In no other moments of her life did she feel so present, so content, so entirely, comfortably, *herself* . . . whoever that was.

After she outfitted Tru with his saddle and bridle, she led him through the big open double doors at the end of the aisle and out to the tree stump that served as a mounting block. The reins were loose between them; Tru would have walked along with her even if she hadn't held them. She climbed onto the stump and swung her leg over his back and settled into the saddle, finding the stirrups without looking down, snapping her chinstrap in place at the same time. She hoisted her left leg forward of the saddle and pulled the girth up one notch tighter, letting Tru walk forward as she made these final adjustments.

He headed in the direction they usually went, down the hoof-worn dirt path that curved along the edge of the paddocks. The sky was bright and nearly white, as though the rain from the night before had bled it of color. The woods loomed at the bottom of the hill. Nic glanced toward the ring, but kept Tru moving along the split-rail fence. On some days she followed the trail that skirted the woods and eventually turned from dirt to sand as it cut down steeply through the bluffs to the beach. On those rides, she held her face up to the strong winds that blew down the coast, and lost the sound of Tru's canter to the thunderous beat of the ocean's waves. Other days, she preferred the quiet embrace of the trails that meandered through the wooded park that ran along the edge of the property. Today, she needed the lush canopy above her, the serenity of moving through woods that grew wild and free. She wanted to see the dirt darkened by rain, the tiny wildflowers that somehow found enough light to thrive.

The air changed in the woods, cooling. Nic zipped up the fleece vest she'd put on over her T-shirt. Tru's hooves pressed into the wet earth below.

Other than a few stretches of trotting and cantering to keep Tru in shape, Nic mostly let him walk at his own pace on these trail rides. He had a nice walk, not too pokey and not too forward either, just a gentle, lumbering stroll, and enough energy in his gait and prick to his ears to let her know that he was alert, checking things out, enjoying himself. Any corrections on Nic's part to speed him up or guide him were so subtle that she hardly knew when she was making them. It was her favorite thing about the physical act of riding: the partnership, at its best, was a form of mind reading, any commands imperceptible outside of horse and rider. It was the only time she felt so immediately and completely understood.

Denny was right; the storm had made a mess of the trails. Tru blew air out of his nostrils and eyed fallen branches. Nic could feel the growing alarm in his body, the muscles tensing below his skin. She tightened her grip on the reins, feeling Tru's fear become her fear.

Do something! The voice, a snarl, cut through her thoughts.

A jolt of adrenaline surged down her body, into her horse.

Tru shot forward.

All Nic had to do was *think* about slowing Tru, and he would have slowed. Instead, she lifted herself a few inches out of the saddle and let her hands move over Tru's neck in time with his stride, giving him his head, not putting the slightest pressure on the bit. Tru's gait opened, lengthening from a canter to a gallop. Nic ducked low branches, felt them snap at her shoulders. The wind whistled in her ears, the forest blurred at the edges of her vision. She flew. She was not free of fear, but there was something delicious about the particular fear that she felt in that moment, the way it expanded inside of her, filling her, leaving no room for anything else. This fear felt like power. She suddenly understood why she had ignored Denny—on some level, she had known that this feeling would only be found here in the woods where she could not be seen.

And then there it was, far ahead: a fallen tree. It cut across the path, rising at least five feet high. Nic thought quickly. She didn't have a lot of jumping experience and had never attempted a fence that size. Her pounding heart brought her back to the soccer field, the searing pain of her shame as she'd stuttered, the hidden eye of the Lurk watching it all—

Jump, said the voice—her own voice. *I dare you.*

Tru's ears were pricked and taut; he'd caught sight of the tree, too. Nic made the slightest adjustments to bring Tru in on her plan. His hooves carved a steady pattern into the trail. Nic knew to count her horse's strides on the way to the jump, measuring the stretch ahead of them with her mind's eye. *Three strides to go*, thought Nic, feeling the distance in her bones.

One.

Two.

Three.

And then they were lifting off the ground, suspended and weightless and free. Ahead, a sliver of sky glittered between the shadowed branches like a reward; when Nic saw it, she felt the relief of finding the thing for which she'd been looking.

Something hard collided with her shoulder, wrenching her from the saddle. There was a loud crack that seemed to come from inside her head, and in response, the earth roared. The trees swirled around her in a wild tangle, softening her fall. The world was bright and beautiful and forgiving. She willed herself, before darkness fell, to try to remember this.

Chapter 5

In a cab on the way to the hospital, my daughter's life flashed before my eyes. It wasn't the version that might have flashed before Nic's own eyes as she fell from that horse, but it was the version of her life that *I* knew, the version that would be imprinted in my memory for the rest of my days. These were the things I thought about in the taxi on the way to the hospital:

Nic at one week old swaddled into an impossibly small bundle, smiling in her sleep, my surprise at the dimple appearing on her right cheek, the dimple that I would press my kisses into for years to come.

Nic as a baby, sleepy and ready for bed, resting her cheek on my shoulder, patting my back with her chubby little hand spread wide and flat as though she were the one comforting me.

Nic's wobbly toddler voice singing, "Row, row, row your boat, life's a butter dream."

The blur of Nic's toothpick legs spinning through the air when she did her first cartwheel down the slope of Bernal Heights Park at age six.

Nic with pneumonia at nine, the liquid green of her feverish eyes, her hand limp in mine, her skin already calloused from gripping reins tight for an hour each day.

Nic's pale face flooding with joy when she opened the gift I'd wrapped for her on her twelfth birthday—Tru's halter.

The sound of Nic's footsteps padding down the hall to my room on weekend mornings, the feel of her warm, soft body against mine when she snuggled into me and whispered the word "doughnuts."

The spark that burned in Nic's intelligent eyes, the ever-burning flame of her many private thoughts.

The beauty that emanated from Nic when she rode, those moments when she revealed her vast hidden reserve of confidence and strength.

Nic's laugh, a bubble of sound, a balloon tied to my heart, tugging it ever upward.

Nic curling against me on the couch, folding her long legs underneath her. The sound of her relaxed sigh making my heart swell with what was, I knew with complete certainty and utter fulfillment, a love so powerful that it felt like a privilege to live my life tending to it.

And now: Nic lying in a hospital bed, thin and pale and still except for the rhythmic rise and fall of her chest, her breathing steady due to the life-support machine that did the work she no longer could.

I forced myself not to recoil from this last mental image. I forced myself to focus on it, to stare straight at her, to not flinch or conjure up some easier scenario. The truth was that I did not know the exact state of Nic's health at that very moment—it could be better than what I envisioned, but it could be worse. Roy was at the hospital with her. Denny Corcoran was there, too.

I needed to call Tyler.

"Everything okay?" he asked. "I just landed in London."

Tyler always picked up when I called, no matter when it was or where he was—whether he was on a business trip, or in bed beside his nice wife, Lonnie, in their nice house in Mill Valley. Lonnie must have loved how her husband always answered the phone when he saw my name on the screen.

I told him what Roy had told me: Nic's horse had returned to the barn without her. Denny had found her in the woods, breathing but not moving. Denny had ridden with her in the ambulance to the emergency room, and Roy had followed in his car.

Tyler was silent. I pictured him standing in the middle of Heathrow Airport, running his hand over his eyes, digesting this news, spinning it in the most optimistic light.

"But she's going to be okay," he said.

"I'm on my way to the hospital. All I know is that she isn't conscious yet. Roy said that they're giving her a CT scan."

"A CT scan," he repeated.

I decided not to wait for him to tell me that he was sure that examining our daughter's brain was a mere formality, something the hospital was required to do for every patient with a head injury, no matter how minor. "Tyler," I said. "You need to hang up and start looking at flights home."

"Right." He sounded relieved that I'd told him what to do. "I'll get on the first plane back. Call me as soon as you know anything else. I'll send you my flight details."

After I hung up with Tyler, I called Simone.

"Hey," she said. "I just stopped by your office. Where are you?"

"I'm on my way to the hospital. Nic had an accident."

"Oh my God. Is she okay?"

"I don't know yet. She was unconscious when the owner of the barn found her. She's getting a CT scan."

"Oh, G.G. What can I do?"

"Just hold down the fort. Run an old show. Let Martin know what's going on."

"Of course. Don't even give it another thought."

"We're pulling into the hospital now. I'll call you when I can."

I tossed cash into the front seat of the taxi and ran inside.

"My daughter is Nicola Clement," I said to the woman behind the desk. I was speaking loudly, and couldn't seem to lower my voice. "She was admitted sometime in the last hour—C-L-E-M-E-N-T."

The woman's long nails clacked against her keyboard. She read something on the computer screen. "Nicola is in the middle of her scan right now. I'll let you know as soon as she is done."

My Nic, *my* Nic, lying alone in some room in a hospital, a machine scanning her brain for injury. Breathing but not moving. She was just a girl. I leaned toward the nurse. She leaned away from me. "I need to see my daughter. Now. You can't keep her from me. She's a minor."

The woman blinked. She lifted her hands from the keyboard and folded them in her lap. "If you go in that room right now, you will hinder your daughter's doctors' efforts to help her." She spoke carefully and not unkindly. "They are evaluating the condition of her brain, and you will slow them down."

"I want to speak with one of them. One of her doctors."

"Of course. I'll let Dr. Feldman know you're here."

I looked over my shoulder. Roy stood near the door, twisting one hand in the other. He looked ill. I spotted Denny sitting at the end of a row of seats near him. I pointed toward them. "I'll be right there," I told the woman behind the desk.

Roy walked toward me as I approached and wrapped me in a

hug. His eyes were wet when he pulled away, the lines in his forehead deeply etched. His hands stayed on my shoulders.

"She's going to get through this," he said.

I nodded but didn't trust myself to speak. Denny stood. His hair was gray, his skin looked gray, everything about him seemed gray. The room shifted and blurred and my hands began to shake. They tightened into fists and one of them landed hard against Denny's chest. The other was about to land on his chin when a big ogre of a security guard swung into view and grabbed the front of my coat so forcefully that my feet lifted off the ground.

"Let go of her," Roy said. The ogre barely glanced at him. My hands were still balled into fists. I might have growled. A couple of people who'd been sitting near Denny stood from their seats and moved across the room.

"It's okay," Denny told the guard. "Let her be. Her daughter had an accident."

The guard looked back and forth between Denny and me. "No one fights in my room," he said, and slowly released my collar.

I stared at the guard and rubbed the back of my neck. Fear and fury roared in my ears. What right did he have to tell me how to behave when my daughter's life was in danger? I might have growled again. He took a step toward me, but Denny moved quickly, edging his body between ours.

"Let her be," said Denny again. Even his voice sounded gray, tired and sad.

The guard eyed me.

I shoved my hands into the pockets of my jeans so that they would have a harder time hitting anyone.

The guard looked at Denny, then Roy, then me again, hard. "There's no next time. Understand? Not in my room."

I didn't answer. Roy put his hand on my shoulder and squeezed.

The guard shook his head, grumbling something, and walked back to his post by the entry. Denny nodded his head toward the row of seats. I still wanted to kick something, or yell at someone, but I sat.

Roy looked down at me. "I'm going to step outside now," he said. "But I'll be right here if you need me." I nodded. The doors of the emergency room whooshed open and then shut behind him.

"She was supposed to ride in the ring," Denny said. His voice was low, muted. "I told her not to go out on the trail today."

I looked at him, surprised. Nic was a rule-follower. A people-pleaser. She wouldn't go out on the trail if Denny had told her not to.

"Tru came galloping back to the barn without her," he said. "She wasn't too far into the woods. I found her pretty quickly. She was on the ground near a big, fallen tree . . . and her helmet was still on. There was a low branch hanging near that fallen tree . . . if she tried to jump, the branch might have knocked her out of the saddle. The way she was lying made it seem like she'd hit her head on the fallen tree on the way down."

I stared at him. "You think Nic tried to jump a *tree*? That doesn't make any sense. She doesn't even like to jump." I hesitated. "Does she?"

"No, I don't think so." Denny swallowed. "She wasn't moving, Gail. She must have been knocked out. But she was breathing. I couldn't do anything but call 911. I didn't take her helmet off. I couldn't risk moving her. Head injuries . . . neck injuries . . . you don't mess around with those." He ran his hand over his face. "I didn't see a scratch on her, but I couldn't wake her up. It was like she was . . . sleeping. Sleeping and breathing and . . ." He stopped himself.

"And what? Don't fucking spare me now, Denny."

He looked apologetic. "She was . . . smiling."

The cry broke free from my chest. Denny put his arms around me. For a moment, I lost myself in his barn scent. It was the same scent that I breathed in to bring me closer to Nic when I sat in the back of Roy's car after work each night. I couldn't stop thinking of my daughter lying unconscious in the woods, smiling. She was somewhere in the hospital, somewhere nearby, but I still wasn't by her side. I wasn't sure how much longer I could stand being separated from her. I sat back in my seat, wiping at my tears, shaking and agitated.

"Tru's fine," Denny said. "He's safe in his stall." The horse was the least of my concerns at the moment, but Denny continued. "Nic will want to know."

I imagined Nic sitting up in a hospital bed, unscathed but for a bit of dirt on her cheek, her brow knotted in concern over her beloved horse. This image arrived like a gift. I took a deep breath. "Right," I said. "Thanks. I'm sorry I hit you. I was angry . . . well, that's an understatement. It was a gut reaction."

Denny was about to say something when I noticed the man in scrubs walking across the waiting room toward us. I stood.

"Mrs. Clement?" he said.

"I'm Nic's mother," I answered, standing.

He shook my hand. "Dr. Feldman. I'm the neurosurgeon in charge of the team that's been treating your daughter. Nicola's condition is stable. That's the first thing you should know."

There was a feeling of air moving through my chest, like a valve had been opened and pressure released. Behind me, Denny made a small, relieved noise.

"You can come back to see her now and I'll fill you in on what we think is going on with her."

What they "think" *is going on with her?* Nic had been at the hospital for over an hour; shouldn't he know *exactly* what was going on with her? Instantly, I disliked him, and loathed the fact that he had more control over my daughter's health—her life—than I did.

I grabbed my bag from the floor. "Thanks, Denny," I said, turning toward him. "I'm sure Roy will give you a ride back to the barn."

"You'll call me later? Let me know how she's doing?"

I assured him that I would call, and then turned my attention to the doctor.

"We're all very glad that your daughter was wearing a helmet," Dr. Feldman said. He pulled open the door beside the reception desk and we entered a hallway that seemed strangely quiet. Another doctor walked by and nodded at Dr. Feldman, smiling. Was she part of the team he'd mentioned? *She wouldn't smile if Nic weren't okay, would she?* If Nic were in danger, surely the hospital would have been a swarm of activity. Doctors racing down the halls, sweating, barking updates and orders to each other. Dr. Feldman didn't seem to be in much of a rush.

"Nic always wears her helmet," I told him. I spoke robotically, the words coming out without much connection to the rushing geyser of worry within me. "She loses the helmet, she loses the horse, that's what I've always told her. She'd wear one anyway, though. That's the way she is. She's a very careful person."

But Denny had said that she tried to jump Tru over a tree. This made no sense. He must have been missing some key part of the story.

"So she's okay because she was wearing her helmet," I continued. I'd meant this to be a question, but it came out as a statement. Dr. Feldman slowed. I needed to be getting closer to Nic, my body insisted on this, so I walked on. After a few steps, I glanced over my shoulder. Dr. Feldman was stopped in the middle of the hall, watching me.

"Mrs. Clement, please wait a moment."

An annoyed sigh slipped from my mouth before I could zip it in. "It's Gail Gideon, actually," I said. Walking back toward him felt nearly impossible; every inch of my being wanted to go the other way, toward my daughter. "Call me Gail. I didn't particularly love being called Mrs. Clement even when I was married to *Mr.* Clement."

Dr. Feldman squinted at me. I'd seen that look before: he recognized me now. But then he peered down at the clipboard in his hand and scribbled a note—my name, presumably—onto Nic's chart right there in the middle of the hallway. In that moment, I warmed to him. He may have walked slow as hell but this guy wouldn't let anything slip through the cracks. Also he was pale and his hair was a bit wild and I took both of these things as good signs—Dr. Feldman was too busy, too intensely occupied with saving lives, for sunlight and combs.

"Gail," Dr. Feldman said. "Why don't we step into my office for a moment before we see your daughter? I can explain more about what's going on with her."

I looked down the hall in the direction that we had been headed moments earlier. Nic was somewhere that way, lying in one of those rooms. I imagined myself breaking into a sprint, yelling my daughter's name, barging into room after room until I found her.

"Listen," I said, turning back to Dr. Feldman. "Can't you tell me here? I really need to see Nic." My voice cracked on her name.

He took pity on me. We moved to the side of the hall, leaving room for others to pass.

"Nicola has a traumatic brain injury and has not fully regained consciousness yet. The good news is that she has responded to stimuli—"

"She woke up?" I cut in, my heart pounding.

"No, not fully. But she's made noises and small movements in response to the administrations of my team. At a couple of points, her eyes opened, but they weren't focused . . . she wasn't awake. She has not spoken. There are no fractures in her skull—we can thank the helmet for that. There's no indication of trauma to her spine. Your daughter does not have a single broken bone. She's breathing on her own." He spoke faster than he walked, but enunciated each word with care. "But the scan did show signs of swelling in her brain, so we are continuing to monitor her closely to determine our best course of action. We need to ensure that the blood supply to her brain is not at risk. If I don't see improvement soon, I'll want to insert a pressure-monitoring device in her brain—"

"What? You want to put something in her brain?" That rush of fear and anger was back, making my ears ring.

"Yes. We'll drill a small hole into her skull—"

Dr. Feldman abruptly stopped speaking and looked down, which was when I realized I was gripping his forearm. I released it. He rocked back on his heels. He didn't understand. How could he? He could have cornered the market on the world's empathy and still not have been able to fathom all that my daughter meant to me. She was the love of my life.

"While she remains in a coma, the device is the best way to monitor her intracranial pressure and ensure that her condition doesn't worsen," he said.

It seemed to me that the lights in the hall dimmed when he said the word "coma," the floor shifting below my feet.

"The scan can only show us so much and we want to be sure we're gathering every bit of information about her condition that we can," he continued. "Brain injuries are complicated, but the procedure to implant the monitoring device is not. Of course, every procedure carries a risk of complication, but it's quite small in this case and—"

"What sort of complication?"

Dr. Feldman considered my question, his brown eyes liquid with a mix of intelligence and exhaustion. "You know what, Gail? Let's not even have this conversation yet. Nicola is young, her blood pressure has remained within normal range . . . I'd like to give her a little more time before inserting the device. She's stable now and we have every reason to hope for the best. Still, it's important that I'm clear about the fact that your daughter is not yet out of the woods."

Ironic, that: "out of the woods." If I had my way, my daughter would never go *into* the woods again. That morning she'd been sleepily spooning cereal into her mouth at the kitchen table and now she was lying unconscious in a hospital bed. None of this made any sense.

I must have looked as bad as I felt because Dr. Feldman indicated that we could now continue walking. He glanced at his notes and then back at me.

"How old is Nicola?"

"Fourteen."

"And she's in good health, generally speaking?"

"Yes," I said eagerly, because it was true. Nic only became ill when she had to do a presentation at school.

"Is there any history of brain injury? Concussion? Any serious horseback riding injuries before today?"

I shook my head.

"Good."

He stopped abruptly in front of a door. Then he opened it.

For a moment, I was relieved. Nic looked like she was sleeping, just like Denny had said. She still had a bit of baby fat that lent a softness to her face, but every day there was less of it. I could see the beauty that she was becoming, and I almost smiled at the sight of my gorgeous daughter sleeping there on the hospital bed, tucked in tightly below blankets as though she were a young child. Her dark hair spilled around her face, her lips formed a perfect pale bow. *What a ridiculous mistake! My daughter fell asleep and they rushed her to the hospital!*

Poor Nic, I thought. *She's going to be mortified.*

Even as I was having this little fantasy in my head, I was hurrying toward her. I stopped my hand inches from her arm.

"Can I touch her?"

"Yes," Dr. Feldman said. "That's the idea. And there's no need to whisper. Let Nicola hear your voice. Let her feel you."

The moment I touched her arm, I began to cry. "I'm here, Nic," I managed to choke out. I was probably squeezing her hand too tightly, but she didn't move, and that only made me squeeze and sob harder. I wanted to throw my body on top of hers, hug her, cradle her in my arms, but I was afraid of hurting her.

I couldn't believe that the sound of my voice had not forced her to open her eyes.

I realized then that I'd been so intent on getting to Nic's side as quickly as possible because on some level I'd believed that I could fix her. I thought that there was no way she wouldn't be okay if we were together. I believed there was magic in the mother-daughter bond, a sort of psychic power that could overcome any obstacle and set all things, no matter how dire, back on their proper course.

But there we were, mother and daughter united, and Nic remained unconscious. I felt wobbly, my equilibrium stolen, but I did not let go of her hand. The nurse, a woman named Stephanie, pulled up a chair for me. I sat, still clinging to Nic's cool, limp fingers.

"There's no reason to think that she can't hear you," Stephanie said.

I nodded. I watched Nic closely, waiting for those flutters of movement that Dr. Feldman had told me he'd seen, but as far as I could tell the only sign of movement was her chest rising and falling below the blanket as she breathed.

"I'll be checking in regularly, and Stephanie or another nurse on the team will be in the room with Nicola at all times," Dr. Feldman said. "I remain optimistic about what the next couple of hours hold for your daughter."

I nodded. I understood what he was saying. Nic had a couple of hours to regain full consciousness on her own, and if she did not, he would *drill a hole through her skull.*

At first, I tried talking to her. I told her that I loved her. I told her that her father was on his way from London and would be with us as soon as he could. I told her that Tru was safe and uninjured.

I begged her to open her eyes. Would I ever see their beautiful olive-green color again?

"Please, Nic," I said. "Please, please, please," I said, as though the words were a prayer.

And then, with Stephanie's permission, I took out my phone and began to play music for her, songs that Nic and I had listened to together for years, songs that she normally couldn't resist singing along with, her voice more pure and lovely than mine had ever been. I sat at her side and held her hand and played the Pretenders' "Back on the Chain Gang" and Siouxsie and the Banshees' "Hong Kong Garden" and David Bowie's "Heroes." I played the Velvet Underground and Cat Power and Cowboy Junkies and the Rolling Stones and Sonic Youth. Nic was raised on these songs. I sang along to each of them, hoping she'd open her eyes and join me.

When Patti Smith's version of "Rock 'n' Roll Star" came on, I turned up the volume and Stephanie didn't bat an eye. In fact, I was pretty sure I heard her humming along. The sun that streamed through the window gave way to softer evening light and then darkness. Nic's pale skin took on a disturbingly peaceful glow, specks of dust shining in the air above her.

I sat by my daughter's side and sang to her, checking the time after each song ended, desperate for her to wake up or, failing that, for time to slow. How would I possibly sign a form that gave Dr. Feldman permission to drill into my daughter's head? It was unfathomable. I scrolled through the songs in my phone, fully aware that it was bizarre that I was more willing to place my faith in music than medicine.

My fingers paused over Janis Joplin's "Piece of My Heart." It was the song that Nic had been born to, playing out of the pitiful little stereo that I'd insisted Tyler bring into the delivery room. If this was the song that Nic had first opened her eyes to fourteen years ago, maybe it could perform the same magic today?

I pressed play.

It had been a while since I'd listened to the song, and I'd almost forgotten how plaintive, how bluesy and broken and lush Joplin's voice was. I leaned toward Nic, tears streaming down my face, and sang. I was so close to her that my breath made the baby hairs around her ear move. I pressed my palm to the perfect skin of her cheek. I sang and cried about breaking off pieces of my heart, offering vital pieces of myself in the name of love.

"'Take it!'" I begged my daughter, wishing it could be that easy. I would crack myself open if it would make her whole.

Nic's eyelid flickered.

My pulse leapt.

"Nic!"

Stephanie rushed to the other side of the bed. "Keep talking to her," she said, picking up Nic's wrist. "Keep singing."

So I did. Janis and I sang together and Nic's eyelid trembled again. Her pointer finger moved in my hand, the sweetest touch I'd ever felt.

And then she opened her eyes.

She blinked a few times and moved her lips. A flicker of confusion passed over her face, like a storm that only makes the sun seem brighter when it finally appears.

She looked into my eyes.

She smiled.

"Hi," she said.

I laughed. "Oh, Nic!" I hugged her, my face damp with the tears that I'd been shedding for hours.

"Hi" had been Nic's first word as a fourteen-month-old, delivered with the same open, joyful smile that she gave me in that hospital room when she finally opened her eyes. "It's the perfect first word for a future extrovert," I'd joked to my friends when she was a baby. I was proud. I thought of Nic as social and chatty right up until the moment that I realized she wasn't either of those things. Or maybe she changed in the months following that first word. Babies change so much, every few weeks becoming someone new. Either way, I soon realized that Nic's bright "Hi!" was—maybe forever—for my ears only.

So when she looked up into my eyes from that hospital bed and gave me her special Nic "Hi," the relief that I felt was staggering. The Nic-sized break in my heart was sealed by Nic herself. The love of my life had opened her eyes and smiled at me. All was right in the world.

And then Nic's eyes flicked away from mine.

"Hi," she said, aiming that same gorgeous, open smile at Stephanie.

My heart seemed to react first, beating out a thunderous warning. When I hit the pause button on Janis's singing, I saw that my hand was shaking. The room sank into quiet.

"Well, 'hi' right back at you, sweetheart," said Stephanie. "You don't know how happy I am to see those pretty eyes of yours. Green, no less!" She leaned closer to my daughter. "Can you tell me your name?"

Nic started to push herself up on the bed, then winced.

"What hurts?" Stephanie asked.

"My head. My side." Nic's brow furrowed as she took stock of her body. She swallowed. "Actually, everything hurts a little and nothing hurts a lot." She smiled. "And my name is Nicola Clement."

My heartbeat thundered again. *Everything hurts a little and nothing hurts a lot.* I'd never heard Nic say something so quick and clever to someone she'd just met.

Even the way Nic had said her own name caused alarm bells to go off within me. She usually said her name as though it were a question, as though she were giving you the option to call her by it or instead pick another name more to your liking.

Stephanie was as charmed as I was concerned. She leaned in conspiratorially to Nic. "I'll up your meds a smidge to tackle that pain problem. Meantime, can you tell me what day it is?"

"It's September . . . something. It's definitely Tuesday." Her confident voice trailed off as she looked beyond Stephanie. Her gaze wandered the room, taking in the blinking machines that surrounded her, the navy sky beyond the window. When her eyes landed on me, there was a questioning look in them. "Or, it *was* Tuesday . . ."

The door swung open and Dr. Feldman walked in.

"Hello," he said, taking Stephanie's place on the other side of the bed. "I'm Dr. Feldman. What's your name?"

Nic lifted her hand and held it out to Dr. Feldman, who shook it gently, smiling. "Nic."

"Very pleased to meet you, Nic. Do you know where you are?"

"Let's see," Nic began, a twinkle forming in her eye. "I'm lying in a hospital bed in what appears to be a hospital room, so . . . I'm gonna go with Disneyland? Final answer."

I sucked in my breath, unable to hide my surprise at Nic's joke. Behind me, Stephanie let out a trill of laughter.

"She's sharp!" Stephanie said.

"I wish my tests at school were this easy," Nic said. She was still smiling, but I noticed that her voice was beginning to flag. She sounded alert, but tired.

"Do you know why you're here?" Dr. Feldman asked. "Do you remember what happened?"

Nic's brow furrowed. She looked at me and I nodded encouragingly and squeezed her hand. "Was I in an accident?" she asked me.

I felt oddly touched by her uncertainty. "You were—"

Dr. Feldman cleared his throat. "What do *you* remember, Nic?"

She looked at him. "Well, I remember being at the barn."

"Good," I said. "That's good, Nic." I couldn't help myself.

"What's the last thing you remember?" asked Dr. Feldman.

Nic looked down at her hands. "I remember grooming Tru . . ." She trailed off.

"Did you go riding?"

"No." Then she hesitated. "Well, I remember brushing Tru, and getting his tack ready . . ."

"And then?" Dr. Feldman asked.

Nic shook her head, uncertain. "I—I don't know. I guess I don't remember anything else." She looked at me, and I looked at Dr. Feldman, and he nodded at me.

"You rode Tru into the woods," I told her, "and Tru went back to the barn without you sometime later. Denny found you unconscious on the ground by a huge fallen tree. He thinks you tried to jump it and got knocked out of the saddle by a low branch." I wasn't sure how I expected Nic to react to this news. A part of me thought she'd deny it, or at least laugh off such a dangerous act as ridiculous, something she'd never do. I didn't expect her to look so pleased.

"Whoa," she said. That twinkle in her eye had returned. Then her smile vanished. "Is Tru okay?"

"Denny said he's fine." I felt a surge of gratitude toward Denny for supplying this information.

Nic relaxed back against the pillows as though this were all that she needed to know in order to feel perfectly at ease. She looked so pleased with herself that I momentarily forgot about her head injury and felt my temper flare. *Why did you ride into the woods when Denny told you it wasn't safe? Why did you try to jump that tree?* I wanted to ask, but managed to restrain myself. Even if I'd asked these questions, she'd have no answers for me. She didn't remember doing it.

"Don't worry too much about not remembering exactly what happened," Dr. Feldman was telling her. "In time, those memories might return to you. For now, let's just focus on what you *do* remember."

He began to ask Nic a series of simple questions: the year, the day of the week, her birthday, the name of her school. Nic answered each easily, confidently, every so often flashing that bold, bright smile at me or Dr. Feldman or Stephanie in what seemed like an intentionally egalitarian dispersal of charm. She passed Dr. Feldman's test, and the many ones that followed through the night, and yet as I listened to my daughter, as I watched her, I could not tell if the shiver that I kept feeling run down my spine was one of relief . . . or fear.

Chapter 6

In the morning, the hospital room was bright and held an air of expectation. Nic wondered how many patients had moved in and out of the bed that she lay in. How many had died there. She made a silent wish for all of these people, without quite knowing what it was that she wished for them. It was strange that she should feel affection for this hospital room, but she did. She had the feeling that her mother's music had somehow seeped into the room's powder-blue walls. The evening before, when Nic had heard her mother singing and had opened her eyes to meet her mother's gaze, the room had seemed to pulse with life. It had been strange to awaken in an unfamiliar place, but she had not felt afraid. She'd had the sense that she was missing something more than the memory of the accident, and that, whatever it was, she didn't need it. She felt lighter without it. The closest she'd ever come to this particular feeling previously was when she'd lost a bracelet that her stepmother, Lonnie, had given her. She'd never liked the bracelet but had worn it every other weekend anyway, knowing that Lonnie fretted over their relationship. For a long time, Nic could envision no end to this situation. And then, one day, the bracelet was gone. Lost. The relief had been so great that Nic had almost cried.

"Hi, sweetie," her mother said now from the chair beside her bed. Nic wondered if she'd slept at all. Her auburn hair, usually full of light, hung limply around her shoulders.

"Good morning." Nic only remembered her bruises when she moved, and as she sat up she had to clench her teeth to keep from crying out.

"Do you want something more for your pain?" her mom asked. "Dr. Feldman should be here any minute."

Nic shook her head. "I'm fine." She wanted to ignore her bruised body and the slight headache that pressed at her temples. These minor aches were especially annoying because otherwise she felt full of energy. She spread her fingers wide atop the thin blue blanket that covered her legs. Her mind was crowded with thoughts. When would she be able to return to the barn? Now that she knew that she had tried to jump a fallen tree in the woods, she wanted to try it again. It didn't seem fair that she had done something remarkable for the first time in her life, and now she couldn't even remember it.

Her mother studied her, looking worried. Nic noticed that her mother's green eyes had the same tiny gold specks in them that her own did. She loved finding echoes of her parents in herself; they made her feel closer to whole, as though each discovery brought with it a twist of a screw, a tightening of her loosely assembled self, making her secure.

"Has Dad's plane landed?"

"Not yet. He should be here this afternoon."

There was a knock on the door and then Dr. Feldman walked in. "Good morning," he said. He pulled a chair over to the bedside and smiled at Nic before looking down at her chart. Nic liked Dr. Feldman. He spoke to her in the same kind, tired, straightforward way that he spoke to her mother and the nurses.

"How did the night go?" he asked. "Were you able to get some sleep? I see you had quite a few visits from nurses checking on you."

She remembered these middle-of-the-night visits only vaguely. "I feel great. Can I go home now?"

Dr. Feldman's smile reappeared. "What's the rush?"

The "rush" is that I have things to do! she wanted to tell the doctor, but didn't. How could she explain something that she didn't understand herself? She only knew that she wanted to leave the hospital. That she felt ready to go. Her fingers tapped against the blanket.

"I have school . . ." She trailed off. A strange sensation fluttered through her, making her head throb.

"You have your doctor's permission to miss school. In fact, he insists on it," said Dr. Feldman. "Let's talk a little more about how you're feeling. Any nausea or dizziness?"

Nic shook her head.

"Headache?"

Her mother watched her closely. Dr. Feldman's pen hovered above his notepad, waiting. The pain in Nic's head didn't worry Nic. It was nothing. She'd ridden Tru through countless clouds of colds and flus, and even once, strep throat! She would never let this little headache keep her from her horse.

"Nope," she said.

Dr. Feldman's pen scribbled against the page. "Have you remembered anything else about the accident?"

Nic felt funny every time she tried to remember riding Tru. The rest of that day was so perfectly clear to her. She thought of talking to Lucas Holt that afternoon and running from him, crying. Oddly, the recollection didn't make her want to cringe. There was a gap in her memory, a dark ravine that she had crossed with much effort (her current whereabouts were testament to this), and the conversation with Lucas Holt was on the far side of that gap, the side that lay safely behind her.

But it *did* feel odd to not remember the accident. How could she not remember something that she had done just one day earlier? Searching her existing memories was like pressing a finger into a wound—it only seemed to make things worse. Nic suspected that if she stopped trying so hard, the memory would eventually surface on its own.

"No," she said. "I still don't remember riding Tru." As the doctor began to make note of this, she quickly added, "But I remember walking into the barn. I remember the tack room smelled good." She shook her head. This memory didn't seem sufficient; the tack room always smelled good. She should try to be specific. "I gave an apple to Peach, the super bitchy mare across from . . ." She faltered. Had she just used the word "bitchy"? Her mother's sharp glance from her to Dr. Feldman confirmed that she had.

"Don't let it worry you," Dr. Feldman said. When he spoke his thick black eyebrows moved very slightly, like boats bobbing on calm water. "Sometimes our brains work to protect us from remembering scary things, such as falling from a horse when you are otherwise alone in the woods."

Nic nodded, but something about his words did not ring true to her. She didn't need her brain to protect her. And shouldn't her own brain know this? How could it work against her?

Dr. Feldman leafed through her chart and said that all of her test results continued to look fine. "I'm optimistic that you should be able to return home this afternoon or evening," he told Nic. "But cognitive rest is key to your recovery. That means going easy on your brain. No school tomorrow or Friday. Take the weekend to rest, too. Stay off your phone and computer for the next few days. Minimal television. Check in with yourself and if anything you're doing triggers symptoms—headache, nausea, dizziness, fatigue, irritability—stop."

"And then I can go back to school on Monday?" Nic asked.

"Nic . . ." her mother began.

"If you're feeling up for it, yes." Dr. Feldman turned toward her mother. "Isolation isn't good for recovery either. Everything in moderation."

"When can I ride?" Nic asked.

Dr. Feldman clasped his hands on top of her chart. "Brain injuries are cumulative. Once you've had one, it's easier to get another, and each injury carries more risk of long-term damage than the last."

Nic swung her gaze to her mother. "I'm not going to stop riding."

"Let's just see how your recovery goes," her mother said, taking her hand. "Give yourself a little time."

"No!" Nic's voice emerged louder than she'd intended. That strange sensation fluttered through her again, that feeling that she was missing something, that feeling of relief.

"Sweetie, this isn't a broken bone. We're talking about your *brain*."

"I'm not going to fall off again. I'll be careful."

"I'm sorry, Nic. I know how much riding means to you—"

"No, you don't!" Her mother obviously did not know how much riding meant to her, or she wouldn't tell her she shouldn't do it. *Take away something else*, Nic silently begged her. Anything *else*.

"I *do* know," her mother insisted. "And I'm sorry. But it's not a risk worth taking. A bump to your head—even a small one—could have much worse consequences next time."

"Then I won't ride. I'll work Tru from the ground using a lunge line. He needs to exercise."

"I'm more worried about you than Tru," her mother said. "Anyway, when Denny called to check on you last night, he promised me that he would take good care of Tru while you recover."

Denny had called her mother? This seemed to Nic like a bear picking up the phone to call a lion.

"You see," said Dr. Feldman. "Your horse will be just fine."

"Tru may be fine," Nic answered. "But *I* won't be until I ride again." Her words emerged smoothly, but she could tell by the way that her mother and the doctor blinked at her, the sudden swell of quiet in the room, that the resolve in her voice had startled them. It was in that moment that Nic realized what else was missing besides the memory of the accident: the stuttering child that she'd carried within her for so many years.

That girl, it seemed, was gone.

Chapter 7

I spotted Tyler in the waiting room, staring out at the parking lot, chewing his lower lip. Nic chewed on her lip when she was lost in thought, but Tyler chewed on his lip only when he was anxious, which meant—since being unflappable was one of his defining characteristics—he did it rarely.

That catch thing happened in my chest. It happened whenever I saw Tyler, whether we were college classmates or lovers or spouses or forty-and-divorced-and-connected-only-by-our-hospitalized-daughter.

I stood very still and studied his profile, telling myself that I was cataloguing the physical traits that he had passed down to our daughter. Dark hair. Long face. Long nose. Long legs. Austere eyebrows. Tyler must have sensed me watching him, because he turned and looked at me and after a beat of time that felt like it held every moment of our shared history, he crossed the room and gathered me in his arms.

He smelled different than he had when we were married, but his body felt the same. I let myself relax for a moment, comforted. I couldn't remember the last time he'd really hugged me. It must have been years. Years of phone calls and emails and text messages about Nic—her behavior, her speech therapy, her grades (always mediocre despite her clear intelligence). Years of polite conversation when he dropped off Nic after the weekends they spent together. Tyler didn't love me anymore—he loved his wife, Lonnie, who was perfect for him, and their two young sons (and what a strange relief it had been to learn that their children were sons and that Nic would continue to be her father's only daughter)—but he would always love Nic. He was a good man. Really, his main fault was glaringly easy to identify: he didn't love me.

We'd been divorced for nine years. Nine years! We'd only been married for seven. This didn't seem possible. In my memory, our married years stretched on and on like a rubber band pulled taut; the years since had felt like the snap of that rubber band, released.

Tyler stepped back from our embrace and I quickly wiped the tears from my eyes.

"How is she?" he asked.

I tried to think of how to describe Nic's current state to Tyler. "It's very strange. She doesn't remember the actual accident, but she remembers everything else. She's smiling a lot. She's happy. She's been chatting with the nurses like she's known them her whole life. Everyone who works here is completely charmed by her. If the hospital ran a contest for most popular patient, our daughter would leave here wearing a crown."

"Leave here? Is she ready to leave already?"

It was just like Tyler to latch onto the most positive thing I'd said. "Dr. Feldman said that as long as she continues to show improvement, we can bring her home later today. But you're not listening to me. Nic isn't acting like herself."

Tyler looked confused. "You said she's smiling and happy. That sounds like our Nic."

"Exactly! That's *our* Nic. But ever since she woke up from the coma, she's smiling and happy with *everyone*. She's not self-conscious at all. She's *different*."

His brow furrowed. "What does her doctor say?"

"He said that a traumatic brain injury like Nic's can cause behavioral changes and lowered inhibitions. He said that in some of these cases, people become reckless, violent, or sometimes just rude. They can't control their impulses. But Nic isn't acting like that, so he isn't worried. He thinks her symptoms are mild."

Tyler's expression relaxed.

"But Nic is *different*," I insisted. "She may not be violent, but she isn't the way she was before the accident. I keep trying to explain that to Dr. Feldman, but he just repeats what he's already said. Now I'm convinced that he's instructed one of his nurses to page him after he's spent two minutes talking to me."

"Giving the doc hell, eh, G.G.?" Tyler asked, smiling.

"Apparently hospitalizing my daughter brings out the beast in me."

"I think perhaps *life* brings out the beast in you." Tyler was still smiling, but his head was cocked as though he were imagining the bullet he'd dodged by divorcing me. If I hadn't been so focused on Nic, I would have taken the opportunity to remind him that he'd *adored* the beast in me right up until the moment he'd decided he didn't. The bullet dodged had been the one *he'd* aimed at *me*, not the other way around.

"Stay on subject," I told him. "Nic wants to go to school. *Our* Nic *wants* to go to school. She also wants to get back to the barn to ride Tru, but that's no surprise. Dr. Feldman explained that a second brain injury could be much worse than the first, and when he told her that riding wasn't a good idea, Nic became really angry." It had seemed to me that the entire hospital had fallen silent for a beat of time after Nic had raised her voice during that conversation, everything shifting off-kilter before righting itself again. "I tried to explain to Dr. Feldman that she never yells like that, and he said I should consider myself lucky. I got the impression that his own teenage daughter hasn't stopped yelling in three years."

Tyler laughed. "I'm sort of looking forward to meeting this Dr. Feldman."

"He also said it might not be the worst idea to let Nic visit Tru."

Tyler's face fell. "No."

"That's how I felt at first. But he thinks it could help her regain her full memory. And, at the very least, that it would give her comfort to see with her own eyes that Tru is okay. Honestly, I hate the idea of her ever getting near another horse, but maybe on this particular subject Dr. Feldman is onto something."

Tyler said he wanted to think about it. I walked him to Nic's room, stopping when we reached the door. "I'll be in the waiting room, okay? Nic will love having you all to herself, and I could use a moment to check in with work."

But now Tyler was only half-listening, nodding and offering a vague wave before pushing open Nic's door and stepping into her room. It occurred to me that he probably felt the same way that I had felt when I first arrived at the hospital; some part of him was convinced that everything would be okay once he was physically reunited with his daughter, because she was the love of his life, too, or one of them (he had so many loves now), and how could she not be okay once they were together?

Love turned us all into fools.

I SANK HEAVILY into a chair in the waiting room and checked the voice messages on my phone. There was one from Richard

Hylan, Nic's English teacher. "Nic is bright," he said, "but quite shy, as I'm sure you're aware. I'd love to chat with you about a few ideas for cracking her shell." Usually I felt a flash of protective fury when I received one of these calls from yet another teacher who would not accept my daughter for who she was, but in that moment I felt disconsolate. *The shell is already cracked,* I thought, feeling worried for my daughter in brand-new ways.

Next, there was a message from Simone, wondering how Nic was doing, and letting me know everything had gone smoothly at the studio the night before. And then a message from Martin Jansen, Talk960's program director, tripping over himself to let me know how sorry he was to hear about Nic's accident, that I should take all the time I needed, that the studio would support me in any way it could. Martin always became increasingly solicitous as I neared a contract renewal date—I didn't think it was likely that he'd caught wind of the interest from ZoneTV, but he must have known that other radio stations were always circling.

There were two missed calls from my agent, Shayne, who had never once in all the years that I'd known her left an actual voicemail message. I'd pushed any thoughts about the television show to the back of my mind—our conversation on the car ride home from the studio only two nights earlier felt like a lifetime ago. But clearly, Shayne was anxious to hear from me. In her world, life-changing decisions were made in a matter of hours, not days.

I draped my knees over the armrest and dropped my feet onto the chair beside me. I'd been wearing the same clothes for nearly forty-eight hours. I was so tired that my eyes burned. My old friend the security guard pointed at my feet and shook his head sharply. I sighed and swung my legs off the armrest, letting my boots land with a loud smack on the floor.

I decided that I felt too exhausted to talk even to Simone, so I sent her a text letting her know that I would be out of the studio for the next few nights while I stayed home with Nic. I would return to the show on Monday. I realized that I'd have to hire our old babysitter, Irene, for Nic again—I didn't want her to be home alone while I was at work. What if she fell and hit her head and there was no one there to help her? I sent Irene a message to ask if she could help out again for a while.

Then I did a quick scroll through my email in-box to see if there was anything that couldn't wait. One particular email caught my eye. I didn't recognize the sender's email address, but the subject line—"Hello from a fan!"—made me believe that the message inside would lift my spirits. I was checking my personal email account, not my public fan mail one, but every so often a fan managed to dig up my personal address. As a public figure, I'd learned years ago that there was really no hiding if someone was intent on finding you.

I opened the email. I should have deleted it the moment I realized what it was, but once I started reading it I couldn't seem to stop.

> You're playing an old show on the radio tonight. I remember this one. I didn't like it the first time I heard it. Now I'm almost enjoying it, because the fact that you're running it, that you're not in the studio right now as I write this email, means that I must have gotten under your skin. I'm glad. When you ruin someone's life, you shouldn't get away with it. You shouldn't get rich on it. You might be able to hang up on me, but I will make sure you can't forget me. You mess with my life, I'll mess with yours. YOU BETTER FUCKING WATCH OUT.

They were the words of the caller from two nights earlier, the show before Nic's accident. Maybe the email was from the same person, or maybe it wasn't. The strange thing about crazy people, I'd noticed in the years since my rant about Tyler had gone viral and I'd become a household name, was that they all shared a similar vocabulary, as though love could be found in a million variations, but hate was just hate, any way you sliced it.

Then again, hatred wasn't always the motivating emotion of my stalker-fans. Jenny Long, for example, had been a different sort of crazy. We'd met for the first time after a show one night when she sprang toward me from the shadows outside of the Hawke Media Building and asked if we could take a photo together. Roy had shot me a warning look, but I didn't feel particularly worried—it wasn't uncommon to find fans waiting for me outside the studio. Jenny had put her arm around my shoulders and as we smiled up at the phone she held in her outstretched hand, I saw on the phone screen that her eyes had filled with tears. Suddenly, both of her arms were around my neck. "I need to talk to you," she'd whispered, her breath wetting the skin behind my ear. "You're the only one who understands." Her grip tightened. While Roy tried to peel her off me, I dug my elbow into her stomach. She'd reeled backwards, her expression morphing from anguish to shocked betrayal. "Please, G.G., you're my best friend," she'd cried. "It's me, Jenny!" A security guard from the building made a belated appearance then, grabbing the woman by the arm as Roy and I hurried toward Roy's waiting car.

"Do you know her?" Roy had asked after we were safely inside the locked car.

"No." The collar of my jacket was damp from the woman's tears. It was only when I wrenched that jacket off my shoulders that I realized how badly I was shaking.

After that night, Jenny Long waited outside of Hawke Media frequently enough that I grew to expect her, and yet infrequently enough that each time she sprang out of the shadows and hurled herself at me it was a surprise. The building's guards knew to look out for her, so she became increasingly stealthy, wearing wigs of different colors. Some nights she waited on the corner and ran toward me at full speed just as Roy opened the car door for me. She was always crying. In her mind, I was her closest friend. She thought that I spoke to her—and only her—through the radio every night. "Please, G.G.," I'd hear her whimper dejectedly as Roy slammed the door behind me. "It's me, Jenny."

After a few weeks of this, I filed for and was granted a restraining order. It worked. I hadn't seen Jenny Long in over a year. I had no idea where she was, or what had happened to her, or if she still listened to me on the radio and believed that I was speaking directly to her alone. Had her obsessive love for me morphed into hatred over the past year? Had she gone from believing that we were best friends to believing that I had ruined her life? Was she now intent on ruining mine? I had no way of knowing.

I blocked the email address, but it was too late. If I'd read that note at almost any other moment in my life, I would have rolled my eyes as I deleted it from both my in-box and my mind. But on that day I was sad and confused and worried about my daughter, who it seemed I was to take home from the hospital forever changed.

The threatening words landed like darts in a soft target, and there they remained.

Roy drove us home from the hospital later that night. I held Nic's hand and watched the side of her face as she gazed through the window. Her expression was placid, but her eyes seemed unusually bright. It might have been the reflection of the headlights of the cars headed south on the freeway.

"Is everything okay, Nic?" I asked her softly. Roy glanced at us in the rearview mirror.

I could have sworn that my lovely daughter stifled a sigh as she pulled her gaze from the apparently mesmerizing sight of 101 in all its heavily trafficked glory. "I'm fine, Mom," she said. "I told you, I feel great."

"But, Nic," I pressed, "do you feel a little off? A little different than you did before the accident?"

Instead of answering, she smiled. "Can you believe I did that? Tried to jump Tru over a tree?"

"No, actually, I can't."

"I think it's kind of amazing."

"Frankly, it makes me want to put you on a leash."

Nic laughed.

"The other day," I told her, "I looked down from my office window and saw a toddler wearing a backpack with a rope attached to it and at the other end of the rope, about four steps behind him, was his mother. She seemed calm. The whole thing appeared very reasonable."

"Mom."

"I'm just saying, one rope attached to your school backpack and so many of our problems could be solved."

Nic shook her head, smiling. She leaned into me and rested her head on my shoulder. A moment later, before I could press her again about how she was feeling, she was asleep.

Over the next few days, Nic and I spent most of our time listening to music and taking naps and eating comforting meals of pasta and stew. I studied Nic, reading into everything she said, examining each of her smiles. It was clear that she knew I was watching her; her mood swung from indulgence to annoyance and back again.

The house was full of flowers sent by Martin (card: "With hope for a swift recovery!") and Shayne (card: "Nic—Feel better! G.G.—Let's talk soon!") and Simone (card: "We love you, Nic!"). Denny called twice to check on Nic. Tyler visited every day.

Nic spoke on the phone with my parents, who had retired to Palm Springs a few years earlier. They were irritated to only learn of her accident days after it had occurred, but were relieved that she was on the mend. My mother offered to come help, but I thanked her and said we'd be fine; anyway, we'd see them soon enough when they visited at Christmas.

Nic called her friend Lila often. On the couple of occasions that I overheard her on these phone calls, I found her mildly conspiratorial tone both comforting and worrisome. She hadn't made close friendships at her old school, so her relationship with Lila was a welcome change. But there was a *knowing* quality to her voice, a certain throaty maturity, that made my breath catch in my chest.

She painted her fingernails red. She must have found the polish in my bathroom. She sang "Piece of My Heart" as she painted her nails, and her singing voice was strong and clear. But this was nothing new.

On Sunday night, Roy arrived with burritos from our favorite Mexican restaurant. Two of the burritos had the extra-spicy salsa that Roy and I loved, and one had the mild salsa that Nic had always preferred. When she asked to try mine, Roy and I watched in astonishment as she ate the entire thing without breaking a sweat.

By the time she went to bed on Sunday night, Nic—*my* Nic,

who usually had to be pushed out of the house each morning—was already itching to go to school the next day. As I'd done for the previous four nights, I lay down to sleep on a blanket on the floor beside her bed, and listened as she begged me to let Roy take her to the barn after school the next day. I told her that her father and I were still discussing it, but the truth was that Tyler had pulled me aside earlier in the day and told me that he'd decided allowing Nic to see Tru was a good idea. His change of heart had not surprised me. With each visit, I'd watched my ex-husband grow less wary of Nic's newfound confidence. He seemed charmed by her poise. By the time he pulled me aside during that morning's visit, he seemed, oddly, *less* worried about Nic than ever before.

Even though I'd agreed we should let Nic return to the barn, it was impossible for me to fully shake the terrible thought of her lying unconscious in the woods, the shock of almost having lost her, and the disconcerting sense that she was irrevocably changed.

I had not been sleeping well, and Sunday night was no different.

The next morning I awoke before Nic and watched her, my heart skittering anxiously, waiting for my daughter to open her eyes.

Chapter 8

The first thing Nic saw when she woke up was her mother's worried expression.

Nic bolted upright in bed, holding her arms out stiffly in front of her. "It's *aliiiive*!"

Her mother released a strangled laugh and swatted Nic's shoulder. "I think I might be ten years older than I was five minutes ago." Her mother *did* look tired. Nic felt a stab of guilt. "Don't forget Simone and the kids are coming over this morning with bagels. They wanted to see you before school."

Nic stretched. Her body no longer ached, but the steady hum of her headache remained. "I'll get in the shower."

"I'll make coffee."

Within moments of her mother leaving the room, Nic could hear her cursing and banging around in the kitchen. She smiled. For as long as she could remember, weekday mornings began with her mother doing battle with the coffee machine.

"Hasn't that thing taken enough abuse from you over the years?" she called on her way to the bathroom.

Her mom appeared at the bottom of the stairs. "Are you sure you want to go to school, Nic? I wouldn't mind spending another day lounging around in our pajamas."

Nic groaned.

"Right, right." Her mother waved her hand in the air dramatically. "Got it. You *want* to go to school. If you happen to see my daughter Nic while you're there, please tell her that her mother loves her."

"Will do!" Nic said, and stepped into the bathroom. She kept waiting to feel anxious about returning to school but the skittering sensation within her felt more like anticipation than worry. Part of this was that she knew, just *knew*, with surprising, delightful certainty that she would never stutter again. Had hitting her head somehow done this to her? Had some off-switch been flicked within her? Or maybe an on-switch? How could she know? She felt grateful and free, nearly giddy with possibility. It was like awakening one morning and discovering that you could fly.

After she showered, she ran her hand across the line of gray and brown shirts that filled her closet and stopped on the yellow dress. *Oh, just wear it already*, she thought. And she did. She twisted her wet hair into a bun and pulled on her favorite shoes, a pair of black Converse high-top sneakers.

She heard the doorbell ring, and then the voices of her mother, Simone, Rachel, and Sam floated toward her. She was about to head down to join them when she caught sight of the bottle of perfume on her bureau. It had been a birthday present from Simone. Even though the scent, a mix of lilac and vanilla, was light and sweet, each time Nic had put it on she felt like she was trying to be someone she was not—someone grown-up, someone who could accept a compliment without blushing or growing tongue-tied. Before, the scent had carried hints of all of Nic's hang-ups, but now it just smelled nice. She sprayed it on the translucent skin of her wrist and then held her wrist to her nose and breathed in. She rubbed her wrists against her neck. This felt like a ritual, womanly and calming.

"Nic!" Simone cried when Nic entered the kitchen. "You're looking gorgeous! Traumatic brain injury becomes you."

Nic laughed. She felt her mom watching her as she hugged Simone and Rachel and Sam.

"I love your dress!" Rachel said.

"Thanks. Mom got it for me."

"Months ago," her mother said. "It looks great."

"You smell good, too," Simone said, winking.

"I'm wearing all of my birthday presents this morning."

"Happy birthday!" gushed Sam, who was seven. His eyes darted around the kitchen, looking for more presents maybe, or cupcakes.

Nic smiled. "No, it was a few months ago, remember? But your mom gave me the perfume I'm wearing today."

"Well, it may not be your birthday, but it *is* your first day back at school, and we thought we should celebrate with your favorite bagels," Simone said. She passed Nic a plate with a toasted bagel slathered with cream cheese. "I'm so relieved you're okay, Nic. We've been worried about you. But look at you! You'd never guess the ordeal you've been through."

"I feel great," Nic said, as much for her mother's benefit as Simone's. It seemed possible that Nic could have entered the room doing a chain of back handsprings, and her mother would still eye her warily, wondering what secret injury she nursed.

When Nic was halfway through her bagel, her mom walked to the far side of the kitchen to refill her coffee, and Simone trailed after her. They put their heads close and spoke in low voices. Nic couldn't make out anything they were saying because Rachel was chattering loudly about some new dollhouse furniture she was hoping to get for Christmas and Sam was busily beating two spoons against the kitchen counter, but the gist of the adults' conversation became clear the moment they returned to the table.

"Nic," her mother said. "Your father and I have decided that you can visit the barn this afternoon—"

Nic's heart soared. "Oh, Mom, thank you, thank you, thank you!"

"Hang onto those thanks for a minute and let me finish. You're not allowed to ride. I don't even want you to lunge Tru. But I know it's important for you to see him, so if you promise me that you will be very careful, and that you won't ride, I'll tell Roy he can take you there after school today."

Nic was dying to ride—five days out of the saddle felt strange to her—but she could see that she wasn't going to get anywhere by pushing back. She put her arms around her mother. "I'll be careful."

"No riding," her mom repeated. "No lunging. Don't even walk into the ring. Denny is going to keep an eye on you."

Nic managed to stop herself from rolling her eyes. She took a large bite of her bagel. She couldn't wait to see Tru, but she wasn't wishing away the school day like she usually did. She wondered if Lucas Holt had written her off after her weird stuttering meltdown or if that small flicker of flirtation between them might still exist. Had he noticed that she hadn't been at school?

She caught sight of the clock on the microwave. *Shit!* she thought. *I'm going to be late.*

"Nic!" her mom said.

"What?"

"You just said . . ." Her mom glanced at Rachel and Sam, then at Simone. They all watched her. Sam grinned. Rachel's glossy pigtails seemed to quiver with excitement.

"You said a bad word," Rachel announced.

"Oh!" Nic laughed. "That was out loud?" She stood and carried her breakfast plate to the dishwasher, feeling all four pairs of eyes move with her as she did.

More eyes followed her as she stepped out of her mom's car in front of the school that morning. Maybe they were excited to catch sight of Gail Gideon, or maybe it was Nic's yellow dress. Or had everyone heard about her accident? The school wasn't that big, making life easy for the kids who thought it was important to know everyone's business. Nic felt those eyes on her and for the first time wondered if gossip was really all that bad. Maybe the interest in one another's lives was natural, maybe even critical, for a community. The idea of someone talking about Nic behind her back had always made her feel cold in her bones and strangely lonely, but now she felt herself grow a little taller. She was *interesting*. Maybe people were talking about her because a part of her belonged to them. *With* them. They felt her absence when she was gone.

Lila jumped up from a bench in the school's foyer when Nic pulled open the front door. "Hey!" she called, and Nic knew that her friend had been waiting for her. "I'm so glad you're back!" When they hugged, Nic felt Lila humming with the anxiety built up from having faced three full days of school without her.

Nic squeezed her back, knowing just how awful it would have been for her if Lila had been the one who missed school and Nic the one left to walk the halls alone—those heart-pounding moments of wondering where to sit at lunch, if anyone would talk to you, if it were possible to go through an entire day without saying a single word.

"Oh!" Lila said, pulling back. "Was it okay to hug you? Does it hurt— Wait, Nic! What are you *wearing*?"

"No, I'm fine . . . and it's called a dress. My mom got it for me. What do you think?"

Lila blinked a few times as though she didn't know what to say.

Nic looked down. "It's not that bad, is it?"

"No, no. I love it. I'm just surprised." She studied Nic, squinting. "You look different."

"I feel different," Nic admitted. "I guess it's the dress." She knew this wasn't true. She'd felt different before she'd even put on the dress; feeling different was what had allowed her to put on the dress in the first place. But she didn't really know how to explain this to Lila. She couldn't even explain it to herself.

"Well," Lila said. "You look amazing." She sounded a little worried about this development.

Nic linked her arm through Lila's and steered her toward their lockers. "So what did I miss?"

Lila perked up again. "Have you checked Instagram?"

"Lila, you know my mom doesn't let me have an account."

Her friend pulled her phone from her bag and began scrolling through the photographs and videos on her Instagram feed. They weren't supposed to have their phones out at school but the teachers never seemed interested in busting girls like Lila and Nic on this rule. The adults of Kirke had bigger fish to fry—one of these bigger fish being the latest despicable Lurk, whose Instagram feed Lila was studying now. For a school so rampant with gossip, it was amazing that the student's identity hadn't yet been rooted out and publicized.

"Here it is," Lila said, passing her phone to Nic when they reached their lockers.

Normally, Nic felt an uncomfortable twist in her gut when

Lila insisted on sharing something from the Lurk's Instagram account. She usually had to force herself to look at her friend's phone, always worrying that the Lurk had posted something about her, something snarky and searing that would burn bright in her mind every time she turned out the lights to go to sleep.

And there had always been another edge to Nic's dislike of the Lurk. For as long as she could remember, she'd felt strongly affected when something struck her as unfair. Who was this person, writing while wearing a coward's cloak of anonymity, skewering unsuspecting schoolmates with furtively taken photographs and cruel remarks? It didn't matter to Nic that most of her peers found the account funny; she thought only of the kids who were strung up for entertainment. What right did someone have to do this to others? She felt each of her classmates' humiliations nearly as deeply as her own.

Now, a sense of indignation outweighed her trepidation. She nearly snatched the phone that Lila offered her. On the screen was a photograph posted on Friday of a dark-haired boy with his head bent toward Jasmine Cane, his arm around her back. The photograph was blurry, taken surreptitiously and on the fly like all of the Lurk's work, but the boy, Nic realized as something clamped around her heart, was clearly Lucas Holt. Below the photograph of Lucas and Jasmine (gorgeous, popular, captain of the swim team), the Lurk had posted a red heart emoji followed by the words "HASHTAG BARF" in capital letters.

Nic gave a choked laugh, half-relieved that the Lurk's comment was more funny than mean, and half-crushed by what she'd seen in the photograph.

Dr. Clay came into view down the hall. "Phone!" she trilled.

Lila grabbed the phone from Nic's hand, tossed it in her locker, and slammed the door.

"Get to class, ladies," Dr. Clay murmured as she walked by.

Nic and Lila headed toward math class.

"You know, Lucas and I had a moment," Lila reminded her.

Nic realized that her friend was talking about the moment when Lucas had first walked into the cafeteria—the moment when Nic had been sure he'd looked at Nic, and Lila had been sure he'd looked at Lila. Nic hadn't had a chance to tell her friend that he'd turned out to be her senior buddy, or that she'd made a fool of herself in front of him, stuttering and running away in tears. Now she told Lila the whole story, but in the telling it became funny, and when Lila laughed Nic found that she didn't mind at all, and even laughed along with her. Neither of them stood a chance with a guy like Lucas when girls like Jasmine Cane existed, and they might as well laugh about it.

"Oh my God, Nic, stop. You didn't really run away, did you?" Lila asked.

"Hashtag barf," Nic said, nodding, and they both burst into laughter again.

Nic was exhausted by the time she dropped into her usual seat in the last row of desks in Mr. Hylan's classroom. Her body ached, and though she did not like to admit this even to herself, the steady thump of her headache had grown with each passing hour of the day. At least she'd see Tru soon. She hoped her excitement about going to the barn would be enough to keep her awake for the next fifty minutes.

Mr. Hylan loved Shakespeare, lived and breathed Shakespeare, drank coffee out of a mug with the words "To caffeinate or not to caffeinate, that is never the question." Nic once saw him walking around the school grounds early in the morning with headphones on, gesticulating dramatically, and she assumed he was listening to a Shakespeare play, probably read by Patrick Stewart. Mr. Hylan looked a little like Patrick Stewart, come to think of it; he was bald with glittering eyes that vacillated from kind to stern seemingly on a whim. Nic suspected that Mr. Hylan believed he could have been a fantastic Shakespearean actor, and that somewhere along the way the world had disagreed, landing him at Kirke.

It seemed to Nic that if Mr. Hylan had been allowed to perform onstage, he wouldn't have tormented his fourteen-year-old students by making them perform Shakespeare in front of their whole class. They were being punished for their teacher's failure.

"Does anyone," he asked, a sigh in his voice, "have any idea *why* I'm asking you to memorize Shakespeare?"

"To torture us?" Nic speculated. She didn't realize she'd said the words out loud; when everyone in the classroom looked at her in surprise, she looked in surprise right back at them. She'd never made a room full of people laugh before—unless you counted a room filled with her mom and Simone, which she didn't.

Lila looked at Nic in the way she'd been looking at Nic all day—worried, and curious. Nic wanted to reassure her friend that she was okay, she was still Nic, she was still her best friend, but she'd never gotten a laugh before, and she found herself caught up in the feeling.

"No, not to torture you—to enlighten you!" Mr. Hylan said, but his rich tenor was no match for the laughter that Nic had created.

AFTER CLASS, SHE stepped into the hall and almost bumped right into Lucas Holt.

"Hey," he said. "You're back." He didn't seem startled to see her. In fact, if she didn't know better, she might have thought he was waiting for her.

"Hey," she said. When Lucas took a step back as though to let her pass, she slung her backpack onto her shoulder and started down the hall. To her surprise, he fell into step beside her.

"How are you feeling?" he asked. "I heard you were in the hospital last week."

"Oh. Yeah, but I'm fine. It wasn't that big of a deal."

"That's not what I heard. I heard you were in a coma. But I'm also learning that the Kirke grapevine has a way of exaggerating things."

"Well . . ."

Lucas put his hand on Nic's arm, stopping her. His eyes searched her face, his expression sharper now, newly alert. "Seriously? It's true? You tried to jump your horse over some huge wall or something?"

How could he possibly know this? How did anyone at Kirke? Lila, she supposed. But how many people at the school even knew who Nic was? She guessed a coma story was dark enough to spread quickly even if the key player was an unknown freshman.

"I don't remember what happened. The owner of the barn found me out in the woods after my horse turned up at the barn without me. I was lying near a tree that had fallen across the riding path, so yeah, I guess I tried to jump it."

"Holy shit." Lucas studied her, impressed.

Something within Nic leapt to life, a flame lit. This was who she could be, if she wanted: someone surprising. Nic realized why Lucas's expression seemed familiar: she'd seen it on the faces of people speaking to her mother.

"Holt!" The crowd in the hall swiftly parted to reveal Hunter Nolan, the boy Nic thought of as Angel Bully, striding toward them. His blond curls bounced slightly with each step; his skin was creamy and unflawed. Simon Pinelli trailed after him. Still halfway down the hall, Angel Bully lifted a set of keys over his head and jangled them. "Holt! You want a ride?"

Lila had told Nic that Angel Bully's black Jeep Wrangler was always parked in the prime spot of the student lot. There were no assigned student parking spots at Kirke, but day after day no one but Angel Bully parked in the spot closest to the school.

"Sure," Lucas called. "I'll catch up with you in a minute."

"Cool," Angel Bully said. "You know where to find me." He eyed Nic as though trying to place her. When he turned away, he bumped into one of Nic's classmates, a quiet boy named Jack, who just that morning had given Nic a pencil when she couldn't find her own. Jack winced as Angel Bully's shoulder collided with his ear.

"Nice shirt," barked Angel Bully, plucking at Jack's white polo.

The sight of Jack's stricken, reddening face made Nic so angry that her fingers began to shake. She almost said something—the word "jerk" was sour on her tongue, begging to be spit out—but she stopped herself. Would saying something make Jack feel better? Unlikely. Would it shame Angel Bully? She doubted it. She'd do something, she decided, but not now. Angel Bully's behavior had always bothered her, but in this moment it made her furious.

Abruptly, she turned away from Lucas and pushed the front door of the school so hard that it flew open. Lucas followed. Outside, Roy leaned against the hood of his black sedan on the far side of the circular driveway. He broke into a smile and waved when he saw Nic. She waved back.

"Who is that?" Lucas asked.

"Our driver, Roy."

"Oh," said Lucas, squinting at Roy. "Cool. Are you heading home already?"

Was that disappointment in his voice? "I'm going to the barn. My doctor said I'm not allowed to ride, so I'll just visit with my horse. I haven't seen him since the accident."

"Is he okay?"

"I think so. I'll know more once I see him."

"Will you let me know?" Lucas asked. "Tomorrow?"

Nic nodded, baffled and flattered by his interest. She wondered how Jasmine Cane would feel if she saw them talking.

"Cool," Lucas said again. He had a smile that did not linger—it flashed and then was gone, leaving Nic unsure if it had really been there at all. "See you later."

Nic jogged toward the car, her yellow dress swishing lightly against her bare legs.

DENNY WAS WAITING for her as she walked up to the barn from Roy's car. Bear sat beside him, panting and beating the ground with his tail as Nic approached. Denny hugged her. He smelled like a horse. He let go pretty quickly and she wasn't sure if it was because he wasn't much of a hugger or he was worried that she was still in pain from the fall.

"I'm fine," she told him preemptively.

"Good," he said. He cleared his throat. "Don't scare me like that again, kid."

It was hard for her to imagine Denny being scared. She might, she realized, be alive because of him. "Thanks for finding me out there," she said, glancing over her shoulder toward the dark line of woods that ran along the far edge of the paddocks.

Denny followed her gaze and was quiet for a moment. "You don't have anything to thank me for, but I sure am glad to see you."

She thought he might ask her why she'd done it, but he didn't. Maybe her mother had already told him that she still didn't remember riding that day. He stuffed his hands into the pockets of his jeans and leaned back on his heels. "Come on, I'll take you to see Tru."

She smiled. "I think I can find him."

"I know you can, but I'm not letting you out of my sight." He gestured toward the barn's open door. "After you."

Nic rolled her eyes. She didn't like feeling irritated with Denny, but she didn't need a babysitter *here*, too—her mother had already told her that her old babysitter, Irene, would be waiting for her when Roy dropped her off at home.

"I'm not going to ride," she muttered, stepping into the barn aisle.

"Nope," he said. "You're not." Denny walked a few steps behind her, his boots loud against the stone floor.

Tru heard them approaching and swung his head over his stall door, and Nic jogged the last few steps to him. His eyes were bright and shiny and his dark coat gleamed. Denny had taken good care of him. Nic breathed out, relieved. How would she ever have forgiven herself if he'd been injured by what she'd asked him to do?

"Hi, Tru," she murmured. She pulled an apple from her bag and he chomped through half of it in one bite. She massaged the star on his forehead as he chewed. She ran her hands over his velvety ears and soft muzzle, feeling his whiskers move with each bite. When she turned, she noticed a sign handwritten in red hanging on the stall across the aisle from Tru's.

DO NOT OPEN DOOR!

Nic recognized Denny's handwriting from the monthly board bills he left in her tack trunk each month. Peach's black eye glared at her from between the stall bars above the sign. She kicked a hoof against the wall and the sound echoed through the barn.

"What did she do this time?" Nic asked Denny. He was leaning against the wall of the aisle. Bear looked up at her from where he lay at Denny's side.

"Bit Javi when he was turning her out. Spun around out in the field and took a chunk out of his stomach. He wound up with stitches and a tetanus shot. I've been taking too many people to the hospital lately." He sighed. "She's a beautiful mare, but she's not long for this stable if she can't learn to trust us. I don't want anyone else getting hurt around here."

It made Nic sad to think of what might become of Georgia Peach now. Her reddish brown mane was a blur caught in glimpses through the stall door. Even the sound of her hooves moving through the straw bedding seemed to resonate with anger. Nic thought of how angry she'd been when Dr. Feldman and her mother had told her she couldn't ride. The way she felt when she watched Angel Bully swagger through the halls of Kirke.

Tru nudged her shoulder, looking for another apple. She moved to slide his door open, thinking she'd groom him.

"Hey now," Denny warned.

She looked at him. "Are you serious?"

"It's safer this way. Your mom and I agree on this. You stay in the aisle; Tru stays in his stall. You can spend all the time you want with him, but there's going to be a door between you."

"That's crazy! What could possibly happen to me in Tru's stall?"

"This is my barn, Nic." Denny's voice had taken on the testy edge that she'd heard him use with other kids, but never her.

There would be no convincing him to change his mind; he was as stubborn as her mother. Worse! At least her mother had a soft spot when it came to Nic's happiness. "Fine," she muttered.

Tru moved back to his flake of hay. Nic hung her arms over the stall door, rested her chin on her hands, and watched him. He seemed to be moving well. He didn't have a single cut. She looked back over her shoulder. Peach shifted back and forth, her black eyes glittering.

"Do you think she'll ever let you ride her?" Nic asked Denny, nodding her head toward Peach.

"Hard to say." He thought for a moment. "But I don't think so. She's eating pretty well and she's gained some weight. Her coat is in good shape now even if she hardly lets me groom her. She must know we're trying to take care of her, but she still doesn't trust anyone."

"Someone hurt her."

He nodded. "I'm guessing Peach was always hotheaded and wound up in the hands of someone with a temper to match. She has a scar on her face from someone jerking a chain across her nose. And more lines on her shoulders from something—maybe a whip, maybe worse. I guess none of that worked the way her owner hoped, though . . . Peach came to us so skinny that I'd say at some point he just started trying to starve her into submission."

Nic winced. She stared at the huge horse shifting and pawing in the stall across the aisle. The scars weren't visible from where she stood, only a big, pissed-off horse with a lot of straw stuck in her mane. "You can't just quit on her."

Denny's jaw tightened. "Believe me, that's the last thing I want to do. But this is a boarding and training facility. I can't have a horse here that might injure other people's horses or the people that work for me . . . or a kid who's here for a lesson."

Nic turned back toward Tru's stall so that Denny wouldn't see the hot, angry tears that suddenly welled in her eyes. She thought of all the years she'd spent watching Denny work with horses, caring for them and riding them. She'd always been amazed that someone so short with people could be so soft with animals. She'd always hoped that someday she would know as much about horses as he did. But now he was giving up on the one horse that needed him more than any other Nic had ever seen him bring to Corcoran Stables.

"And what kind of life will she have if she stays?" Denny said. "I have to think of that, too. Cooped up in that stall because we don't trust her to be turned out with the others. Always by herself. Horses aren't meant to live like that. No one is."

"So you're just going to get rid of her? All because she doesn't behave the way you want her to?"

"Listen—"

"No," Nic interrupted. Tru snapped his head up from the flake of hay he was working on, and eyed her, worried. Nic reached out to him and murmured quietly that she was sorry. She just didn't feel like hearing any more about how hard it was to keep a horse that didn't play well with others. "Are you going to stand there watching me the whole time?" she asked Denny without turning around.

"I'm not sure yet."

A few minutes later, the phone rang in the office. Nic could feel Denny's hesitation. "I'm not going anywhere," she said, without looking away from Tru.

"Stay out of Tru's stall. I mean it."

Nic turned and snapped her hand off her forehead in salute. She'd never done this before.

Denny's eyebrows knit together. The phone kept ringing. He narrowed his eyes at Nic one last time and then strode off, boots echoing as he walked the length of the aisle and stepped into the office.

There was no one else around. Tru pulled mouthfuls of hay from his flake and chewed peacefully. Nic, as though drawn to her, peered toward Peach's stall. The horse had not stopped moving since Nic had arrived; she seemed agitated by the girl's presence.

Nic took a second apple from her bag and crossed the aisle. She opened Peach's stall door just wide enough to slip inside. Peach was a few hands taller than Tru, but it was her expression as much as her size that gave Nic the impression that the horse towered over her. Tru had a soft, honest eye, but this horse's eye was hard, a glint of danger in the shadowy stall. Peach breathed quickly, smelling the apple. Nic's head thrummed.

And then a strange thing happened. The sounds of the barn—the horses eating and shifting and breathing all around them—fell away, and it was just the two of them.

Nic held out the apple. Peach watched her. The horse drew up her head and flared her nostrils, huffing out hot bursts of air. Nic thought Peach was just about to step forward and take the apple when they heard the sound of laughter. She glanced through the bars of the stall to see if someone was coming, and in that instant Peach flattened her ears against her head and came at her, teeth first. Nic stumbled backwards and felt the wind knock out of her as her shoulder slammed into the stall door. Her knees buckled and she fell to the ground, the apple dropping from her hand into the straw bedding.

Peach swayed above her, breathing hard. Nic's heart hammered in her chest. She could feel the heat that poured off the horse. She saw the fear in the horse's eye and tasted it in her own mouth.

Nic knew fear. She knew that fear became a mask you could not remove. Below the horse's fear, below Nic's own fear, there was something else waiting to be discovered.

Nic slowly stood.

Peach watched her, chest heaving.

"I see you," Nic said. She used her voice in the same way that she held bridle reins: light and sure. Medicine hidden in honey. She heard the softness and the strength in her voice, and the horse heard it, too.

Peach lowered her head to the ground and found the apple. She bit into it, watching Nic.

And then there were footsteps outside the stall, two sets of them, and voices. Nic pressed herself against the wall where she would not be seen. Peach moved toward the stall door and looked out into the aisle, her teeth grinding through the last bite of apple.

"That horse isn't right in the head," said one of the voices. It was Javi, the barn hand that Peach had bitten during turnout. Javi was great with the horses, beloved by their owners, and it had always seemed to Nic that he had a special affection for the least favored horses at Corcoran Stables. It was strange to hear him speak so negatively, so decisively, about Peach. She heard him take a step closer to the stall. Peach stretched her neck and snapped her teeth together, making contact with the bars on the stall door. Nic sucked in her breath.

"Jesus!" Javi cried.

There was a loud guffaw. It was Pat, another barn worker. "Damn, Javi," he said. "She's got your number."

"Not for long, she doesn't," Javi said. Now he sounded sad. "Someone pushed that horse too far and she's never coming back."

Their steps retreated and faded away as they continued down the aisle. Nic knew Javi was wrong about Peach; the horse was not made of anything worse than fear. She wished that she could put her hands on Peach so that she could massage the tension from her powerful neck and pull the straw from her mane, but she knew the horse wouldn't allow it. Still, she made Peach a silent promise of help, and in return the horse turned a cold eye on her, ears flattened.

"Hey," Nic whispered. "That won't work with me again."

It was true; she wasn't afraid of Peach. At least, not much. Was it because of the accident? Because she'd hit her head? Was there something wrong with her? Nothing *felt* wrong. She felt like she'd been carrying a weight for years, and now it was gone. She grew tall. "Make room," she told Peach. "There's only one way out." She made a slow shooing motion with her hands and clucked her tongue and Peach tossed her head defiantly but backed away from the door. Nic slid it open and stepped into the aisle.

She was standing in front of Tru's stall, rubbing her sore shoulder and entertaining secret plans, when Denny returned from the office. He seemed distracted, maybe even amused; he didn't say a word when Nic momentarily forgot herself and kicked a clump of straw from the bottom of her sneaker.

Chapter 9

The first thing on my agenda when I returned to the studio Monday afternoon was a meeting that I'd arranged with Hawke Media's head of security, director of Information Technology, and Simone and Martin. There weren't enough seats in my office for everyone, so Martin stood by the window and Adam, the security guy, crossed his arms and leaned against the back wall. Simone and Rebecca from IT sat in the pair of armchairs that faced my desk.

The lowering sun reflected off the windows of the building across the street at a blinding angle, so I lowered the shades as I hurried through a couple of answers to questions about Nic's health. Over and over again, I had to stop my mind from returning to the sight of Nic appearing in the kitchen wearing the yellow dress that I'd bought her for her birthday, looking as bright and shiny as a new penny. I was certain that if I lingered too long on thoughts about my daughter I'd end up running from the building, hailing a cab, and racing down to Corcoran Stables to stop Nic's fragile, perfectly imperfect brain from getting anywhere near a horse.

Instead, I leaned my elbows on my desk and said, "I think I have a stalker."

Rebecca immediately straightened in her chair. "I scan your in-box daily," she said. "I'd say you have fifty stalkers, minimum. More during the holidays."

"The holidays are particularly hard on stalkers," chimed in Adam from security. I could see that he was excited to have been included in the meeting; there was a vein in his neck that appeared intent on breaking free of his skin.

Martin, ever delighted by the effect that crazed fans had on ratings, failed to stifle a grin. When he realized I was watching, he lifted his fist to his mouth and tried to mask his joy with a spectacularly fake sneeze.

"Allergies," he murmured. "My apologies."

I chucked a box of tissues at him, certain that his reflexes would be dulled by his glee at Rebecca's stalker news. (Fifty stalkers! Jesus. I knew there was a good reason why I hardly ever checked my fan email account.) The tissue box thudded against Martin's shoulder and fell to the ground.

"I know that *some* of us believe that stalkers make excellent listener bait," I said, "but I think there might be one in the mix who needs to be taken more seriously." I reminded them of the call we'd received during the show the previous week, and told them about the heavy-breathing phone call to my home line and the email with the unnervingly similar threat that had been sent to my personal email account. "It's not much to go on, but it could be the same person. If it is, I'd prefer we get a handle on the situation sooner rather than later."

Adam was vigorously nodding. "I'm with you one hundred percent, Ms. Gideon. The best defense is a good offense."

"That's not the saying," Simone said.

Adam ignored her. "We can beef up security at the building, but I also want to be out there catching this guy." He knocked Rebecca's chair with his foot. She turned to look at him, startled. "Any leads from IT? We need to work together on this."

"Leads?" she sputtered. "I was sitting right here in this office with you when we learned of this guy's existence thirty seconds ago."

Adam released a disdainful scoff, as though this were no excuse, and began to pace the length of my office.

"*Woman's* existence," said Simone.

Everyone looked at her.

"That caller last week sounded like a woman," she said. "But who knows. There are devices you can use to change the sound of your voice. There's even an app you can buy for a cell phone." It seemed to me that Simone was the only one in the room who was truly worried.

"So it could be anyone!" Martin said. He quickly spread a tissue across the lower half of his face—but not quickly enough to mask his grin. "Achoo!" he said. When he lowered the tissue, he looked thoughtful, and a little disappointed. "Or maybe it's just Jenny Long again?" Martin held Jenny Long in great contempt; a woman too crazy to hide her crazy long enough to make it on air could never be a boost for ratings.

"Who knows?" I said. "But I don't think so. This person hates me. Jenny was a 'stan.' "

"A 'stan'?" asked Rebecca.

"Short for 'stalker-slash-fan,' " explained Adam, still pacing. "This new asshole isn't a true stan because he isn't a *fan*. He's just an old-fashioned *stalker*." He shook his head in disgust.

"Do you still have that email?" Rebecca asked me. "I should be able to trace it to an IP address. We can give that information to the police."

"And me," Adam said.

Rebecca rolled her eyes. "What do you plan to do with an IP address, Adam?"

Before he could answer, I told Rebecca that I'd already deleted the email and blocked the sender from contacting me again.

She shrugged. "Send me your log-in information for your personal email account anyway. I'll get to the bottom of it."

"Good," I said. "Threats come with the territory—I know that by now. I simply prefer *empty* threats. Let's all just go about our business on a slightly elevated level of alert." I sighed. "Adam, *please* quit pacing." He stopped abruptly, military style, and turned on his heel.

"What about when you're at home?" he asked. "You should think about having security there, too. For you and your daughter. If this person has your home phone number, he or she probably knows where you live."

I considered this. Over the years, many people in my life had suggested I hire a bodyguard, or at minimum a security guard for our home. I had always resisted taking their advice. Even though I was a household name, I wasn't a household face. I believed this protected me. I wasn't regularly recognized and stopped by fans on the street. I'd been interviewed on television and in magazines, but I wasn't a movie star. I was, mostly, a voice on the radio. Of course, all of this would change if I accepted the offer from ZoneTV, but until we crossed that bridge I wanted my daughter to continue to live a normal life. Nic—or at least the old Nic—would be mortified to have a bodyguard shadowing her every move. Did I really want to let one mouth breather scare me so badly that I turned our lives upside down? And the person who had called my home had not actually said a word when I answered the phone—he or she might not have anything to do with the person who had emailed me and called during the show. And even if they *were* all the same person, she could live across the country for all I knew.

"Let's hold off on that," I told Adam.

I hoped I wouldn't regret the decision.

After the meeting, I called Corcoran Stables. The phone rang eleven times before Denny picked up. *Eleven times.* I could have boiled an egg faster than the time it took that man to answer the phone.

"Corcoran Sta—"

"Is Nic there? How does she seem?"

"Oh, hey, G.G.," Denny answered. "Sure, she's here. She seems fine."

The knot in my chest loosened.

"Actually," Denny said, "I'd say she's better than that. She seems strong. Surprisingly strong, given how serious that fall was."

I leaned back in my desk chair. "She's desperate to ride."

"Yeah, she's made that pretty clear. But for now she needs to take it easy. She'll ride again, just not yet."

I mumbled some agreement, but the truth was that I could not imagine allowing Nic back on a horse.

"You're doing the right thing by letting her visit Tru," Denny said. "It's good for her to be around horses. She could be spooked by the accident, but instead she's itching to ride again. That's a brave kid."

"She's working every angle to get herself back in the saddle. On the way to school this morning, she announced that she'd spent an hour online yesterday researching the therapeutic benefits of horseback riding for patients with traumatic brain injuries. She wasn't even supposed to be on the computer."

Denny's laugh was a low rumble of a sound, truck tires over gravel. "She's always been stubborn, in her own way. I remember a few years ago, back before she got Tru, when she was riding one of our lesson horses, George, who absolutely refused to do a flying lead change." He paused. "A flying lead change is when a horse does a midair change of the leg that's leading his canter gait, switching from left to right, or vice versa."

"Oh. Right," I said. I was glad for the reminder. The afternoons when I'd ridden horses at Corcoran Stables felt like a lifetime ago.

"Well, George just refused. Some horses never learn how to do it under saddle. If you wanted him to change leads you had to bring him back down to the trot and then back up into the canter again on the correct lead. But Nic got it into her head that he was perfectly athletic and smart enough to master the flying change. She kept asking to ride him, and I'd see her out there in the ring day after day after day working that horse through his gaits. She'd even ride him bareback, thinking he might come to understand what she was asking if he could feel more of her legs and seat. She must have been, what? Ten, eleven years old."

The name George rang a distant bell, but I couldn't remember Nic telling me this story. Still, I could picture the scene as clearly as though I'd seen it with my own eyes: stone-faced Nic, long hair whipping the air behind her, skinny legs wrapped around the barrel of a horse, a blur of sky behind them. My heart thudded with pride.

"Did she get him to do it?" I asked.

"Of course. It took some time, but your girl was bound and determined and she taught old George a new trick. He's been one of our most popular lesson horses ever since. 'Point-and-Shoot,' the kids call him now, which basically means that he's very easy to ride. All thanks to Nic. So I'd say that stubborn streak you're talking about? It's not so new."

It had never really occurred to me that after all these years, Denny knew my daughter well. But of course he did. He'd watched her grow up.

"I guess she's just been stealthily stubborn until now," I said.

"Are you really surprised? The apple doesn't fall too far from the tree, does it?" I could hear the smile in his voice. "You used to butt heads with my mom every single week about which horse she put you on for your lesson."

"For good reason! She always put me on the ponies."

"You were so tiny, G.G. Those ponies were the right fit for you."

"But I wanted to go fast, really fast, and those ponies . . ." I trailed off, hearing myself. "Oh God. Your mom was totally right."

"You felt the need for speed . . . and my mom felt the need to see you live another day."

I shook my head, laughing. "I can't believe you remember that."

"I also remember that you used to groom your horse with your Walkman on your hip, Patti Smith blaring through your headphones. You never realized how loudly you sang along with her. Or maybe you didn't care."

"Oh, your mom must have loved that," I said. A memory flashed through my mind of Denny's salty, no-nonsense mother asking my mom if I was ever quiet, and my mom answering with a rueful *no*. My mother liked to say that someone must have been looking out for her when she wasn't able to have another child—as it turned out, one was plenty.

"I think she knew she wasn't going to have to put up with you for long," Denny said. "A thirteen-year-old who belts out something about how the night belongs to lovers while she's brushing a pony's forelock doesn't really scream 'lifelong rider.'"

I laughed. Thirteen. I'd dropped out of riding lessons entirely soon after that, devoting my afternoons to hanging out with boys, talking with friends about boys, thinking about boys. Boys, boys, boys. And music, of course. Always music. My life had a sound track back then, each important moment punctuated, molded, celebrated by song. It felt good to be reminded of the girl I'd once been. For the first time since I'd learned that Nic had been in an accident, I felt relaxed.

I wasn't sure that Denny and I had ever had such a long conversation before. He'd always struck me as sort of gruff, but on the phone he was straightforward and funny. And he remembered a lot about me. That was another surprise. A lot of my listeners believed that they knew me, really knew me, just from hearing me talk on my show, but this was different. Denny had known me when we were young. I'd known him, too, of course, but I suddenly realized how *little* I'd known him. I'd hardly noticed him back then—he was only a year or two younger than me, but those years mean something when you're a kid.

I tried to dig up some long buried memory of Denny back then, but found nothing. "How are your parents?" I asked instead. They'd retired years ago to property that they owned in Idaho, leaving the Pacifica stable to Denny.

"They're doing well. Still riding every day."

"Tell them I say hello."

"I will." That smile was back in his voice. I had the sense that he was imagining the face his mother would pull when she heard my name.

"Well," I said. "I should let you go."

"Yeah, okay. All is well here. Try not to worry."

"I'm a mother, Denny. I *run* on worry. And coffee."

"And music, if memory stands."

I smiled. "Yes."

"Alright then. Goodbye for now. If I were a betting man, I'd say I'll be hearing from you again around this time tomorrow." He was teasing, but the warmth in his voice kept me from minding. He'd called me twice after Nic left the hospital to check on her, after all. He was no stranger to worry.

"As long as Nic is stuck on Corcoran Stables," I told him, "you are stuck with me."

"YOU'RE ON AIR with Gail Gideon. Tell me everything, starting with your name."

"Oh my God, I can't believe I'm actually speaking to you, G.G.! I must have called a million times!"

"Millionth time's a charm. What's your name?"

"Right, right," the caller said, laughing. "I'm Paulina."

"Hey, Paulina. What's going on?"

Paulina and her boyfriend had been dating for four years, and what had once been a passionate love affair had fizzled into a roommate situation . . . for Paulina. The boyfriend, apparently, still felt the heat.

"I think he's going to ask me to marry him," she said. She wanted me to tell her if she should say yes. She still loved him, but her feelings had mellowed. Was that normal or a bad sign?

"Here's my gut feeling," I said. "I think you're calling me because you think, mistakenly, that I'm anti-marriage." From the engineering booth, Simone looked at me, curious. She was my best listener, really. In a lot of ways, I was always just chatting with Simone. "I don't know where people got this idea. I'm not anti-marriage; I'm anti-*bad*-marriage. Marriage that makes you someone that you're not.

"But you think I'm going to tell you not to marry this guy, don't you? And since you've called me one million times, waiting for the chance to hear me tell you *not* to marry this guy, to give you permission to say no, then I don't think you actually need my advice at all. I think your actions—calling me over and over again, trying to get through—tell you everything. Do you see what I mean, Paulina?"

"Right," she answered slowly. "Riiiiiiiight." She began to cry. "I can't marry him. I can't."

"Listen, we all *know* what we want. That's the crazy thing . . . we all already know. Don't ask *me* what you want, ask *yourself* what you want. The ultimate power is learning how to listen to *you*. And then of course you have to have the guts to do whatever it is that you really want to do. What's stopping you? What's scaring you?"

"I don't know. I guess . . . I don't want to be alone."

"Hell no you don't!" I felt warmed up now, the creaks from being away from the show for six nights worked out of my system. I leaned into the mic. "It took guts to admit that, Paulina. Sometimes, being alone sucks. But if the alternative is forcing a relationship that doesn't make you happy, then that sucks, too. Sometimes I wonder if choosing to be alone instead of choosing an unfulfilling relationship is one of the bravest things we can do with our lives. It's not an easy choice."

I thought of Tyler choosing to leave me. It would be so much easier to hate him, but I never would. It was torturous to care for that man the way that I did, to even, in some small way, *admire* him for leaving me.

"When I need help feeling brave, I listen to music. I'd play you something right now if I could. A song that would make you jump around. A song that would slide onto your skin like armor and pour into your veins like liquid steel. Then, once you were ready for battle, I'd tell you to ask *yourself* what you want. I'd tell you to own the decision. It's yours to make. You're ready.

"Ah!" I said abruptly. "I just thought of it. The song you need. 'Nowhere to Run' by Martha and the Vandellas. Do you know that song, Paulina?"

"No," she said. "I'm not really into music."

I smiled. "Paulina," I said, laying the rasp on thick. "You are one serious straight shooter. Never have I ever had a caller blow so little smoke at me. No music for you. Got it. There's something else, then. I know there is. What do you do when you need a shot of courage?"

Paulina laughed. "I listen to you, G.G.!"

In the booth, Simone grinned at me. If you were lucky, you found something to help you through the rough patches in life. For Simone, it was radio. For me, it was music. For Nic, it was horses. For this woman, Paulina, it was *me.* I was deeply aware that this was an honor, and I did not want to let her, or any of my listeners, down. Still, throughout the show that night I kept returning to thoughts of the girl that Denny had reminded me I had been; a girl who never stopped listening to music, a girl who craved more horse, more speed, more everything.

Chapter 10

On Tuesday, Mr. Hylan asked the class to break into groups of four to practice presenting the Shakespeare monologues he had assigned them. "I don't want to add any undue pressure," he intoned, "but you should know that I have a surprise up my sleeve that will make the day of your final performances even more exciting. Let's just say, preparation is your friend, my friends."

Nic and Lila paired up and then Jack Myeong asked if he and Noah Clarke could join their group. The rest of the class had already gathered into foursomes.

Lila looked at the boys and, with a smile that only Nic could have identified as sarcastic, said, "Excellent. We're the Dream Team."

Mr. Hylan sent each group to a different location on campus where they could practice without disturbing other classes. Nic's group was assigned the front steps of the school.

"I'll be coming around to check on you," Mr. Hylan said. "So do not 'wear out thy youth with *shapeless idleness*.'" He delivered this last line in his serious Shakespearean actor voice, hands lifted dramatically skyward.

"That poor man," said Lila, shaking her head.

They sat on the front steps and one by one read the monologue that Mr. Hylan had assigned them. Lila volunteered to go first. She stood and easily recited one of Puck's monologues from *A Midsummer Night's Dream*. What she lacked in theatrical talent, she made up for in sheer speed.

"You have it memorized," Jack said when she'd finished. "I don't have mine memorized yet."

"I don't either," Nic assured him.

"I think it was really good," Noah began quietly, "but maybe you could just, you know . . . slow down a little. If you want."

Nic smiled. Suggesting Lila slow down was like suggesting an earthquake stop shaking your house.

"I'll go next," Nic said. She pulled the printout of her monologue from her backpack. She'd been assigned one of Juliet's monologues from *Romeo and Juliet*. In a flash, she thought of herself stuttering in front of Lucas and her pulse momentarily quickened. But that wasn't going to happen again! She reminded herself that she had tried to jump Tru over a fallen tree. She couldn't envision it—when she tried, the girl riding Tru was just a blur. But it *had* been her. Nicola Clement. And if she had done that, surely she could read a few lines of Shakespeare out loud. Besides, only Lila and Jack and Noah were present. Why should she be nervous?

She took a deep breath and read her lines easily. When she was finished, Lila clapped.

"That was so good!" Lila said. Nic heard the surprise in her friend's voice, and she didn't blame her for it. Nic was surprised herself.

"I have no critique," said Jack. "It was perfect."

"Ditto," Noah said. "Great job. Except, you know, you need to memorize it."

"But you still have lots of time," Lila said.

Nic grinned. She was relieved to be done, but more than that she felt as though she'd achieved something.

"I'll go next," Noah said reluctantly. He spent several long minutes digging through his backpack. Nic and Lila exchanged a glance. Finally, he looked up from his bag. His cheeks were burning pink. "Someone stole my monologue."

"Noah," Nic said softly. She understood how he felt. She'd gone to bizarre lengths to avoid public speaking herself, once making herself so sick with worry that she'd literally thrown up.

"No, seriously," he said. "It's that guy Hunter Nolan. He keeps stealing my homework." His voice dropped and he looked away. "I've seen him do it."

"Hunter Nolan is a senior," Lila said. "Why would he want a freshman's homework?"

"Oh, he doesn't really want it. He just does it for shits and giggles," Jack said. Nic noticed that Jack's skin, too, had become mottled. "I never leave my backpack in the halls anymore." He glanced at Noah. "You should use your locker."

Nic stared at Jack. "He's done this to you, too?" She didn't really need to ask. It was not hard for her to imagine Angel Bully stealing homework from the boys' bags.

"He does it to everyone," Noah answered for his friend. "All the freshmen guys. It's our warm welcome to Kirke." He barked out a short, bitter laugh.

Nic slammed her hand against the stone step.

The other three looked at her in surprise.

Her eyes smarted as pain shot from her hand up her arm.

Her head thrummed as though in answer to the pain in her palm.

"He shouldn't get away with that," she said, thinking, *And he won't.*

When the seniors arrived at Dr. Clay's Freshman Connection class, Lucas walked right up to Nic. "Hey," he said. "Should we go to our spot?"

Their "spot"? She looked up at him, blinking. "Sure," she said. She stuffed the handout Dr. Clay had given the class into her backpack and slung the bag onto her shoulder. "I just hope it's true that lightning doesn't strike the same place twice."

"Lightning?"

"Disaster," Nic said, walking with Lucas into the hall. "Our first meeting was a disaster. You must have thought I was . . ." She trailed off, not really interested in saying the rest of this sentence out loud. He must have thought she was completely off her rocker. She'd babbled about meatball subs and Tru and . . . oh God, had she mentioned her therapist? She had. And she'd stuttered over the word "predictable" so that she'd ended up barking the word "dick" at him about sixteen times. And then she'd sobbed and run away. All in all, she'd really put her craziest foot forward for the new guy, and yet here he was, offering her that flash of smile, the one that exposed his sharp canine teeth and made her want to run her fingers over his lips. They looked remarkably soft.

"I thought that you seemed the opposite of boring," Lucas said. They moved in a stream of freshman-senior buddy pairs that were headed toward the soccer field, but somehow Nic felt as though they were alone.

She had to remind herself not to stare at him. "I like your spin on it. I figured you thought I was weird."

"Oh, I do." Lucas rearranged his face so that he looked serious. "For the record, I think you're super weird." He said this as though it were a compliment.

Nic looked down, her mouth twisting into a smile.

They sat under the same tree they'd sat under a week earlier. The moat they'd dug in the grass with their fingers during that meeting was still there. Nic inched away from it, turning her body so that it ran alongside instead of between them.

"I've been avoiding the meatball sub," Lucas said. "Thanks for the tip."

"Beware the tacos, too. I think it might be the same meat."

"'Beware the tacos,'" he repeated. "Noted."

Nic felt him studying her. It didn't bother her. In fact, she liked it. Had anyone ever studied her before? She'd watched so many people . . . all that time, was it possible someone had been watching her, too, and she'd been too wrapped up in her own mind to notice?

"How's your horse?" he asked.

"He's okay. But there's this other horse at the barn who was abused before she came to Corcoran and I . . ." Nic stopped herself. Why was she telling him about Peach? She'd hardly spent any time with Lucas, but she realized that she felt oddly close to him. In a way, the fact that their first conversation had been a complete disaster almost put her at ease. He'd seen her at her worst and he seemed to like her anyway. Still, Nic felt it would be a betrayal to tell him about the promise she'd made to help Peach. If anyone found out that she'd gone into Peach's stall, she might not be able to do it again.

Lucas waited for her to say more.

Instead, Nic dug around in her backpack and pulled out the crumpled handout from Dr. Clay. "So, do you know about this list of questions we need to answer? Apparently, I'm supposed to find out at least one of your deepest, darkest secrets by the end of class today." She pretended to read from the paper. "'True or false: Lucas Holt's favorite TV show is *The Real Housewives of Atlanta.*'" Nic looked up and gave Lucas a questioning look.

He shook his head and laughed. "False."

She looked back down at the paper and pretended to continue reading. "'For fun, he enjoys baking oatmeal raisin cookies.'"

"Wrong again. Let me see that list." He reached out to take the paper from Nic, but she held onto it. Their eyes locked. Lucas's smile slowly spread. Nic let go of the paper.

To her surprise, Lucas began to ask her the actual questions that Dr. Clay had written. She answered mostly honestly, wondering if he knew that she was Gail Gideon's daughter and if because of this he already knew some of her answers. She told him about her family (parents divorced, two half-brothers), where she was born (San Francisco), her hobbies (riding), her favorite class (here she lied and said English, when as of that exact moment Freshman Connection had taken the lead), her favorite color (green).

"Like your eyes," Lucas said.

She nodded, flushing, and took the paper from him. "Your turn."

Lucas told her that his parents were in the process of getting a divorce. He and his mom and his two younger sisters had moved to the area from Brooklyn. Lucas's dad still lived in the house they'd all lived in together.

"My mom grew up here and always wanted to come back," he said. "She told my dad he could have the house if he let her take me and my little sisters to live in California. She was always yelling at him about how being his wife had made her lose track of who she really was, and the only way she'd be able to find herself again was if she went back home. Anyway, my dad jumped on the deal, and even sweetened it for my mom by pulling some strings to get me into Kirke. I think my mom is kind of in shock about it all now—it's like she got exactly what she thought she wanted, and now she's confused about how it happened. Our house in Brooklyn is worth a ton of money so basically my dad traded his family for a golden real estate ticket. And every day he gets up and brushes his teeth in the bathroom that he shared with my mom for like twenty years. He chose to stay in the place where his family imploded. How fucked up is that?"

Nic had not expected such an outpouring of information. The bitterness in Lucas's voice upset her. She wondered what she could share with him that might make him feel less alone.

"My mom and I still live in the house where we all lived together before my parents got divorced," she said.

Lucas stared at her. "Why?"

Nic could see the pain in his face. She had no idea why she and her mom had stayed in their house after her parents divorced—she'd never really thought about it before. She could hardly remember her dad in that house; maybe her mom didn't either. "I don't know," she admitted. She could not help but feel she was somehow failing Lucas with this answer.

"Maybe your mom wanted to stay because she didn't want you to feel like everything was changing . . . like your whole life was over," Lucas said, looking away. "Parents are always worried their kids are going to kill themselves."

"I was five," Nic said. She was pretty sure that her parents had never worried that she might kill herself, and she was now just as certain that Lucas's parents had. "I don't really remember my parents being together."

"Lucky you," Lucas said sharply.

Nic was quiet.

He ran his hand through his dark hair. Nic watched him take a deep breath. When he turned back to her, his eyes were softer. "Sorry," he said.

Nic looked down at the hand he'd put on top of hers. Her pulse jumped below his touch.

Inside, the buzzer announced the end of class.

"There are three more questions," Nic said.

"I guess some of my secrets will have to remain a mystery," Lucas answered, that flash of smile restored.

ON THE WAY to the barn, Nic asked Roy if they could stop at the supermarket so she could buy a bag of carrots for the horses. Inside, she found herself slowing to a stop in front of a small display of inexpensive children's toys.

Back in the car, she tossed a bag of pretzels to Roy.

"Find what you were looking for?" he asked, eying her in the rearview mirror.

She nodded, knowing that her smile could not possibly hint at her plan since she hardly knew it herself—it was vague still, a glimmer of sunlight behind slowly clearing fog.

In her bag was a Matchbox Jeep Wrangler, a miniature version of Angel Bully's car.

SHE FELT PEACH watching her from the moment she stepped into the aisle. The horse seemed less agitated today, and quietly followed Nic's movements with her eyes. Nic worried Denny would notice the horse's curiosity, but he didn't. She grabbed a soft brush from her tack trunk and silently brushed Tru's head from the aisle. As he had the day before, Denny leaned against the wall beside Tru's stall. Bear lay at his feet, breaking the quiet with his steady pant.

"You probably have a lot to do," Nic said.

"Nope," Denny answered.

Just when she was beginning to worry that her time at the barn would run out before she had a chance to sneak into Peach's stall again, the phone in the office rang. Denny straightened. Bear looked up at Denny and thumped his enormous tail against the stone floor. "Keep an eye on Nic," Denny told the dog. He gave Nic a stern look before setting off at a jog toward the office.

Nic studied Bear. Bear studied Nic. A long, skinny line of drool ran from his lip to the floor. Nic could not be entirely sure that the dog did not have a way to communicate with his master. Denny had a way with animals that at times seemed to border on mystical.

She decided to risk it.

With the leafy stalks of two carrots sticking out of the pocket of her jeans and the soft brush still in one hand, she slid open Peach's stall just wide enough to step inside. The horse flattened her ears and started to turn away. Nic realized she was about to get kicked.

"Peach," she said. "Look." She held out one of the carrots.

Peach stopped. Her ears flicked forward, her eyes suddenly less hard than bright. She snatched the carrot from Nic's hand and began to chew. As she ate, Nic took a step closer. Then she took another step. The horse watched as she approached, but other than her teeth grinding and her ears flicking, she didn't move. Nic felt sure that deep inside, Peach wanted her there, and had been waiting for her. There was something between them, a connection that Nic had never felt with another horse. She had needed horses before, to comfort her and distract her and sometimes challenge her—but this time, this horse needed *her*. Nic suspected that on some level Peach knew this.

She reached up and placed her outstretched hand on Peach's neck. She spoke gently, reassuringly, confidently all the while, and felt the horse listening. She began to move her hand down the horse's neck, stroking below her mane, lifting her hand before she reached the scars on Peach's shoulder. The horse relaxed below her touch, the taut, sensitive skin below her coat gradually softening.

"There you go," Nic murmured. She lifted the brush and began to use it instead of her hand, slowly brushing the length of Peach's body. She kept up a steady stream of murmured praise for the horse.

After a few moments, Peach sighed. *Okay*, the horse seemed to be saying.

"I won't let you down," Nic replied. But to do this, she knew, she had to ride her.

Suddenly, just outside of the stall: the sounds of Bear scrambling to his feet, barking, and setting chase after some unseen barn intruder—a bird or a squirrel or a mouse.

Peach startled. Then, in a flash, she reached back toward where Nic stood at her side and snatched the second carrot from Nic's pocket, her teeth striking Nic's hipbone.

Nic winced and stumbled away. From the office, she could hear Denny tell Bear to quiet down. She hurried from the stall, hip throbbing. When she stood again in front of Tru's stall, she turned back to look at Peach. The horse watched her between the bars. Denny was out of the office and in the aisle now. Nic willed away the tears that smarted her eyes.

I see you, she told the horse with her mind. She pressed her hand against the pain at her hip. *You didn't mean to hurt me.*

Chapter 11

On Wednesday morning, I tossed my phone into Nic's lap and started the car. She was supposed to be at school at nine and as usual we were running late. The battlefield that was San Francisco at rush hour waited for no one. I took a strange pleasure in navigating the predictable morning gridlock with Nic at my side; during those thirty to sixty minutes, Monday through Friday, our fates were intertwined.

"Find something that will appease the traffic gods," I said to Nic, nodding toward my phone.

She scrolled through my playlists, and before long, the car's speakers filled with the sound of Janis Joplin wailing about the pieces of her heart.

I grinned. "You know, this was playing in the hospital room when you were born."

"And when I woke up from the com . . . I mean the concussion," she answered, just managing to correct herself before she said "coma." She was working hard to use language that downplayed the seriousness of her accident in the hopes that I could be convinced to disregard Dr. Feldman's recommendation that she refrain from riding. Despite her bravura, I'd noticed that she winced as she walked down the stairs from her bedroom that morning. No matter what she said, her injuries—brain and otherwise—were not fully healed. She wasn't riding anytime soon.

"Right," I said. "Your *'concussion.'* The concussion that left you unconscious and in a *coma* for four hours and stole at least as many years from my life."

"Drama queen." I didn't have to look at Nic to know she was smiling.

"Head case," I shot back.

"Mom! I can't believe you're joking about my battered head."

"Oh, so *now* it's battered?"

Nic laughed. "No. It's not. I'm fine."

I shook my head but could not help laughing along with my daughter. How could I? There she was in the passenger seat of my car, wearing a bright red T-shirt that I hadn't even known she owned, laughing and healthy. I felt so lucky that she was there beside me, where I could reach out and squeeze her hand.

"Hands on the wheel, please, Mom."

I sighed and returned my hand to the wheel. I began to sing along with Janis. To my delight, Nic joined in.

After a moment, she stopped. I felt her eyes on the side of my face. "Do you ever miss playing music for people?" she asked.

I glanced at her. "What do you mean? I play music all the time."

"Not on the radio, though. Not the way you used to. You have such a cool music collection but no one ever gets to hear it."

"Oh. Well, first of all, thank you. Second, *I* hear it. *You* hear it. Simone and Damien and Rachel and Sam hear it when they come over. Roy hears it in the car, as much as he might wish he didn't."

Nic began braiding the dark hair that fell over her shoulder. She could do this practically in her sleep, her fingers nimble from hours spent plaiting Tru's coarse tail. "Yeah," she said, "but we're just a few people."

"You're the only ones who matter to me."

I felt Nic looking at me again. I considered telling her about the ZoneTV offer and how excited I was about the prospect of reshaping the career I'd carved out for myself, but something stopped me. She was in a good mood, and I suppose I didn't want to ruin the moment.

"Anyway," I said, "I haven't played music that I actually *like* on the radio in a billion years. Not since college."

"But you hosted that show when I was little. I remember. *Love Songs After Dark*."

"I didn't play any of the music I really like on that show. It was all cheesy love songs."

"But 'Piece of My Heart' is a love song."

"Well—"

"You once told me," Nic persisted, "that *all* songs were love songs."

"Did I? I don't remember that. Anyway, Hawke Media wouldn't agree."

"Oh." The Rolling Stones' "Sympathy for the Devil" was next on the playlist. Nic turned up the volume. "They don't know what they're missing!" she yelled over the music.

Nic sang along with Mick Jagger. I'd seen him perform the song live, slipping on the persona of the devil for the few minutes that the song lasted and then shedding the persona just as quickly as he moved on to "Brown Sugar" and "You Can't Always Get What You Want" and "Satisfaction."

I glanced at my daughter. Her eyes were bright, her hair loosening already from the hasty braid. She seemed happy. And a bit wild, too: hopeful and complicated and *teenaged.* I recognized myself in her. For a few minutes, I ignored the constant throb of my worry. I gave in to the music that filled the car, the drum that had always matched something deep inside of me beat for beat.

Who could resist being a devil for a moment or two? Not me.

She's right, I thought. *Hawke Media doesn't know what it's missing.*

WHEN I WAS young, I thought punk music was about being young. I thought it was about rebelling against everyone always telling you what to do (and *how* and *where* and *when* to do it). To me, being forced to follow other people's rules *was* childhood, so I guess it was only natural that I heard the rebellion in punk and rock and thought it was the domain of the young. Now, I knew better. Or, maybe, I continued to be every bit as self-centered as I was when I was young, and therefore I had to expand my interpretation of punk so that I could remain sure that those songs that I loved were still, in the end, about me.

Either way, after that conversation with Nic in the morning, I spent the rest of the day thinking that punk rock was actually about freedom. Freedom from expectations, freedom from the past, freedom from convention, freedom, yes, from the rules placed on us by others, but also freedom from ourselves, the freedom to shed the roles that we've adopted and that might no longer fit, the freedom and the fire to grow and change and, sometimes, break free.

The first thing I did after Roy dropped me off at Hawke Media that afternoon was shut the door to my office so I could blare Patti Smith's *Horses* album. Moments later, my agent's number appeared on my office telephone line, which I knew meant that she'd become serious about tracking me down.

"What in the hell?" she said when I picked up. "What is that god-awful noise?"

"That, Shayne, is music."

"Music, music, music . . ." she repeated slowly. "Ah, yes! I remember music. It used to be a moneymaker, didn't it? When was that? The nineties?"

I laughed despite myself; I had always found her very agentness endearing. Shayne somehow managed to poke fun at herself while completely embracing her own quirks. I could perfectly imagine her at eighty years old, making the same snarky jokes, having the same greedy impulses. If anyone could remain happily the same over the decades, it was my agent, the one and only Shayne Deacon.

"Is this," she asked, "the kind of music you can only listen to at an exceedingly high volume? Perhaps the nuances aren't discernible until the windows begin to rattle?"

"Yup," I said. Still, I pointed the remote at the stereo and turned Patti down a few notches.

Shayne asked how Nic was doing and I told her the truth: I wasn't sure.

"That's great," Shayne said. "Have you been thinking about the ZoneTV offer? You got my message that Simone is part of the deal now, right? She'll be a senior producer."

"Thanks for moving on that," I said. "But I'm not sure how interested Simone is after all. And . . . I don't know, Shayne. I need to make sure I make the right decision. Not just for me, but for Nic."

"How could this not be the right decision? Radio is a steppingstone to television! You're on an upward trajectory! If you think you make a difference in people's lives now, wait until you see your reach when you're on television. It's a whole other *galaxy* of influence. Hop on this ride, Geej. You won't regret it." I heard Shayne cover the phone and holler for her assistant. "What are your plans this weekend?" she asked me, her voice suddenly loud again in my ear. "Will Nic be with you?"

"No. It's her weekend with Tyler."

"Fantastic. Lev Curtain is going to be in San Francisco and he wants to meet you in person. Apparently he is really excited—I guess he's been a fan of yours for years. Your one male fan, Geej! You'll finally get to meet him!" Shayne barked out a laugh. "But seriously. What do you think? Can I give my assistant the go-ahead to make the arrangements?"

What else did I have planned that weekend? Nothing.

"Sure," I told Shayne. "Send me the details."

After we said goodbye, I turned up the music so loud that Martin eventually swung by my office and asked in his particular groveling, fake-apologetic way if I would turn it down.

DENNY PICKED UP the phone after a few rings.

"Nic's fine," he said.

I smiled. "Hello."

"I knew you'd want to know that before anything else."

"I appreciate it. Are you busy?"

"No."

He'd also said this when I called him the day before, and I didn't believe him then either. I'd been to the barn enough times to know that Denny Corcoran was always busy. No matter what I saw him doing—whether it was throwing down hay bales from the loft, or hosing off a horse in the wash stall, or standing in the center of the ring as a row of children on ponies circled him—I always had the sense that it was just one of hundreds of things that he would do that day. I was sure the enormity of the task of keeping a property like Corcoran Stables running was part of the reason Denny always seemed so brusque—he didn't have the time to use ten words when two would suffice. So when he told me he wasn't busy, I knew that he wasn't telling the truth, but I was glad. The other thing that I'd noticed about Denny was that no matter what he was doing, he seemed to center himself on that one thing, giving it his full attention. And if there's one thing I'd never shied from, it was attention.

As we had for the last couple of days, Denny and I spoke first of Nic, how she appeared stronger and more determined by the hour. She had a buzz of vitality about her now that made the memory of her lying in a hospital bed just one week earlier seem impossible, more like a scene that I'd pulled from a nightmare than something that had actually happened.

"I don't know if I ever really thanked you for finding Nic and making sure she got to the hospital quickly," I said to Denny. "When Tru came back to the barn without her, she might have been anywhere, but somehow you knew where to look."

"You don't have to thank me," he said. Then he added, "In fact, maybe I'd rather you don't. I think my chest is still bruised from the gratitude you pummeled me with in the hospital waiting room."

My laughter was sudden and surprised. "Sorry about that. Scared and angry are a dangerous combination for me." I was quiet for a moment. "But, really, how did you know to look for Nic out there? You told her not to ride on the trails. Doesn't she usually listen to you?"

"She does. She's a good kid . . ."

"But?"

"I don't know. There was something about the way she looked at me when I told her that the woods were a mess and I wanted her to stick to the ring. It wasn't as though I knew in that moment that she was going to ignore what I'd said . . . but when Tru came back without her, I started running right down into the woods."

I'd been returning, more and more lately, to my memory of the night before the accident, when I'd tucked Nic into bed and the look in her eyes had made me wonder what she was thinking about, and if she were planning something. The memory pained me now. "Did she seem upset when she got to the barn?" I asked Denny. "The way she looked at you when you told her to stay in the ring . . ."

"If you're asking if I think she had something on her mind when she went out into the woods, the answer is yes. But if you're asking if I think she meant to hurt herself . . . no, G.G. I can't possibly know that for sure, but my gut tells me that wasn't her intention."

I released a long breath I hadn't known I was holding. Then I groaned. "If she wasn't trying to hurt herself, then trying to jump that tree was just being stupid for the fun of it. I'm so angry with her, but it's hard to be mad at someone for something she doesn't even remember doing. She still doesn't remember riding that day."

"Maybe it's better this way," Denny said. "Sometimes anger gets you somewhere, and other times it just gets between you and where you need to go."

I opened my mouth to respond and then shut it, realizing I had nothing to say. I'd always attributed so much of my drive to the anger that I felt, but now I found myself wondering where I might end up if I truly let go of that anger once and for all. What if I stopped chasing some notion of proving my worth and instead simply followed my heart? What would come next? Where would I go? Who would I be?

AFTER THE SHOW that night, I pushed through the building's front doors and Roy immediately fell into step beside me on the sidewalk.

"I ordered a limo to take you home," he said, gesturing toward the black car idling by the curb.

I slowed and looked at him. "A limo? Why?"

He hesitated. "Someone smashed my headlights. But don't worry, I'll have them replaced by tomorrow. Jasper from Bay Limo is going to get you home tonight. He's a good guy. I've known him since—"

"Wait," I said, cutting him off. "Someone smashed your headlights while I was in the studio?"

"Yeah. I was waiting in Pinecrest Diner, having dinner like I always do while you're on air—great show tonight, by the way. When I got back to my car, the headlights were broken."

"Was anything stolen from the car?"

Roy shook his head.

There was no one else on the street with us. I looked up at the high-rise buildings that lined the sidewalk, the office lights that glowed in the gray night sky. Any number of people might have been looking down at us. I usually loved San Francisco at night, but suddenly I felt vulnerable.

"Don't worry about it, Ms. Gail," Roy said, reading my mood. "It's San Francisco. Stuff like this happens all the time. I'll have the car back to tip-top shape tomorrow."

"Do you think whoever did it knows that you're my driver?"

His brow furrowed. "I wouldn't worry, Ms. Gail. This was just some jerk. How could he know the car had any connection to you?"

I swallowed. "Remember Jenny Long? She saw us together. She'd know which car was yours."

"Jenny Long?" Roy asked. "She's back?" We simultaneously scanned the street around us.

"I don't know. Maybe." If Jenny Long was back and she'd been following Roy's car, then she knew not only my schedule, but Nic's, too. She knew the location of our home, Nic's school, Corcoran Stables.

The words of the email I'd received in the hospital flashed through my mind.

You mess with my life, I'll mess with yours.

Chapter 12

It seemed to Nic that her mother's knuckles gripped the wheel with increasing intensity on the Thursday morning drive to Kirke. Periodically, her mother would narrow her eyes and glance at the rearview mirror. She'd seemed out of sorts all morning—even her fight with the coffee machine had been louder and more profane than usual. And before they left the house, when Nic pointed out that her mother was still wearing pajamas, she'd distractedly thrown on her faux-leopard-fur jacket. Nic still remembered the afternoon several years earlier when her mother had found that jacket in a thrift store and had shrieked like someone who'd won the lottery. Her mother was probably richer than most, maybe all, of the Kirke moms, but with her vintage, tattered, rocker wardrobe, you'd never know it by looking at her. Right now, with that matted-fur jacket and her ever-present, never fully removed smudges of black eyeliner around her green eyes, she looked like a wild cat poised to strike its prey, all of her energy coiled into something small and tight and dangerous.

"What's going on?" Nic asked after her mother jerked the wheel and sped past a hefty black minivan.

Her mother looked over at her. Nic had the sense that she'd forgotten she was in the car. "Sorry," she said, shaking her head. "There's just . . ." She trailed off, thinking, and then tried again. "There's something going on at work right now."

"Aaand . . ." Nic prodded.

Her mom gave a little shrug, but Nic could tell that she was just trying to downplay her mood. "Honestly, it's a lot of stuff that you don't need to worry about, okay?" she said. But then, when they pulled to a stop in Kirke's circular drive, her mother leaned over and kissed her cheek and told her to be careful.

"Mom, it's been more than a week since the accident. I'm fine." Nic meant this, too. Even the headaches had, at last, faded, just as Nic had always believed they would.

"Right. Well. I don't just mean at the barn. At school, too. Don't wander off alone anywhere. Do a buddy system thing with Lila or someone."

Unlike her mother, Nic was in a *good* mood. She'd managed to sneak into Peach's stall again the day before, and the horse had stood still long enough to let Nic pull the straw from her chestnut mane. Sure, she'd tried once to nip Nic, but a few words from Nic had put an end to that behavior. Nic felt sure that they were getting somewhere. If Denny gave her another window of unsupervised time that afternoon, she planned to attempt to give Peach a proper grooming. So she was willing to indulge her mother's tendency to overprotect.

"Sure," she said. "If I slip into a coma in the computer lab, I'll make sure my buddy notifies you immediately."

This was the kind of joke at which her mother would typically laugh. Today she just sighed. Nic slid back into the car and wrapped her mother in a hug.

"Buck up," she said. "You'll figure out this work thing. You've been kicking ass your whole life; why stop now?"

She kissed her mother's cheek, nudged her chin upward with one finger so that her mother went from openmouthed surprise to closemouthed surprise, hopped out of the car, and strode toward Kirke's front door.

THAT AFTERNOON, NIC was washing her hands at a sink in the bathroom when she heard someone crying in one of the stalls. She hesitated, taking longer than usual to dry her hands. The crying continued.

"Is everything okay?" Nic called out finally.

After a few sniffles, a small voice answered. "No."

"What's wrong?" When the girl didn't respond, she asked, "Can I help?"

The stall door opened and Nic recognized the red-haired girl who emerged as a junior. She didn't know the girl's name, but she remembered that during Kirke's first monthly assembly of the year she had received a standing ovation for some achievement in swimming—the state championship, maybe?

The red-haired girl in the bathroom wiped at her eyes. "It's not a big deal."

Nic noticed that she was holding a phone. "Did you get bad news?" she asked.

That was all it took. Something in the girl broke; she released a shuddering sob and handed her phone to Nic.

On the screen was an Instagram post by *TheKirkeLurk7* showing a photograph of a girl swimming. The Lurk's caption: Proof that chlorine pickles the brain. Nic peered closer at the screen.

"That's you?"

The girl nodded. She took back her phone and stared at the

photograph. Her eyes were red-rimmed, her long eyelashes damp with tears. "I should be a senior," she said quietly. "I got held back."

"So you could swim?" Nic had heard they did this sometimes for guys who played football, but she'd never heard of swimmers taking an extra year.

The girl chewed on her lip. "No. Because they didn't think I was ready for senior year . . ." She hesitated. *"Academically."*

Proof that chlorine pickles the brain.

"Oh." Nic didn't know quite what to say after that. She felt a pang of empathy so sharp that it made her ribs hurt. "What's your name?"

"Bridget."

"I'm Nic."

The girl's eyes widened. "*You're* the coma girl?"

Nic started to say that it was really just a concussion, but changed her mind and instead nodded. Being known as the coma girl seemed a slight improvement over being known only as Gail Gideon's daughter. She was proud of her mother and her show, but Nic thought that maybe it wasn't so bad to be known for something she herself had done, even if it was that she had fallen off a horse and wound up in the hospital for a couple of days.

"Wow. Are you feeling alright now?" Bridget asked.

She seemed to truly want to know. This girl whose intelligence had just been publicly ridiculed was wondering how *Nic* was feeling. Bridget was sweet and sensitive and a champion athlete . . . what right did someone have to hide behind the internet and throw insults at her? She'd done nothing to deserve it.

"I feel great. Better than ever." Nic motioned toward the phone. "Listen, anyone who makes a comment like that obviously doesn't know you at all. Try not to let it bug you."

Bridget sniffed and nodded. "I know. It's just you wait and wait for the day that the Lurk says something about you, because you know that he will eventually . . . and then he does and you know everyone is out there in school reading it . . ." She pressed her lips together, unable to finish the thought.

There was a ball of rage gathering heat in Nic's stomach. "Not for much longer," she said.

"What do you mean? It's been going on for years. It's not going to stop."

"It will," Nic said again.

Bridget looked at her. "Maybe," she said, with a small shrug. Then she turned to her own reflection in the mirror and took a deep breath and shook out her arms the way that swimmers always seemed to do before a race. She appeared, if not fully recovered, at least a little less upset than she'd been when she'd first emerged crying from the stall.

As Nic followed Bridget out of the bathroom, she dug around in her bag until her hand closed around the Matchbox Jeep. She didn't know quite what she was going to do about the Lurk yet, but there was one plan that she *had* figured out.

NIC HAD BEEN keeping tabs on Angel Bully and knew that he never closed the lock on his locker (it seemed to Nic that that open lock was less a sign of a tight-knit community than a bully's perpetual taunt). During lunch, when the hall was empty, she opened his locker and pulled out his backpack. Moving quickly, she unzipped the bag and reached inside. She felt a wave of disgust that hit like nausea, as though she were feeling around inside of Angel Bully himself and not just his bag. The feeling disappeared the moment she found what she was looking for.

"What are you doing?"

Nic spun around. Lucas stood in front of her, his head cocked.

"I—I dropped something."

Lucas squinted at her. The way he blinked, languidly, made Nic want to stroke the curl of his eyelashes with her thumb. "In Nolan's backpack?"

Nic shrugged. "Busted." The truth was that she did not really care if Lucas knew what she was doing—as long as he didn't try to stop her. She reached into the pocket of her jeans and pulled out the Matchbox car.

Lucas took the toy from her, fingers grazing her palm. He turned the car over in his hand. "This was in Nolan's bag?"

"No." Nic held up her other hand, the one that held Angel Bully's car keys. "These were." Angel Bully's key chain held a small wooden charm with a turtle carved into it, the sort of thing you could pick up at the airport on the way home from a tropical vacation.

Lucas grinned. "What do you have in mind?" he asked.

They walked together to Angel Bully's car. It was parked, as always, in the first spot of the parking lot, the one marked with a big white number 1. They were within view of several classrooms; all any teacher had to do was look outside and they would see Nic and Lucas next to the Jeep.

"Do you want me to drive?" Lucas asked. It was a reasonable question. He had his license; Nic did not. She'd never driven before. Also, Lucas was ostensibly Angel Bully's friend; if they were caught, Lucas could say he had permission to drive the car.

Nic shook her head. She unlocked the car and slid into the driver's seat.

Lucas climbed into the passenger seat. They exchanged a half-giddy, half-nervous glance as they buckled their seat belts. "Have you ever driven before?" he asked.

"No, but how hard could it be? Angel Bully does it every day."

Lucas raised his eyebrows. "'Angel Bully'?"

Nic flushed, running her hand over her eyes. "Oh. Yeah. That's what I call Hunter. He looks like an angel, but . . ."

". . . he acts like a bully." Lucas laughed. The darkness that she sometimes saw in his gaze, weighing on his thoughts, melted away. It was the first time that Nic had heard actual joy in his laughter. "It's catchy. I like it."

Nic tapped the canvas roof with her fingers. "Should we take the top down?"

Lucas shot a nervous glance toward the school building. "That could take a while."

She smiled. "I'm kidding." She slid the key into the ignition, then hesitated, her hand frozen on the key chain's wooden turtle charm. For the first time since she'd devised this plan, she felt her confidence falter. She really had no idea what she was doing.

You'll be fine, said the voice in her head—her own voice. She realized she had not heard more than a peep from this voice in nearly a week.

She felt Lucas's hand on her shoulder. He pointed at the pedals at her feet. "Brake is on the left. Gas is on the right."

Nic swallowed. "Okay."

"Put your foot on the brake while you turn the key."

Nic followed his instructions, feeling her heart jump as a Taylor Swift song suddenly blared over the sound of the engine. Lucas turned the volume down but left the music on.

"Keep your foot on the brake and shift this gear into reverse," he said, patting the gearshift. "Then lift your foot off the break and slowly press the gas pedal."

Nic put the car in reverse, looked over her shoulder, lightly pressed the gas pedal, and inched the car out of the parking spot.

She realized that driving didn't feel entirely unfamiliar—the halting movement reminded her of backing up a horse.

"Okay," she told Lucas, putting her foot on the brake. "I need to get out for a second."

After he showed her how to shift the gear back to park, she opened the door and hopped out. In the now-empty parking space, right on top of the big white number 1, she placed the Matchbox car. When she got back in the Jeep, Lucas was smiling. She drove with increasing confidence down the school's long driveway. Driving felt very adult. She looked for the turn signal, couldn't find it, and turned anyway, out onto the road.

"You're a natural," Lucas said. Out of the corner of her eye, Nic could see that he gripped the door.

At the next intersection, she turned right for no other reason than that it seemed easier than turning left. It was a quiet road and she pulled onto the dirt shoulder, stopping the car alongside a thick green line of hedge. She turned off the ignition. Outside, glinting clouds of dust rose from the tires. She and Lucas looked at each other and grinned.

"Do you do this kind of thing a lot?" he asked.

She shook her head and laughed. "No."

"I don't believe you. That seems like an easy lie for a vigilante."

Vigilante. He had not asked why she was doing this, but he clearly understood. He approved. Perhaps she should have known this when he'd fallen into step beside her at school, but it was only now in the car with him that she felt he was participating not just for the fun of it, but for the reason behind the act, too.

He leaned his head against the seat and looked up at the soft roof of the car. "Nobody should get away with doing that much damage on a daily basis," he said, as though reading her thoughts.

"Right," Nic said. "And some other kids should have a shot at that prime parking spot."

Lucas rolled his head to the side to look at her. "Is there more up your sleeve?"

"Maybe. It depends how much it takes for Angel Bully to change his ways."

A car drove by and, as if they'd choreographed it, Nic and Lucas slid down in their seats. Maybe they would be like Bonnie and Clyde mixed with Robin Hood, Nic thought. It seemed more fun to do this kind of thing with a partner. Lila wouldn't have had the stomach for it (she was already worrying about her college applications), but Lucas, clearly, did.

They were still low in their seats when Lucas said, "So is your mom letting you ride yet? You sure seem of sound mind to me. Not crazy at all."

Nic smiled. "No. Not yet."

"If you want to ride, I'm sure you'll find a way." Lucas stared through the windshield. "I think sometimes adults forget how much it sucks to have someone else making all of the decisions about *your* life for you."

"She just wants me to be safe." It did suck, of course, but Nic knew that her mother did not take any pleasure in telling her what to do. On the contrary, making parental decrees always seemed to chip away at something inherent to her mother's character, lessening her. Nic hated to be the one to do this to her. Lately, even before Nic's accident, it had seemed to Nic that her mother's spirits were a little low. Nic preferred her mother bold and brash, the brightest flame for miles; she liked to think of her as having all the answers. In that way, at least, she supposed she was just like her mother's listeners.

Lucas shifted in his seat. "Sometimes," he said, "I feel like I'm walking through life with these invisible strings attached to my feet and there is an adult at the other end pulling the strings, making me go wherever *she* wants me to go."

"Where would you go if you got to decide?"

"Back to New York."

"To live with your dad?"

Lucas's dark eyes moved over Nic's face. She sensed his thoughts roiling. He gave a sort of half-shrug. "I don't care who I live with," he said unconvincingly. "But my school there had an art program just for seniors. I was supposed to go this year. I submitted my portfolio. My parents didn't know. My dad was busy with . . . his life." He said this as though his father's life had nothing to do with his own. "My mom was busy . . ." He trailed off, his eyes searching Nic's face again. She could feel the anger simmering in his gaze. "She was busy figuring out her next move: how to get us out of there and 'find herself' again. By the time I told them I was accepted to the program, it was too late. They told me they were separating and I had to move to California with my mom and my sisters. Everything had already been decided. And ever since we got here, it's like my mom can't figure out what to do with herself. She turned all of our lives inside out and I don't think she really knows why. She can't decide if she's really happy or really angry about how everything turned out. Her mood changes by the hour."

Nic was quiet for a moment. "What was in your portfolio?"

He looked at her. "Drawings, mostly. Photos of some mixed-media stuff I've done."

"I'd love to . . . I mean, could I see some of it sometime?"

Lucas shrugged. "Sure. How about now?" He twisted in the seat, took stock of the debris in the backseat of the car, and reached for a crumpled paper. Once smoothed against his knee, they saw that it was an essay written in Spanish, every other word circled in red ink, a large red D at the top along with an invitation in English to rewrite the essay and attempt to improve the grade.

"Tsk, tsk, Angel Bully," Lucas said.

Nic felt her first thrum of compassion for Hunter Nolan.

Lucas found a pen in the glove compartment. He turned the paper to its blank side and, just before he touched pen to paper, glanced at Nic. She thought he seemed nervous; she smiled to reassure him. He looked back at the paper and began to draw. He moved the pen in fast, short strokes. It was hard to imagine how anything could grow from those repetitive little lines. Lucas's lips were pressed tight together and his face seemed hard, like something chiseled from stone. Nic looked back to the page and there, magically, a horse was taking shape, a dark burst of beauty and speed. Nic sucked in her breath. A horse and a rider now, too, her hair a long stream behind her, rippling across the page. The pair leapt upward into a sky, a magical sky, a sky churning, now, with fireworks.

Nic felt dizzy.

She remembered this: the beauty of the sky. The burst of color and light that surrounded her. The roar of the earth. She remembered, now, as she had not before, how it felt to ride Tru through the woods on that day, feeling that strange mix of fear and determination. She remembered the fire in her stomach, the burn of humiliation. How gentle the fall had seemed, how forgiving the ground.

She remembered soaring toward a kaleidoscope of tree branches overhead; she remembered the light that had shined through the darkness.

Lucas lifted the pen from the paper. Slowly, he pulled his eyes from his drawing and looked at Nic.

She placed her hands on either side of his face, and then, surprised as much by his cool skin as by what she'd done, almost withdrew them. He stopped her, lifting his own hands to hold hers against his face. He watched her. He waited.

Nic leaned forward and kissed him. It was her first kiss, there in the front seat of Angel Bully's car. Her first kiss with this curious, angry, sad, gifted boy. Her first kiss, ever. She felt his hands in her hair, and then his tongue searching her mouth. Below her thumbs, below his skin, the hard press of his cheekbones.

When they pulled away from each other, the air outside the car still sparkled with dust, as though somehow the dizziness she'd felt had stirred not just her, but everything.

Chapter 13

A couple of hours after dropping Nic off at school on Friday morning, I received a call from Karen Tyson, Kirke's Head of School, and turned right back around.

"This doesn't make any sense," I said after she told me why she'd called me in. I sat across the desk from Karen in her office. With her fluffy gray hair, round face, and sweet smile, the woman was almost absurdly adorable. Part of my confusion lay in her delivery; in her upbeat, peppy way, she'd just rattled off a story about a car being stolen. The other part of my confusion was the simple fact that I could not shake the feeling that *I* was in trouble . . . and the prospect of being reprimanded made me defiant.

Karen repeated her story: someone had driven a senior's car out of the parking lot without his permission and left a toy car in its place. "I wouldn't say any crime occurred—though of course, *technically*, it did," she said with an incongruous wink. "But this was obviously a prank. Hunter found his car parked around the corner from the school, less than a mile away."

"And Hunter's sense of humor? It never turned up?"

The edges of Karen's perpetual smile wobbled. "I'm afraid not."

"Nic doesn't even know how to drive," I said. "I don't see how she could have had anything to do with this."

"I understand that. It seemed unlikely to me, too. Nic generally keeps her head down . . . in a wonderful way! But, the thing is"—Karen lowered her voice—"she was seen driving the car."

I stared at her. "No. That's not possible."

"Julian Towne is sure that he saw her."

"Driving that boy's car?"

"Yes."

Julian Towne was Kirke's dean of students. I'd met him several times. He didn't strike me as the sort of person who would make up something like this. "What does Nic say?"

"Well, that's part of the problem . . . she won't say anything at all."

I was speechless. If Nic wasn't willing to say that she had *not* done this, I was pretty sure that it meant that she *had* done it. But why? Who was this Hunter kid? I'd never even heard her mention his name. And *driving*? She didn't have a license! How did she manage to drive the car off school property? What if she'd been hurt again? I was itching to jump from the chair and scour the school until I found my daughter and got some answers, but Karen wasn't through with me yet.

"If she can't offer an explanation, all I can do is consider the information that I've been given." Karen held up her fingers, ticking them off as she spoke. "One: yesterday afternoon, Hunter Nolan's keys were stolen from his locker and his black Jeep Wrangler was removed from the school property without his permission. Two: yesterday afternoon, Julian Towne saw Nic driving a black Jeep Wrangler down the school's driveway."

She leaned back in her seat and pressed her fingertips together. "Luckily, Hunter's parents don't want to press charges, but Kirke can't simply ignore something that happened on school grounds. Normally, an incident like this might warrant a suspension, but this car business seems out of character for Nic, and I know that she's still recovering from a serious injury . . ." She trailed off and looked at me encouragingly, her gray bulb of hair moving along with her slight, prodding nod.

I shot forward in my seat. "Yes! Yes, this is completely out of character for Nic. She's been experiencing some behavioral changes since her accident last week. Her neurosurgeon told us that acting out isn't entirely uncommon following a traumatic brain injury. But this is definitely not normal behavior for her. I hope you'll offer some leniency, given the circumstances."

Karen nodded, satisfied, her smile reinstated. "I'm going to give Nic in-school detention for two weeks." She lowered her voice again. "Basically, it's study hall instead of free period. Not the end of the world, but the kids do seem to hate giving up their free time."

"Fine by me. Thank you for your understanding. Believe me, Nic and I will be having a long chat about all of this."

"Good." Karen pressed her lips together, thinking. "Let me ask you something. These behavioral changes that the neurosurgeon mentioned . . . they wouldn't put her at risk of being a danger to herself, would they? Or others?"

Well, let's see, I thought. *She has no idea how to drive and yet yesterday she apparently spent the afternoon joyriding in a stolen car.*

I flashed Karen a smile. "I don't think so."

This was somehow all she needed to hear. Maybe it was a liability thing. Or maybe she was allowing special privileges to Kirke's most famous parent. I had no idea.

She stood and walked me to the door. "This isn't the time or place, but I can't resist telling you that I was a huge fan of your show."

"Oh? '*Was*'?"

She nodded. "I'm sure your current show is great, too—it's certainly a big success, isn't it?—but I have to admit it's not quite my thing. I was really a fan of your old show."

"Love Songs After Dark?"

Her brow wrinkled in confusion. "No. No, I don't think that's what it was called. It was the show you hosted as an undergraduate at Reed. I was the dean of residential life at the school at the time. I don't think our paths ever crossed, but I can tell you that I stayed up late way too many nights listening to your show." She leaned in close, whispering conspiratorially. "I still listen to Hole every night before bed. Their music relaxes me. Courtney Love! What a sparkplug!"

I laughed. Who could have guessed that jolly, gray-haired Mrs. Tyson had grunge in her heart?

"I haven't met a fan of that show—or a fan of Courtney Love, for that matter—in a very long time."

Karen winked. "Oh, we're out there." At the door, she hesitated for a moment, and then asked if Nic had a boyfriend.

"I don't think so," I answered, surprised.

"I only ask because there was a boy in the car with her. Julian didn't have a good view of him, so we're not sure who he is. And, as I mentioned, Nic won't tell us anything. It doesn't seem fair that she'll get detention and the other student won't, but unless Nic tells us his name, we don't have a choice in the matter."

I tried not to smile too broadly at the news that my daughter refused to snitch on a friend. So far, this was the only piece of the story that made any sense to me at all.

I FOUND NIC in the cafeteria, a large room with gleaming wood floors and arched windows and terrible acoustics. The air roiled with the hormones of all of those teenagers. I spotted Nic sitting at a table with her friend Lila. She saw me then, too. I was glad that I wouldn't have to cross the cafeteria and draw attention to her. She said something to Lila and walked toward me. I could tell by the slope of her shoulders that she knew why I was there.

"Let's talk," I said. We walked out of the school and sat on a bench by the front entrance. Nic tucked her long hair behind her ears. In the sunlight, her pale skin was as luminous as a pearl. Her beauty made my heart contract. I wondered about the boy in the car.

"I hear you can drive," I began, lifting an eyebrow.

"It's—it's a long story," she said.

"Am I going to like it?"

"I don't know." Despite how talkative she'd been lately, she seemed unsure how to begin.

"Did you steal a car from the school parking lot?"

"No! But I did . . . *move* a car."

"Oh, Nic. Why?"

She slowly found her words. She told me about Hunter Nolan, a senior boy who bullied the meekest of the freshman boys, humiliating them and stealing their homework. "He never does anything so big that the teachers notice," she said. "But half of my class is terrified of him. It's not fair."

"He sounds awful," I said. I could see where this was going. Nic had always had a strong sense of fairness; I'd just never seen her act on her views in this way before. Was this one of those impulses that her brain was no longer able to control?

"He is, Mom! He really is. And he always parks his car in the same spot—the best one in the lot. The spots aren't assigned, but he thinks he owns the school. Nobody ever challenges him on it." She took a breath. "So I found his keys and—"

Here, I interrupted. "You 'found' his keys?"

She bit her lip. "I found his keys . . . in his backpack . . . in his locker."

"Nic."

"I know. I know! But, Mom, moving Hunter's car is like a drop in the bucket compared to what he's done to some of the nicest guys at Kirke. And all I did was park it around the corner. There's not a scratch on it. He probably thought it was stolen for an hour at most before one of his minions spotted it."

"And the Matchbox car?"

She shrugged, catching her lip between her teeth to stop her smile. "That was just for fun."

I laughed. I couldn't help it. Should I have reprimanded her? Yes. But I'd never been great with discipline. If I'd had a kid who needed a lot of rules and regulations, maybe I would have had to change my parenting style over the years. But I'd rarely needed to take on the uncomfortable mantle of authority with Nic.

"Mrs. Tyson is giving you in-school detention for two weeks," I told her. "It's during your free period."

"Okay."

I knew she wouldn't mind the punishment. Her sense of fairness applied to herself as much as anyone else.

"Listen, Nic. All I ask is that next time—if there must be a next time for this sort of behavior—you steer clear of committing actual crimes. I would miss you too much if you went to juvie."

She rested her head on my shoulder. I felt for the millionth time that it was not possible to love anyone more than I loved this girl. We looked out at Kirke's green playing fields. The sky was cloudless. I pressed the moment into my memory, hoping it would remain there forever.

"So, what happened this morning?" I asked, curiosity getting the better of me. "Did this Hunter kid park in his usual spot?"

"No. Another senior took the spot." She didn't lift her head to look at me, but I heard the pride in her voice.

"Well, hallelujah. Someone knew to dump salt on the kid's wound. If I had to guess, I'd say that's probably the real reason he reported the whole thing to Mrs. Tyson this morning." I looked down at Nic's glossy dark hair. "Would this other senior by any chance be the boy who Mr. Towne saw in Hunter's car with you?"

She sat up then. The sun caught the flecks of gold in her green eyes. "Maybe."

"Who is he?"

She didn't answer.

"I suppose he taught you how to drive."

She still didn't answer.

"Nic," I said, "an older guy isn't—"

"There's no reason for him to be in trouble, too," Nic interrupted. "The whole thing was my idea."

My daughter, the ringleader. I worried for her sweet, young, brave heart, wishing I could protect it from the wounds that lay ahead. I didn't really mind what she'd done with that bully's car because what harm had she done other than to a young man's swollen ego? But . . . what if this were just the start? What if her brain could no longer tell the difference between a good idea and a bad idea? How could I both support my daughter *and* protect her? I didn't want to take anything away from her, and certainly not the thing that she loved the most, but given the circumstances, what choice did I have?

"The thing is, Nic, you can see how this kind of thing doesn't exactly make me excited about the prospect of you riding again, can't you?"

"No! What do you mean? Taking Hunter's car had nothing to do with riding."

"It seems like you're acting on your instincts, and you're not necessarily thinking about all of the consequences of those actions. You were trying to teach this kid a lesson, but you were also, technically, stealing a car . . . there could have been serious consequences for that action that you were lucky to avoid. You could have gotten into much more trouble—or worse, been hurt. What if the next time you make a questionable decision, you're on top of a horse?" I reached for my daughter's hand, but she pulled away, her cheeks pink with rage.

"So you don't trust me! That's why you won't let me ride!"

"It's not that simple, Nic. The accident—"

"Mom," she said, interrupting me. "I remember it now! Riding Tru into the woods."

I stared at her. "You do? When did this happen?"

"Yesterday. It all came back to me." She took a deep breath. "At school on the day of the accident, I met this guy and when I tried to talk to him . . . it was horrible, Mom. I was stuttering and I couldn't stop. I started crying and then I ran away from him and I hid in the bushes."

"Oh, Nic," I said. I put my arm around her but she didn't seem particularly upset. Her voice was full of emotion but there were no tears brimming in her eyes. "You remembered all of that yesterday?"

"No, I remembered that part already, but now I remember that it's why I went out into the woods. At least I think that's why. I don't think I even really knew why I was doing it when I did it. I knew I should listen to Denny and stay safe, but I was just sick to death of being me."

I swallowed. "Sweetheart, were you trying to hurt yourself?"

She looked at me and shook her head. "No. But I was so embarrassed and so mad and frustrated. I needed to do *something*.

And I guess maybe there was some part of me that thought that if I got hurt doing it, that would be okay. It would be worth it. Because I just had to do something big. I needed to." She closed her eyes for a beat of time and then opened them again. "I don't know if I can describe it any better than that."

I felt like a weight had been placed on my chest, and it was hard to breathe. All that time, I hadn't realized how trapped she felt within her own anxieties. That she would be pushed to do something so dangerous just to prove her worth to herself, or worse, to some guy—

"I'm sure you did plenty of dumb stuff when you were a kid, too, right?" Nic asked, interrupting my thoughts. She looked at me hopefully.

"Oh, well . . ."

Now it was my turn to close my eyes and take a breath.

Jumped off a bridge into a rushing river (the shockingly cold water . . . that delicious intake of breath when I broke free of the surface). Allowed a boy who had been drinking to drive me home (the car's headlights swinging across the divider line and back again . . . the relief when I stepped out of the car, safely home). Swallowed a pill that a strange girl in a club gave me (and danced all night . . . and lived to tell the tale). Ran away from home to spend a weekend with the guitarist of a local band that I loved (had lots of very fun sex . . . and returned home with good stories for my friends).

I did not do any of those dangerous things because I wanted to die. I did them because I wanted to live.

"A few," I said to Nic.

She grabbed my hands. "Let me ride, Mom. Please. I remember the accident now. I'm better!"

I sighed. "Let's talk with Dr. Feldman about it at your appointment next week. If he says it's okay, then . . . maybe."

Nic yelped and gave me a quick hug. "Thanks, Mom! I better get back to school! See you later!"

"I said 'maybe,' Nic!" I called, but she was already slipping through the front door of the school.

I stood from the bench and looked around, blinking. Why did I feel like I'd just been hit by a Nic-shaped bus?

As I walked back to my car, my phone vibrated in my pocket.

Where's Roy? the text message read. The number that sent it wasn't listed in my contacts.

I looked over my shoulder at the school. Three girls now sat on a bench near the one on which Nic and I had sat. They looked away as soon as they saw that I'd noticed them; one stifled a giggle. Another one hushed her. They were harmless; just some teenagers excited to recognize me—I would have been the same way at their age, studiously pretending not to care.

I looked past them toward the school building. Its windows were opaque in the sunlight.

Among the few other cars parked along the circular driveway, I now noticed that a woman sat in the driver's seat of a silver Mercedes. My breath caught in my chest at the sight of her thick, dark hair. Jenny Long's hair, underneath her rotating assortment of wigs, had been thick and dark like that. The woman was looking down (at her phone?) and her hair hung around her face, blocking her profile from my view. I jogged toward the car, but as I did the car suddenly started and drove away, turning at such an angle that I could catch only a quick glimpse of a New York license plate.

I told myself that there were many women with thick, dark hair, that it was far-fetched to believe that Jenny Long would be driving a Mercedes with New York plates.

I called Roy. "Are you okay?" I asked him, still staring in the direction the car had driven.

"Sure," he said. "Just meeting a friend for lunch before I head down to pick up Nic after school. Why? What's wrong?"

"Someone sent me a strange text. And I'm not sure, but I might have just seen Jenny Long."

"Are you alone? Do you want me to come get you? Should I call the police?"

I looked around at Kirke's stretch of playing fields, the empty spot where the Mercedes had been parked. "No. I'm fine. Sorry to worry you, Roy. I'll see you later today."

I probably should have called Tyler next to let him know about the latest developments with Nic, but as I got in my car I found myself dialing Corcoran Stables. I'd spoken with Denny for long chunks of time every day that week, but this was the first time that I was calling without the intention—or maybe, if I were being honest with myself, the *pretense*—of checking in on Nic. It was earlier than I usually called and I had no idea if he'd be at the barn. I was relieved when he picked up the phone.

"Hi, Denny, it's me. G.G." I started the car and drove out of Kirke, switching the phone call to my car's speakers.

"Hey," he said. "Nic isn't here yet."

"I know—I just saw her at school, actually." I told him that Nic now remembered trying to jump the tree, and that somehow her admission had led me to telling her that I would consider letting her ride again. "I don't quite know how that happened," I said. "But do you think she's ready?"

"Oh, G.G., I don't think I should answer that one. Physically, she seems fine . . . but if you're asking me to tell you that she won't fall off again, I can't. In fact, I'd be more comfortable assuring you that she *will* fall off again. Hopefully she'll never have another serious accident—but if you ride, you fall. It's part of it." Denny paused. "I'm sorry. I know that's not what you want to hear."

Even though my heart sank at his words, I didn't entirely mind hearing them. My life was full of people telling me what I wanted to hear. "Do you think there's any chance Nic will decide riding just isn't for her? Maybe take up knitting instead? I'm guessing avid knitters don't often find themselves in comas."

Denny laughed. "Now I know what to get her for Christmas."

I told him about the prank that she'd pulled with the senior's car.

"But Nic doesn't know how to drive, does she?"

"No! So whether it's on a horse or behind the wheel, she seems set on putting herself in harm's way . . ." I trailed off, suddenly at a loss for words. "Sorry, Denny. I'm not sure why I called you. This isn't your problem."

When Denny spoke, he'd sprinkled some grit into his voice. "Tell me everything, Caller," he said, "starting with your name."

I smiled. "You've listened to my show."

"Everyone has listened to your show. You're famous, G.G."

"For better or for worse," I said, thinking of the threats I'd received.

"You don't like being famous?"

"I like connecting with people. I like showing people their strengths on the days that they feel weak."

"But?"

"Oh, nothing." I was aware that there were few things more annoying than someone whining about the downside of success, so I'd decided long ago to keep my complaints to myself. "What about you? Do you like running the stables?"

"Sure," Denny said after a moment. "It's what I always wanted to do . . ."

"But?"

"No, I was just thinking that it's been surprising, actually. I wanted to run the place because I like working with horses, and this piece of land . . . it's a place that lives inside of me, if you know what I mean. I belong to it. I learned every inch of it when I was a kid and I've never forgotten a single one. And if I didn't take over the place when my parents retired, who knew what the next owner would do with the land? Develop it, probably. No more horses. No more kids learning to ride at Corcoran Stables.

"Anyway," Denny said, "that's the part that has surprised me: the kids. Seeing how much most kids really want to *work*. Some of them come on days they don't even have a lesson and ask what they can help with. They want a purpose. They want to feel like they're making a difference, like they're important. I guess I didn't realize how universal that feeling was—and how young it starts—until I took over the stables.

"And Nic, you know, is the best of the bunch. Your daughter is a hard worker." I could tell that from Denny, this was particularly special praise. "And she really connects with the horses. You have to have both to be a good rider. You can't be all drive and no compassion. You can't do battle with a horse. Well, you can . . . and sadly, you can win. But that sort of victory makes you a bully, not a rider. To be a rider you need to be focused on a goal, but never so narrowly that it's all you see. You can't lose sight of the big picture."

"Which is what?" I asked, perhaps a bit breathlessly. Denny's voice, pouring out from the speakers, had settled around me like a blanket. The freeway traffic, as though in deference to our conversation, was remarkably light, the usually maddening drive almost peaceful.

"The big picture is the partnership. It's finding a way to make the horse whole, and the rider whole, so they can be even greater together. The rider can't be so fixated on pushing the horse that he forgets to push himself." Denny paused. "I'm talking a lot. Sorry. I don't usually do that. Ever, really."

I laughed. "Occupational hazard, for me." I'd learned years earlier that there was something about talking on the phone that encouraged confidence—there was a sense of remove as well as an intimacy. It was the reason my listeners called in to my show and spilled their secret desires and lifelong regrets. It was why after hearing my voice on the radio night after night, some listeners came to believe that I was their best friend or their lover . . . or someone worth passionately hating.

"Maybe you should write a book," I told Denny. *"Zen and the Art of Horseback Riding."* I was only partly joking. He'd discovered something true, something good, a stalk of wisdom that grew completely organically within the life he'd chosen to live, and through teaching he'd found a way to share it with his corner of the world.

"That could be a problem. I'm not always so Zen."

"I have trouble believing that." I'd seen Denny gruff and grumbling, but never truly mad. There was something grounded about him; it was difficult to imagine how anything could knock him off balance.

"It's true," he said. "Right now I'm torn up over an abused horse that I took in thinking that I could turn her around. I'm not getting through to her. She doesn't trust anyone, and she's injured a few of my workers. She's one thousand pounds of angry. I can't have a horse like that at Corcoran, but the idea of sending her away . . ."

"You feel like you're failing her."

"Yeah, I do."

"I'm sorry. Maybe this is one of those times that you were talking about . . . when you need to focus on the big picture. And the big picture isn't just this particular horse, right? It's the safety of all the kids and the workers and the other horses. It's the whole of Corcoran Stables."

"Right." Denny cleared his throat. "Okay, your turn. It's only fair. What keeps you up at night?"

"Nic," I said easily. "Worrying about her safety. Worrying that the life I've chosen has made hers harder than it needs to be."

"Really?" Denny sounded surprised. "But Nic is thriving! She's an amazing kid. And strong. Patti Smith would sing something here about how you've given that kid a pretty big banquet of love to feed on."

I blinked away the tears that sprang to my eyes. I'd spent so many years fielding comments from teachers about how shy Nic was—teachers who mislabeled her as an unengaged student—that I felt incredibly moved to know that Denny knew her—accepted her, admired her, loved her—as I did. I'd known Denny most of my life, but we'd only a week earlier begun having conversations that lasted more than a minute or two. Still, I couldn't deny the connection, the level of comfort that seemed to exist between us, ready to be tapped into if we chose to turn toward it, toward each other.

"I guess there's something else that keeps me up at night, too," I said, slowly. "Sometimes I feel like I'm the woman who plays Gail Gideon on the radio. She's me . . . but there's more to me, too. She's the Gail Gideon everyone expects. It can feel . . ."

"Tiresome?"

"Predictable. And confining." I'd never told anyone this before. Immediately, I felt a sliver of regret. Complaining chafed. I was a problem solver, not a whiner. And there were so many silver linings to my work that even the darkest clouds glowed.

"But," I said, "I *love* having fans. I'm not afraid to admit that fans make me feel good about myself. I didn't get a lot of positive feedback as a kid." I thought about all of the crazy stunts I'd pulled as a teenager, the things that I could not imagine confessing to my daughter. "Then again, I wasn't the easiest kid to love."

"I knew you as a kid so now I know you're lying."

"I promise I wasn't fishing for a compliment, Denny."

"Then I'm afraid you've wandered into the wrong lake, G.G."

I laughed. Whatever fear I'd felt upon seeing that text and the Jenny Long lookalike had washed away.

"Hey," he said. "What are you up to on Saturday night? I'm planning to make some mediocre spaghetti. I'd love to share it with you."

"Mediocre spaghetti sounds amazing," I said, because oddly, it really did. But I was having dinner with Lev Curtain from ZoneTV on Saturday night. "Unfortunately I have plans already."

"How about Sunday then?"

"Nic comes back on Sunday after spending the weekend with her father. Since I work nights during the week, it will be our only dinner together for two weeks."

"Right. No problem."

"It's not that—"

"No, really, G.G., I totally understand."

I had the sense that he *did* understand, but was disappointed nonetheless. I was disappointed, too, and frankly didn't want either of us to give up quite so easily. With my schedule, if I was going to date someone, we needed to think out of the dinner-date box.

"What about lunch?" I said. "People eat spaghetti for lunch, don't they?"

"I'd eat it for breakfast if I could. I'm showing that mare I was talking about earlier to a trainer on Saturday so that won't work . . . but how about noon on Sunday?"

"Perfect," I said. When I glanced in the rearview mirror, I realized that I was beaming.

It was only after I hung up with Denny that I began to question whether dating my daughter's beloved riding teacher, a man she saw more often than she saw her actual father, was really going to be so perfect after all.

Chapter 14

That afternoon Nic was reading in a window seat in the library when Lucas slid onto the cushioned bench beside her.

"So," he said. "What's the word? Are you being shipped off to military school?"

"Fat chance," Nic answered. "My mom would never let me be shipped off anywhere. She needs to monitor my every move."

"Tell her they have microchips for that these days." He put his hand on her neck. "She could slip one right here, just below your skin. My cousin had one put in her dog."

"Seriously, I think she'd love nothing more." Nic closed her book. "I have in-school detention."

"Not bad. What about me?" Nic heard a tremor of anxiety in his voice.

"I didn't tell them you were with me."

Lucas raised his eyebrows.

"You really thought I'd tell on you?" She was a little hurt. Also, she still felt the warmth of his fingers where he'd touched her neck. When she lifted her hand to feel the spot, her hair fell in front of her face.

"I didn't think you would." He brushed her hair away so he could look at her. He smiled. "I owe you."

Nic looked at Lucas, the Clyde to her Bonnie. She thought about how she'd felt when she saw him pull his car into the spot that Angel Bully usually took. A new plan was forming. It would have to wait a couple of days, though—she'd be at her father's house in Marin all weekend. And when she returned to her mother's she'd have to find some way to get rid of Irene, the babysitter who had been staying with her again while her mother was at work. But she'd find a way.

"You owe me, huh?" she said to Lucas, and smiled.

"What is going on with you and Lucas Holt?" Lila asked later that day. "I saw you guys sitting together in the library, looking *very* cozy."

"I like him," Nic said. "I kind of think . . . he gets me."

"Wait a minute! Did you guys hook up?"

Nic blushed. "We kissed."

"Holy shit, Nic! You're making out with the hottest senior in school! First, you stole Hunter Nolan's car, and now you're *banging Lucas Holt*—"

"Oh my God, Lila!" Nic shook her head and laughed. "We kissed. That's all."

"Om sha*lom*," Lila said, long and low, impressed. "Go on with your bad self, Nicola Clement. That's all I have to say to that. And by the by," she added, "I hope you realize that the Lurk is going to have a field day with this." She took out her phone as though she thought something must have been popping up on the Lurk's Instagram feed even as they stood there.

Nic felt a wave of worry. She didn't want anything posted about her and Lucas being together. It could get back to the teachers or

Mrs. Tyson and then someone would figure out that he was the boy Mr. Towne had seen with her in Angel Bully's car. Lucas had seemed pretty desperate not to be found out; Nic suspected his mother wasn't as forgiving as hers.

"What's on there?" she asked, taking the phone from a startled Lila.

"Oh, nothing new."

The Lurk hadn't posted anything since the photograph of Bridget swimming from the day before. Seeing that post again made Nic's blood boil anew. She remembered the girl's tears in the bathroom, the sweet way she'd asked how Nic was feeling even as she cried.

"Ugh," Nic said, tossing the phone back at her friend. "Those pictures make me sick!"

Lila looked down at her phone, surprised. "The Lurk really hasn't been that bad lately. Could be worse."

THAT AFTERNOON, WHILE Denny was helping the hands turn out the horses from the lower barn, Nic slipped into Peach's stall. After five days of this, the horse no longer snapped her teeth or even pressed her ears back against her head when Nic approached. Peach still watched her closely, but the trust growing between them felt as solid as a bridge that Nic crossed each afternoon.

But the horse still lashed out at anyone else who came near her, and Nic knew that Denny was trying to find her a new home. She didn't know exactly why Peach had chosen to trust her and not Denny or even Javi, both of whom easily established relationships with most of the horses that came through the barn. Nic wondered if maybe whatever abuse Peach had experienced, she'd suffered at the hand of a man. Maybe only a girl could save her.

That afternoon, for the first time, Peach let Nic lean against her.

Nic draped her arms over the horse's back, imitating the weight of a saddle. She breathed in the horse's smell. She took in the power of the horse, her huge, solid body, her scars, her majestic neck and beautiful head, her long, lovely eyelashes. In her mind, she told Peach that she would not see her for two days while she was at her father's, but that she would be back on Monday. Peach pressed her muzzle against Nic's arm and released slow, warm, calm breaths that dampened Nic's skin.

As Roy drove Nic home, she sank deep into the backseat. She felt overwhelmed with gratitude for Peach, for the honor of their bond, for the courage that it took for her to accept an offer of kindness.

An offer of kindness.

Nic sat up, pulled her phone from her bag and downloaded the Instagram app. The reason that people felt emboldened online was that it was very hard to catch someone who could not be seen. Perhaps, she thought, if used in the right way, anonymity could be a good thing.

She hesitated for only a moment before setting up her own Instagram account. The twinge of guilt that she felt was slight. Her mother had asked her not to sign up for social media because she worried about Nic's safety, but Nic didn't plan to use Instagram as a place to share personal photographs or information. The whole point would be for her to be anonymous. Still, it was another secret. Two weeks ago, Nic had told her mom everything. Now she was sneaking into Peach's stall, driving cars, kissing a seventeen-year-old boy, and signing up for an Instagram account when her mom had explicitly asked her not to join any social media.

Username?

Nic thought, then typed "KirkeKudos."

She felt Roy's glance in the rearview mirror. "How's it going back there?" he asked.

"Great," she answered. "Just working on a school project." It wasn't a lie—not even a *white* lie. She flashed Roy a smile.

"On your phone?"

Though he seemed more curious than suspicious, Nic didn't trust herself to do more than nod. Had her mother told Roy that Nic wasn't allowed on social media? Nic made her best attempt to seem innocently busy. She felt Roy's gaze a beat longer before he returned his attention to the road.

They'd received their school directories just that morning. All day, kids had complained about their photographs. The murmured chorus of self-loathing had bothered Nic. She still thought that her own school photograph made her resemble a vampire, but the fact was that she had very pale skin and she might as well accept it and move on. Now, she pulled the directory from her backpack and flipped through it until she landed on Bridget's page. She took a picture of the girl's photograph with her phone and uploaded it to the new *KirkeKudos* account. She studied the photograph, then began to type a caption for it.

> Bridget: Your kindness and your integrity give you a beautiful glow that warms all who know you. You are disciplined, powerful, and you dream big. We see you, Bridget, and we think you rock. Kudos.

How would anyone find the post, she wondered? The point was for everyone who saw *TheKirkeLurk7*'s posts to see hers, too. She wanted to drown out the Lurk's posts with something better, messages that would build up her peers instead of tear them down. She thought for a moment and then added the hashtags "kirkekudos" and "kirkeschool" at the bottom of her photo caption. Then she posted it.

The angry heat within her waned a little, pooling into a golden light that made her think of the dress that her mother had given her. Maybe she would go shopping when she was staying with her father that weekend. Her wardrobe had so little color.

She spent the rest of the car ride searching Instagram for schoolmates to follow, and watching as her own account's followers list grew.

Chapter 15

When Shayne told me that Lev Curtain wanted to meet for dinner at Beretta in the Mission, I was surprised. I'd expected he'd pick one of San Francisco's fancier restaurants in one of its shinier neighborhoods—Farallon in Union Square or Spruce in Presidio Heights or Acquerello in Nob Hill. Those were the sorts of restaurants where people who wanted me to sign contracts generally wooed me, I suppose acting on a misguided assumption that famous people felt most comfortable sitting in front of small portions of expensive food. Still, I usually signed the contracts, because contracts meant *more* (more reach, more money, more middle fingers to the memory of my parents' lack of belief in me), but the truth was that those fancy restaurants made me acutely aware that I was doing business with people who did not know me at all.

Beretta, however, was one of my favorite restaurants in the city. It had great pizza, an interesting cocktail menu, and was dark and loud, which was how I preferred my public spaces. I'd probably mentioned my affinity for the place a half-dozen times on my show, so the fact that Lev Curtain asked me to meet him there told me that he—or one of his assistants—actually did tune in on occasion.

I was in for another pleasant surprise when the Beretta hostess led me through the restaurant on Saturday night. A man was seated at the table already, but I didn't think that there was any way *he* was the head of programming for ZoneTV. Instead of an expensive suit, this guy wore a white T-shirt that showed off the sleeves of faded tattoos that covered his arms. He wasn't Los Angeles buff either, but thick in a way that made me think he prioritized steak over kale. A slight stubble of gray emerged from his buzzed head. I wondered if he was Lev Curtain's security guard. Maybe Lev was in the bathroom. Or waiting outside in his car, making imperative calls about ZoneTV's new slate of reality shows.

But then the man caught sight of me approaching and sprang nimbly to his feet.

"Gail Gideon!" he boomed in a voice that contained so much gravel that by comparison when I responded, my own gritty voice sounded practically sweet.

"Lev Curtain?"

We shook hands. Around us, diners were in various states of staring and pretending not to stare. "Sorry about blowing your cover," Lev said, leaning toward me and lowering his voice as much as it seemed he was capable. "I got excited. I'm a fan."

"My agent mentioned that," I said. We sat down at the table. "I thought she was just being good at her job."

Lev's laugh was like the crack of a whip. "Shayne *is* a good agent. She held my balls over the coals to get you more money."

"That sounds unpleasant."

He shrugged, a twinkle in his eye. "Not as much as you might think." He gestured at the drink in front of me. "I remembered the show where you mentioned that you enjoyed this place's Kentucky Mule, so I took the liberty."

Now I was truly impressed. We clinked our glasses and I took a long drink. The delicious burn of bourbon and ginger slid down my throat. Over the rim of the glass, I considered Lev's bulky form and felt a shiver of excitement for all of the food that I suspected we were about to order.

IN THE END, we somehow managed to polish off two and a half pizzas while talking nonstop about everything, it seemed, except *G.G. (Fall in love with the single you!).* When Lev said he was into live music, we talked for an hour about the shows we'd seen, which bands were better in the studio and which were better in concert. And then Lev mentioned that he'd gone to college in San Francisco and had extensive knowledge of the city's dive bars. He recommended a few that I had never heard of, and I made a mental note to check them out.

"The thing I *used* to love about dive bars," he said, "was that they played music I didn't hear almost anywhere else, and the drinks were cheap." He lifted his drink—we were on our third round—and took a sip. "Now, I love that they're the only place that I can go where I'm never the oldest guy in the room. There's always some salty old bastard in the corner, grumbling about how he doesn't need to be cut off, he's *perfectly fine, goddammit.*"

"I love that guy," I said.

It was only when the pizzas were cleared that Lev leaned back in his seat, wincingly patted his belly, and said, "I want to fly you down to the lot sometime soon so I can show you around, maybe toss around some set ideas. I'm thinking we design something that's a little edgy, very G.G., but, you know, accessible enough for a wide range of viewers."

Accessible. I appreciated what Lev was saying, but at the same time I had always felt that my radio show was a success for the very reason that I did *not* try to change myself to appeal to anyone or everyone. My draw was my authenticity. The piece of me that I shared on the radio was just that: only a piece of me. But that piece was, truly, me.

I pictured an even more watered-down version of myself sitting in an expensive leather chair that some design assistant had rubbed ever so carefully with sandpaper to make it look lived-in. At Hawke Media, my studio had ugly maroon walls and a matching carpet. The bathroom was papered in concert posters. Years ago, I'd draped a pelt of gray fake fur over my rolling chair, and ever since Simone had referred to it as the Rat Throne. I'd never felt quite as fondly about the studio as I did in that moment when Lev spoke of creating an *accessible* set.

"I've never worked in front of a camera before," I told him.

He shrugged. "Just think of the camera as your studio mic. Anyway, I saw your Barbara Walters interview last year—you're gorgeous and the camera loves you."

I wanted to take the compliment to heart—I hated when women couldn't accept a nice word about themselves—but I was suddenly questioning if Lev's casual T-shirt and talk of music and dive bars was the real him. It wasn't hard to imagine how his cropped gray hair would play in a glitzy corner office, his tattoos covered by a shiny suit, his sizable bulk suddenly less bar bouncer and more corporate shark. My mind wandered back to the comments Nic had made earlier that week about my music collection, and how Hawke Media didn't know what they were missing.

"What about music?" I asked abruptly.

"The show's music? We'll have something new created for you. You'll have approval."

"But what if I wanted to incorporate music into the actual show format?"

Lev seemed puzzled. "Like an in-studio DJ? Like the dance intros Ellen does?"

I shook my head. The truth was that even I didn't know exactly what I meant, but I knew that I didn't mean dancing around the studio like Ellen DeGeneres. I already felt like *The Gail Gideon Show* was confining, and I was beginning to realize that *G.G.* the television show would have even tighter parameters.

Perhaps sensing that he was losing me, Lev leaned forward, his forearms pressing into the table. "Listen, we'll figure out a way to make this show reflective of you and your message. Nobody wants to turn you into someone you're not. We want you because you're *you*. You'll steer the ship. You're the boss here, G.G."

I nodded, but, frankly, by that point I smelled bullshit. The person who was the boss was the person who signed the check; the employee was the one who cashed it.

When I got home, I grabbed a beer from the fridge, pulled PJ Harvey's "Rid of Me" from my wall of music and placed it in the stereo, kicked off my boots, and lay back on the couch. If I didn't take the offer from ZoneTV, what would I do? Now that I'd admitted to myself that *The Gail Gideon Show* no longer charged me the way it once had, it was harder than ever to imagine signing the upcoming renewal contract with Hawke Media. I could do nothing for the rest of my life and be fine financially, but that idea appealed to me even less than manning the helm of an accessible ZoneTV talk show.

I'd almost drifted to sleep when my cell phone rang. For a moment I felt uncomfortably aware that I was home alone. On Friday, Rebecca, the director of Hawke Media's IT department, had told me that the threatening email that I'd received had been sent from an Apple store in Burlingame, a suburb south of the city, and the text that I'd received at Kirke had been sent from an app that blocked the senders' contact information. So basically all we knew was that at least one of my charming stalkers was in the Bay Area.

I picked up my phone, and felt a wave of relief when I saw Tyler's name on the caller ID.

"Did Nic steal another car?" I asked. I'd filled him in on Nic's run-in with the Kirke law on Friday.

He laughed. "No," he said. "Not as far as I know. She seems great, actually, other than the near-constant sulking."

"She's still sulking? I thought she turned a corner when I told her we'd see what Dr. Feldman said about her riding again."

"Riding? No, this seems to be about having the babysitter around at night again. She hates feeling like she's taken a step back in terms of the amount of freedom and responsibility she's allowed. Obviously if I had my way, she'd be trailed by a babysitter *and* a medical team for her entire life. But, G.G., the way she spoke up for herself today, pleading her case . . . She was calm and thoughtful and articulate and it took every ounce of restraint that I had not to interrupt her with hugs every other minute."

I released a sound that was half-laugh, half-sigh. This was one of the things I missed most about Tyler: being able to co-parent with him, to share in the admiration of and the concern for the person that we had created together.

"I know exactly what you mean, but I'm still not sure she should be left home alone right now." I told him about the call to the studio, the email, the text, and Roy's broken headlights. As I listed these events, I heard how loosely connected they sounded and began to question myself. Was I making this all into a bigger deal than it actually was? Had Nic's accident spooked me into worrying about things that I would have previously blown off?

"You have to go on living your life, and so does Nic, but I think a bit of security would put both of our minds at ease," Tyler said. "What if we had a guard outside the house? That way, we'll know someone is keeping an eye on things when you're at work, but Nic won't feel as though we're treating her like a little kid who needs a babysitter."

I knew Adam, the head of security at Hawke Media, would agree with Tyler, and I had to admit that in that very moment I wouldn't have minded if a security guard were keeping watch outside. I told Tyler that I'd arrange to have someone in place by the time Nic arrived home from the barn on Monday.

He sounded relieved. "Nic is going to be so happy. I'll tell her now. They're all down in the family room watching a movie."

They. Nic and her brothers and Lonnie. I didn't think that I would ever get used to the idea that Tyler and Nic had another family. I didn't begrudge Nic this; she loved them and they loved her and I wanted my daughter's life to brim with every kind of happiness, even the kind that excluded me.

I said goodnight to Tyler and put down my phone.

The CD had finished playing. The house was silent. I drank the final sip of my beer and went to bed.

ON MY WAY to Corcoran Stables the next day, I called Simone to let her know that I'd decided not to take the ZoneTV deal.

"Really?" she asked. "Are you sure? You're going to sign the renewal with Hawke Media?"

"No."

"Oh." In the bit of silence that followed, I imagined my friend contemplating herself out of a job.

"I'm ready to tackle something new," I said quickly, "but whatever that is I think we should do it as a team. We built *The Gail Gideon Show* together. I don't want to take this next leap without you." What I meant was that I loved her. One of the things I enjoyed most about my job was that I did it with her. But she was my best friend, and she already knew all of this.

"What do you have in mind?" she asked.

"I don't know. But I've been thinking a lot about music."

"Music . . . ?"

"That's all I have so far."

"Okay," Simone said, laughing. "We'll figure it out."

"I don't doubt it."

When she asked what I was doing that day, I admitted that I was on my way to Corcoran Stables.

"Isn't this Tyler's weekend with Nic?"

"Yes. I'm going to see the owner of the barn. We're having lunch."

"You're having lunch with the owner of the barn."

"Yup."

"Wait a minute," Simone said. "Is this who you've been talking to all week before we go on air? The calls that keep making you late for production meetings?"

I laughed. "I call the barn to check on Nic, and then I find I can't get off the phone with him! It's the strangest thing. I've known him for years . . . since I was a kid."

"I can't believe you're just telling me now! What's his name?"

"Denny."

"Stop it."

I laughed. "No, really. That's his name. Denny Corcoran."

"I'm picturing Robert Redford in *The Horse Whisperer.* Please tell me I'm right."

I thought of Denny, his softly graying brown hair and his olive skin and the lines that etched his forehead. I didn't even know what color eyes he had—I'd never noticed. But I knew for sure that he didn't look like Robert Redford. He looked better. Why had it taken me so many years to realize this?

"Yes, of course," I told Simone. "He looks just like Robert Redford."

She let out a low whistle. "Thank God," she said. "You *desperately* need a real man. In fact, I think you should exclusively date cowboys from here on out. A cowboy couldn't possibly give a shit about you being famous. He'd happily live in your shadow . . . until the cows come home! And he'd be perfectly comfortable *riding* your coattails!" She was laughing so hard she barely managed to choke this out.

"I have to go," I said, smiling. The turn for Corcoran Stables was just ahead. "But for the record, Denny doesn't own any cows."

In all my years visiting Corcoran Stables, I'd never been to the Corcoran house. I'd never even seen it. At a certain point the driveway forked; one road led to the barn, and the other led up a slight hill toward the house. As the road curved upward, and just before a line of trees blocked the view, the ocean was visible in the distance.

It turned out to be a pretty two-story Victorian farmhouse with a wraparound porch and a crisp white gabled roof that cut into the blue sky. Denny's muck-crusted boots were on the mat in front of the yellow door as though he'd stepped right out of them and walked inside. The whole thing looked like a postcard.

I heard a dog bark. Denny opened the door before I even had a chance to knock and I felt my heart do a little fishtail-flick thing that I hadn't felt in a long time.

"Hey," he said. "You made it." He held open the door, smiling out at me from below a Giants baseball hat that was faded to gray and frayed around its edges. He might have had that hat for years, or it might have just barely survived a single horse trampling. Denny's mammoth black dog was at his side, wagging his tail and grinning up at me. Behind them, I caught glimpses of honey-colored wood floorboards and a staircase with a curving white banister.

Denny held open the door wider and the dog padded out to sniff my boots. "You know Bear, right?"

"Sure, but this is our first formal introduction." He was an easy dog to pet since he came up to my waist.

"Alright, Bear, go find your own girl." Denny took hold of Bear's collar. "Come on in. This spaghetti isn't going to eat itself."

I unlaced my boots and stepped past Denny into the hall. He shut the door behind me and then neither of us seemed to know quite what to do with ourselves. After a moment, I stood on my toes and put one hand on his shoulder and lightly kissed his cheek. It was . . . disappointingly awkward.

"Thanks for the invitation," I said.

"Thanks for coming," he said.

I was seriously considering walking outside and calling him on my phone so that we could have the sort of conversation that we'd been having all week. But then Denny rocked back on his heels, smiled, and said, "Maybe the business of eating will help."

I nodded. "I'm starving."

As I followed him down the hall, I caught a glimpse of the den, a cozy-looking room with a large fireplace flanked by worn leather armchairs. Above the fireplace was a beautiful black-and-white photograph of a horse's face. Its eyes were dark pools reflecting specks of light.

When we walked into the kitchen, I heard Patti Smith on the stereo and smiled. Rain began to batter the window. We looked at each other, surprised. A moment earlier the sun had been out.

"Strange to have so much rain early in the season," said Denny, almost to himself, which was when I noticed the sheet of dough stretched across the kitchen counter.

"Is that homemade pasta?"

He grinned. "It's a hobby." He gestured to the small round table in the corner of the kitchen where a bottle of wine stood between two place settings. "Have a seat, pour yourself a glass of wine . . . this will only take a minute."

"Denny," I said. "I'm a lot of things, but I'm not a spectator." I rolled up my sleeves and washed my hands in the big white sink. "Teach me everything you know."

And he did. Well, not everything. But he taught me how to flatten the dough between the pasta machine's rollers and how to swap out the rollers for cutters and send the flattened sheet back through the machine and then catch the cut ribbons of pasta in my open palms. We moved together side by side, linked by spaghetti, from the pasta machine to the pot of boiling water and let the spaghetti roll from our hands. The entire time, I felt acutely aware of his body, strong and warm beside mine. Two minutes later, he pulled the pasta from the water with tongs and spun it around in a large porcelain bowl with a few hunks of butter, a sprinkle of parsley and black pepper, and a healthy spoonful of grated Parmesan cheese. The pasta was still steaming as he portioned it into two bowls and set them on the table. He took off his hat and hooked it on the back of his chair, then ran his hand through his hair. The rain drummed the window. Denny poured the wine. I wondered how many women—the other divorced mothers of his riding students, perhaps—had been treated to this display of culinary magic. I decided that it didn't matter. None of them were there now. It was just the two of us. And Bear snoring beside the table.

We clinked our glasses together.

"Thanks for having me," I said again.

"Thanks for coming," he said again.

I'd like to say we smiled at each other, but in truth, we grinned.

The pasta was so good that we were forced to eat in silence for a full minute before either of us could say another word.

"How was the thing with the horse yesterday?" I asked. "Is that trainer going to take her off your hands?"

Denny looked momentarily troubled. "No. He was willing, but I could see it wasn't going to be any better of a match than she and I are, and I didn't want him getting hurt."

I raised my eyebrows. "You were worried about the trainer?"

"She's a difficult horse. She needs something particular that I can't give her and this other guy couldn't either. I just hope I can help her. She can't stay here much longer. It's not safe."

I nodded. We spoke a little more about this horse named Georgia Peach, and then Denny told a funny story about a family he'd taken on a trail ride down to the beach that morning and how the father had spent the whole time swearing in French about how much his ass hurt—apparently Denny knew a bit of French—and then we talked briefly about Nic and how badly she wanted to ride again. And then after an ever-so-short conversational lull, I decided that all of the unknown parts of Denny's life needed to be unveiled immediately.

"Have you ever lived anywhere but here?" I asked him.

"I went to college in Colorado. And after college, I had a little place in San Francisco that I lived in until my parents retired. Then I moved back here."

"You've worked here since college?"

He nodded.

"Never anywhere else?"

"It's the family business. And I've always loved the land. This has always been what I wanted."

No wonder he always seemed so sure of himself. He'd figured out early in life exactly what he loved most, and he'd never let it go, never compromised it. "Smart man," I said.

He looked at me as he took a sip of wine. "I bet you feel that way about music."

"Yeah," I said, sitting back in my chair, feeling happily full. "I do."

Denny stood and moved our plates to the counter and then rummaged around in a cabinet. He returned to the table with two small squares of chocolate so dark they looked black.

"I refuse to call it a meal unless chocolate is involved," he said, handing me one of the squares.

"Really?" I asked, fascinated. "Even breakfast?"

"Breakfast more than any other meal requires chocolate. I drop it in my coffee." He sat down again and popped the chocolate in his mouth.

"Were you ever married?"

He looked at me steadily. "No."

"But you've dated?"

Now he smiled. "Yes. I've dated. I just haven't . . ." He hesitated, thinking. "I guess I never found someone that I couldn't live without."

"Oh, Denny." My temper inexplicably flared. Wasn't he old

enough to know better? "That's because there *isn't* anyone that you can't live without. She doesn't exist. People go on living and breathing even after their hearts are broken by those they love. Even when you think you can't possibly live without one particular person, you can. You do. There is *no one* that you can't live without, even the love of your life." I regretted the words even as I said them, sure that he guessed exactly whom I was really talking about. Why had I said all of that? Why was I thinking of Tyler?

Denny was quiet, studying me. "Okay," he said, finally.

I held his gaze for a beat of time and then dropped my head into my hands and laughed, mortified. "Sorry." *Nice work*, I told myself. Who wanted to date someone who believed she had already met and lost the love of her life?

"It's okay," he said again, but I could tell that wherever we'd been heading moments earlier, whatever we were about to hold in our hands and share, had now slipped out of reach.

Denny cleared his throat, but I spoke before he could.

"It's getting late," I said. "Nic should be home soon, and I bet you have a million things to do around here." He didn't argue. I put my napkin on the table and stood. "This was really nice. Thank you."

He looked up at me for a moment, then stood. "It was." He unhooked his hat from his chair and slid it on his head, pulling it low to his eyes. Which, I finally noticed, were a deep cornflower blue.

Chapter 16

Nic didn't enjoy pitting her parents against each other, but for her plan to work, she couldn't have a babysitter watching her every move. She had not foreseen that her mother would install a security guard in place of the sitter, telling Nic that a threat she'd received during a show had made her want to be overly cautious. But Nic didn't really mind the guard—she could work around him.

If Nic had had her way, Lucas would have come to get her on Monday night, but he wasn't able to slip out from under the watch of his mother, who was apparently in a particularly frazzled state of mind that week, until Thursday, when she had a meeting with her book club. Every afternoon, Nic sneaked into Peach's stall and told her of her plans. She felt the horse listening, her beautiful body growing still as Nic brushed her. Every night, Nic posted positive messages about her schoolmates on the *KirkeKudos* Instagram account she had created. She was happy to see that not only were her posts receiving supportive comments, but that the comments on *TheKirkeLurk7*'s feed seemed to have swung in the other direction. Not cool, someone had commented on the Lurk's latest post, an image of a sophomore football player unattractively stuffing a dripping, overstuffed hamburger into his mouth. Let it go, KirkeJerk! someone else commented.

Finally, on Thursday night at nine o'clock, just as they'd planned, Nic received Lucas's text message.

I'm here.

She pulled back the curtain in her bedroom window and peered down at the street. The security guard sat on their front steps, smoking. There was no sign of Lucas, but that, too, was part of the plan: he'd parked around the corner.

Nic set the house alarm—a habit ingrained in her by her mother—and left the house through the back door that led from the kitchen to the yard. The fence that separated their yard from their neighbor's was eight feet high. She'd never tried to climb over it before, but she was pretty sure she could do it. She could envision it in her mind—her arms reaching up and gripping the top of the fence, her leg swinging up and over. Her mom believed that if you could truly picture yourself doing something, you could probably do it. Her mom didn't know that Nic had read her book, *Number One Single.*

Nic had never spent time in the yard at night. She was surprised to find it was a little spooky, but she didn't want to draw attention to herself by turning on the outdoor lights. In the back corner of the yard, she jumped up and grabbed the top of the fence. Pulling herself up and over was harder than she'd thought it would be and she landed with a thud in the neighbor's yard, setting off a motion sensor that flooded the yard with light. She sprinted to the next fence and wrenched her body over it. By the time she made it through the next yard, the next fence, and then dropped down onto the sidewalk, she didn't know which was pounding louder: her head or her heart.

Lucas's car was double-parked halfway down the block. Nic slid into the front seat.

"Hey," he said. He looked surprised, which was when she realized that he had not really believed she'd do it. "You okay?"

She took a deep breath, trying to calm herself. Her body felt a little strange, a little . . . delicate. It had been more than two weeks since she'd done anything so active. "I'm fine," she said. "Thanks for doing this."

"It's okay. I owed you one."

His smile didn't help the situation with her pounding heart.

Lucas began to drive. "So why do you have a guard outside your house? Is your mom a diplomat or something?"

"No, she has a radio show. Her name is Gail Gideon."

Lucas glanced at her. "Really? Your mom is G.G.?"

"Yeah."

"Whoa."

He didn't seem overly impressed by Nic's famous mother, and she was glad.

The city soon fell away, leaving only the dark freeway, the starless sky, and the lights of other cars. In the quiet, Lucas told her about his friends in Brooklyn, his favorite coffee shop there, the art store where he bought his supplies. He talked about how instead of looking for the nursing job that she claimed to want, his mom now sat around the house all day reading self-help books and talking with a friend she'd left behind in Brooklyn who still saw his dad and knew all about the women he was now dating.

Nic told Lucas about Peach, how badly the horse needed her help, that she'd been abused, that if not her life itself than certainly her *quality* of life depended on someone breaking through to her and finding a way to make her trust people again.

Eventually she pointed out the exit and they veered off the freeway. Nic had thought that she had memorized every bend of the route, but the dark threw her. She was beginning to worry that she'd missed the turn when the car lights swung over the white-and-green Corcoran Stables sign. Instinctively, she reached out and put her hand on Lucas's arm.

"There it is!"

Lucas slowed and turned into the driveway, stopping in front of a large metal gate that blocked their entry. Nic had never seen the gate closed. In fact, she'd forgotten there *was* a gate; during the day, it was always open, half-hidden by the shrubby bushes that lined the driveway.

Lucas turned off the car's engine. He peered out at the gate. "Any idea if there's a camera on that thing?"

Nic got out of the car to take a look, all the while wondering if Denny was watching her on a video screen in his house. But she didn't see anything attached to the gate that might have been a camera. Lucas walked up beside her.

"I think we're fine," she said. The gate was easy to walk around; it was meant to deter someone from pulling up to the barn with a trailer to steal horses. Other than their shoes crunching against the dirt driveway, and the distant rhythmic hush of the surf pounding the shore, all was quiet. They walked until the driveway split; in one direction, the road veered toward Denny's house; in the other, toward the barn and indoor arena. A narrow strip of woods separated the structures. They hurried toward the barn.

The horses shifted in their stalls when Nic slid open the door. A string of whinnies moved down the aisle. The light in the area of the barn where Peach and Tru lived seemed especially bright, and she hoped that Denny wouldn't notice it glowing through the trees if he happened to look through his window in the direction of the barn.

Tru hung his head over his stall door and snorted a greeting. "This is my horse, Tru," she told Lucas. He stroked the side of Tru's head in the awkward way of someone who wasn't entirely comfortable with horses. Kind, forgiving Tru leaned into his touch and Lucas took a step back, surprised.

"Don't worry," Nic told him. "He wouldn't hurt a fly. That one, on the other hand . . ." She nodded in the direction of Peach's stall. Peach was weaving back and forth behind her bars, ears flattened. More than any other horse in the barn, she seemed agitated by their arrival. Nic walked over to her. "It's alright," she murmured. "We're here for a ride." The horse stilled. Her ears flicked forward, listening.

Nic felt Lucas at her side. He was looking at the sign on Peach's stall, the one that read DO NOT OPEN DOOR! "Are you sure—" he began. Peach's hoof smacked hard against the wall and they both jumped back, startled.

But Nic didn't have time to reassure him that Peach didn't behave like that when it was just the two of them—at any moment, Denny could find them and ruin her plans. She hurried down the aisle, leaving Lucas standing halfway between Peach's stall and Tru's stall. In the tack room, she zipped on her chaps. They felt loose; she'd lost some muscle during her time out of the saddle. Her helmet was missing from its usual hook—she realized she hadn't seen it since the accident. Maybe it had cracked when she fell and someone had thrown it away. She took another helmet from a hook—it was a bit small and made her head throb for a moment, an unwelcome reminder of what had happened the last time she'd ridden. She balanced her saddle on her hip and slung Peach's bridle onto her shoulder. With her free hand, she pulled her grooming box from her tack trunk.

Nic told Lucas to stay near Tru's stall while she brought out Peach. The horse stood very still as Nic entered her stall, slipped a halter over her head, and attached the lead rope. Nic could not help but believe that Peach somehow knew that tonight was important. Once out on the cross ties, though, Peach began to anxiously dance around and blow air from her nostrils. Her hooves were loud against the stone aisle and Nic had to keep reminding herself that Denny could not hear them from his house. She brushed Peach and picked her hooves clean. When she lowered the saddle pad and saddle onto Peach's back, Peach tossed her head and gnashed her teeth.

"Easy, girl," Nic said, stroking the horse's muscular neck. Peach tossed her head a few more times, but stopped gnashing her teeth long enough to allow Nic to slip off the halter and guide the bridle's bit into her mouth. "There we go."

As she walked the horse down the aisle, Nic worked to assert herself into the leadership position. With Tru, she felt she had a partnership, but with this mare, someone needed to be in charge. Nic wrapped her fingers around the reins and held her right fist close enough to Peach's chin that she could feel the hairs around her muzzle twitching. Peach tried to set the pace, high-stepping, weaving and dancing. Her hooves kept knocking against Nic's paddock boots. After they walked into the ring, Nic asked Lucas to shut the gate behind them. He stood there, seeming a bit lost, looking in over the gate from the barn aisle. Nic forced herself to ignore the feeling of his eyes following her. She had to think only of Peach now.

Peach skittered and danced and wouldn't stand still at the mounting block.

"Easy, girl." Nic managed to lower herself onto the saddle before Peach shot forward, nearly leaving her behind. She sank into her heels and let her tailbone melt heavily into the saddle and adjusted her fingers on the leather reins. As she drew Peach to a reluctant halt, she felt the horse's muscles shifting beneath her legs. She couldn't let Peach move forward on her own; it had to be a command from Nic. She waited a few more moments until it was clear to Peach that they were stopped because Nic wanted to stop, and that now they were moving forward because Nic wanted to move forward.

Being back in the saddle soothed something within Nic. Peach was a very different horse than Tru—bigger in every way—but Nic felt an uncanny sense of familiarity in Peach's movements. Maybe she had dreamed of riding her.

She could feel the horse's energy building as they walked. When Nic asked Peach to trot, the horse bolted forward and bucked, but Nic had sensed that she might do this and was prepared. She'd always had a good seat and it served her well now . . . she stuck like glue to that horse's back as it rippled and shook and twisted. Peach dropped her head low, ripping the reins through Nic's hands and in the same moment shooting her back legs powerfully out and up. Nic hardly moved. She gathered the reins and with them, the horse, below her, turning her sharply again and again. Peach was forced to slow. Nic rewarded her by pressing her forward off her leg into a more energetic trot. She moved the horse unpredictably, zigzagging across the ring, sparking Peach's curiosity. Peach was interested now, her mind as engaged as her body; she listened.

Nic saw that the overhead lights threw quivering shadows against the footing in the ring and she moved her body, anticipating and adjusting Peach's reaction to the sight, communicating reassurance and confidence. They moved in large circles, small circles, serpentines, and diagonal lines. Sometimes Nic sat, slowing the trot; sometimes she stretched the trot longer and posted up and down in the saddle.

The horse's coiled power was new to Nic. Tru's energy was accommodating; Peach was a singular force.

Nic sat in the saddle and asked for the canter. The horse moved beautifully; her canter was strong and smooth. They moved around and around the ring, switching directions, flying through lead changes, never slowing. Peach's energy uncoiled as she tired. Nic moved her up and down through her gaits, cutting through the ring in tight, round arcs.

Nic thought of what she wanted to do and Peach did it.

They were together now, dancing.

Nic felt full of joy and strength. She'd never loved riding as much as she did in that ring, on that night, with that horse. There was, suddenly, magic in the air.

No one else had been able to do this. Not Denny. Not Javi. Only Nic.

She slowed Peach and finally trusted the mare enough to give her a long rein. Peach stretched her neck low as she walked, cooling down after the hard ride. Nic emerged step by step from the world they had created together.

She noticed Lucas, still standing by the aisle gate. He looked different. Nic couldn't put her finger on it, but something in his expression had changed.

It wasn't until they'd driven all the way back to Bernal Heights that Lucas told her what he was thinking. He turned off the car engine. It was eleven o'clock at night. Nic's mom would be home from the studio in an hour. Lucas leaned his head back against the seat and turned to face her. She felt as though she could sit there looking into his dark eyes forever.

"I can't believe I thought you were pretty before," he said then. He seemed mildly disgusted with himself.

Nic felt her chest constrict painfully. She looked down into her lap, blinking.

"Oh, no," he said, straightening in the seat. He lifted her chin so that she looked at him again. "That came out wrong. You are *so* beautiful, Nic. I've known that from the first moment that I saw you in the cafeteria. It's impossible to look at you and *not* see that you're beautiful. Your beauty is a fact. It's like . . ." He broke his eyes away from hers and glanced through the car window. "It's like that stop sign. It just is. It's there. You can't deny it exists because it's right in front of you, stopping you."

Nic felt her mouth twitch into a smile. "My beauty is like that stop sign?"

Lucas looked at her so intently that her smile fell away. "I used to think so," he said. "But then I saw you tonight, riding that horse, and now . . . it's not just that I see how beautiful you are. Now I see the things that you can't see just by looking at you." He reached out and took her hands in his. "You amazed me tonight. You shouldn't let your mom tell you that you can't ride Peach. You shouldn't let her control you. This is *your* life."

He leaned his head toward hers and kissed her. When they parted, Nic felt breathless. He held his arms around her. She rested her chin on his shoulder, felt the side of his face against the side of her face. He smelled good. She breathed him in.

"We seem to have a thing for cars," she said. She felt his smile against the side of her cheek.

"I'd have a thing for you anywhere."

She pulled away and looked at him. "Let's test that theory," she said, and invited him inside.

For a moment she thought he might say no.

"Are you sure?" he asked. She told him that she was.

They helped each other over the eight-foot fences, darting through the neighbors' yards, unsuccessfully trying to stifle their laughter as the neighbor's motion-activated floodlights blinded them. They arrived, breathless, at Nic's back door.

"Never a dull moment with you, Clement," Lucas said, grinning.

Now that she felt comfortable touching him, she couldn't seem to stop. She kissed him. "We seem to have a thing for yards, too," she said when they separated again. She pulled up a loose brick from the patio and plucked the back door key from its hiding place. Inside, she had trouble thinking of anything but the pressure of his hand on her lower back, and fumbled with the alarm code.

They moved from room to room, holding hands and kissing.

"We seem to have a thing for kitchens," Nic said, laughing.

"We seem to have a thing for couches," Lucas said.

"We seem to have a thing for hallways," Nic said.

When he finally left through the back door, she had just enough time to shower off her horse scent before her mother came home from the studio. Nic was so exhausted that she almost fell asleep with the hot water streaming over her, her muscles sore from riding, her lips tender from Lucas's kisses.

Chapter 17

You appear to be in tip-top shape, young lady!" Dr. Feldman said, looking over the results of the series of exams that Nic had taken that morning.

Nic looked at me, her eyes bright. I knew exactly what she was thinking, knew exactly the question that was poised on her tongue. But I had my own questions, and I beat her to the punch.

"Is it possible that these tests could miss something? That there could be a lingering injury or change that you can't see on a scan?"

"It's not impossible, but it's unlikely. The results show that the swelling in Nic's brain has completely dissipated." Dr. Feldman looked back and forth between us. "Why do you ask?"

"Nic still isn't . . . quite herself." I turned to Nic. "You'd agree, wouldn't you? It's important that Dr. Feldman has all of the information."

"Sure," Nic said agreeably. I was relieved that she didn't seem bothered that I'd brought up the subject. I'd noticed that she'd been trying and failing to suppress a smile all morning. My best guess—since she only pressed her lips together and shrugged when I asked about her buoyant mood in the car—was that she expected Dr. Feldman would give her clearance to ride.

"Why don't you tell me a little more, Nic?" Dr. Feldman prodded.

She puffed out her bottom lip, thinking. "I guess it's mostly that the things that used to worry me, or scare me, don't anymore. I remember how I used to feel, but I don't feel that way now."

"It's the not-being-scared part that worries me," I said. "She had an incident at school where she stole a—"

"Mom!" Nic interrupted. "You said you yourself did plenty of things when you were—"

"But I was a very different girl than you are, Nic, and—"

"Maybe we're not as different as you think," my daughter said. Her arms were crossed in front of her chest in a way that suggested they might never uncross again.

"That might be, but I still want to be sure you're not at risk of doing something dangerous. If your doctor thinks there's anything we can or should be doing to alleviate some of the personality—"

"I just want to ride again!" Nic's voice cut into the room, urgent and sharp. Dr. Feldman had been flicking his gaze back and forth between us, but now it landed squarely on Nic. "I remember the accident now, Dr. Feldman." She told the doctor what she had already told me—she'd ridden Tru into the woods despite Denny's warning and tried to jump over a fallen tree. "Since I remember, that means I'm healed, right? I can go back to riding horses now?"

The doctor sighed. "I can only repeat what I have said before: a second head injury would likely have more serious repercussions than the first. Your scan looks good, Nic. You're healed. What you do with your healed brain is up to you and your parents."

Nic beamed triumphantly. She turned to look at me. I wondered if she'd even heard what Dr. Feldman had said about the risks of a second injury. I could hardly believe what I was about to say, but what could I do? Take away the thing that she loved most in the world? I had a terrible feeling that if she were able to choose how she would die, she would choose dying on horseback in the same way that I might choose dying listening to music. In the end, of course, this didn't matter at all. We didn't get to choose how we died, only how we lived.

"Okay," I told her. "You can ride Tru tomorrow. I'll go with you."

For a split second, she hesitated, and in that moment I immediately regretted my decision. Had she, somewhere deep inside, hoped I'd refuse? But then she was hugging me tightly, and there was nothing more I could possibly say.

On the drive to the barn on Saturday, Nic kept shifting in the passenger seat, too excited to sit still. Her energy only fed my own nerves—I was still uncertain about my decision to let her ride . . . and I was also nervous about seeing Denny. We'd spoke a few times that week, but it had seemed to me that our conversations had become stilted since our date. I wondered whether being face-to-face would make things between us more or less awkward.

It turned out that in the week since I'd been to the barn, fall had arrived. Sometimes it took leaving the city to notice these things. The long dirt drive to the barn was speckled with fallen yellow leaves; the bright sunlight reflecting off of them made the driveway seem to glow. I parked and opened the door, surprised by the chill in the air. I would have liked to have taken a moment to enjoy the beautiful day and the view of bright green pastures that surrounded us, but Nic was already jogging away from the car, so I hurried after her into the barn.

"Hey, Nic!" one of the barn hands called down the aisle. "Denny asked you to go find him at home when you got here."

Nic was having trouble containing herself. Her boots were clicking an eager tap dance against the aisle's stone floor. "Can you get Denny?" she asked me. "I'll start grooming and tacking up."

I was happy for the excuse to be able to see where I stood with Denny without Nic watching. "Just don't get on until we're back . . ." I called after Nic, but she'd already ducked into the tack room.

I left the barn and followed the dirt driveway toward Denny's house. His boots stood guard by the door. I knocked and he appeared in the doorframe moments later, a silver thermos in his hand.

"Hey, G.G." he said. The ease and warmth of his voice immediately relieved me. "I ran out of coffee at the barn and had to come home for a refill. Would you like some?"

"Sure." I pulled off my boots and padded into the house after him.

In the kitchen, Denny reached high into a cabinet for another thermos, his faded flannel shirt stretching across his back. "Milk? Sugar? Chocolate?" he asked.

I smiled, remembering his sweet tooth. "Black is fine." He handed me the thermos, and I took a sip of the hot, strong coffee. "That's delicious. Thanks."

He raised his eyebrows. "Really? I'd add milk and sugar to milk and sugar if I could." As if to emphasize his point, he lifted the top off the sugar pot and popped a sugar cube into his mouth, smiling as he crunched into it. He held up the pot, wiggled it. "I can't tempt you?"

"You can, actually," I said. I plucked a cube of sugar from the pot and dropped it into my mouth.

I could have sworn his eyes twinkled with delight as he crunched through that sugar cube. There was so much that I still didn't know about him, so much that I wanted, I realized, to know. I felt a mix of excitement and impatience. Was it really possible that I hadn't felt this way since Tyler? I'd had so many first and second and third dates, countless fizzled flirtations . . . all that time waiting to feel as strongly as I felt about a man who had been happily remarried for years.

I felt Denny watching me. He cleared his throat. "Last weekend—"

"I know," I cut in, shaking my head. "It was all going so well, and then I said some things that I shouldn't have said."

He leaned back against the kitchen counter and crossed his arms. "I got the impression that you're hung up on someone else."

"I'm sorry." I managed to suppress the urge to walk over to him and uncross his arms. "I used to be hung up on someone else. My ex-husband. It wasn't my decision to get a divorce. But we did, nine years ago, and he's been remarried for a long time. I'd like to meet someone else. I'm open to it. I just haven't."

Denny smiled, lines deepening around his blue eyes. "Until now."

I couldn't stop myself: I set the coffee thermos on the counter, walked over to him, uncrossed his arms, and held onto his hands. "Until now."

He looked down at me for a beat of time, and then in a remarkably deft move, he turned both of us around so that I was the one leaning against the counter. He burrowed his fingers into my hair, holding my gaze just long enough that I felt a shiver of anticipation run down the length of my spine. And then he kissed me. His hands moved down my back, pulling me toward him. The space between our bodies melted away. He lifted me onto the counter and I wrapped my legs around him. I felt hungry for him . . . it was nearly impossible to pull away. But I did, finally.

The way he looked at me, his gaze liquid with desire, almost made me forget why I'd stopped. But then understanding flooded his face.

"Nic," he said.

I nodded. "She's at the barn, waiting for us."

Denny took a deep breath. He leaned in and gave me one final kiss and I took hold of his shirt to make it last longer.

"I wanted to do that last week," he said when he pulled away. "But you ran out of here too quickly."

"I won't make that mistake again." I slid, reluctantly, off the counter.

Denny moved his hand over his face, as though trying to re-adjust to the light in the kitchen. I was beginning to see that the gesture was a habit for him; he managed to make it seem vaguely philosophical. "So this is the big day. Nic must be excited."

"Do you remember those little rubber Super Balls?"

He squinted at me. "Sure. I had a collection of them when I was a kid."

"Imagine one bouncing around a small city house—off the walls, off the stairs, off your *face* at six o'clock in the morning. That has been Nic today."

He smiled. Desire still warmed the air between us, pulling us toward each other. He wrapped his arms around me again. "She's a great rider," he said in my ear. "She's going to be okay."

Despite Denny's reassurance, I felt an uncertainty that bordered on dread building within me as we headed back toward the barn. When we arrived, the aisle was empty. Tru was still in his stall. I checked for Nic in the tack room and she wasn't there. When I stepped back into the aisle, Denny was staring at an open stall across from Tru's.

A young man suddenly sprinted into view at the open door

at the far end of the aisle. "Denny!" he yelled. "You better come quick!"

For a moment, from the edge of the barn looking down toward the large ring, it could have been any pissed-off horse and determined rider. But then the familiarity of the rider's dark hair, her tall, thin body leaning as the horse bucked and twisted below her, registered like a slap.

"Nic!" I cried, and began to run toward the ring.

Denny grabbed my arm. "Wait," he said. "Just walk. We don't want to spook Peach . . . or distract Nic."

The name Peach rang an alarm. Wasn't that the horse Denny had been talking about last weekend? The one he'd said was dangerous? I sucked in a frightened breath.

"She's okay," Denny murmured as we moved toward the ring. "She's stuck on that horse like a tick."

Nic was cantering the horse in increasingly tight circles. As I watched, the horse abruptly tossed her head and released a series of irate bucks. I winced with each jolt, but Denny was right: Nic seemed glued to the saddle.

"Did you know about this?" I hissed.

"Of course not. I would never let her . . ." His voice trailed away as he gripped the top rail of the fence, his eyes pegged on Nic and the mare. They were at the far end of the ring, still moving in circles. It took everything in my power not to yell out to Nic, but I was too scared of surprising her or the horse to raise my voice.

After several excruciatingly long minutes, Peach seemed to lose interest in killing my daughter. She moved into a canter now, tracing an invisible figure-eight pattern in the sand of the ring. Each time the pair crossed through the center of the eight, Peach lifted off the ground for a beat, swapped the direction of her lead midair, and landed smoothly on the new lead: a flying lead change. Moments earlier the horse had seemed ugly with rage, but now she was transformed: powerful and beautiful, too, the slope of her neck and neatly tucked nose almost regal.

Even on that huge, gleaming horse, Nic looked strong. They looked like a match. I thought back to the many times that I'd watched my daughter ride Tru and the quiet loveliness that I'd seen in their partnership, the care they took with each other. Nic and Peach were different. I could practically hear Nic thinking the whole time that she rode. Peach pushed her, dared her. I could see this horse suffered no fools; lower your guard for a moment, and she would seize her advantage. Nic rose to the challenge. I'd never seen her ride so well. I'd probably never seen anyone ride so well.

The hairs on my arms tingled.

I was absolutely furious with my daughter, but I could not deny what I was seeing. I thought back to Nic's urgent pleading in Dr. Feldman's office. There was an urgency and intensity to how she rode today, too—and to how Peach responded. It was impossible to watch them and not feel moved.

The horse turned down the centerline of the ring, still cantering. Nic looked in our direction, but didn't seem to see us; her physical gaze was pinned in the direction she wanted her horse to move, but her focus was centered somewhere deep inside of herself. When they reached the dead center of the ring, Peach halted without any visible command from Nic. My daughter's eyes focused; she smiled at me. Then she leaned forward to murmur something in the horse's ear and stroke her neck. Peach walked on. Nic let out the reins a few inches, giving the horse room to stretch her neck. They stopped at the rail in front of us.

"What were you thinking?" Denny asked her. There was an angry growl in his low voice.

Before Nic could answer, Peach lowered her head almost to the ground and sighed loudly. Some emotion that I didn't understand moved over Denny's face. He lifted his hand and stroked Peach's forehead twice.

"She's a good horse," Nic said simply.

"She's not safe," Denny responded, but there was doubt in his voice. If I heard it, Nic surely did, too.

"She almost bucked you off!" I said, finally trusting myself to speak.

Nic laughed. "Oh, that? She was a little fresh at first the last time, too. She just needs to blow off steam before she gets to work. I *let* her buck." She abruptly clamped shut her mouth, but it was too late.

I stared at my daughter. "What do you mean *last time, too*?"

She began to play nervously with Peach's mane. When she looked up again her eyes were wet with tears. She pressed her lips together.

"Nic," I said, forgetting for a moment to keep my voice low. The horse jerked up her head and gave a surprised snort, pinning back her ears and glaring at me from glittering black eyes.

"Mind your manners, Peach," Nic said. "That's my mom." My daughter's voice was almost unrecognizable—it was clipped and authoritative, but gentle, too, a beast with a soft belly. The horse seemed to hear all of it. Her ears perked and rolled to the side, listening. "Mom, please don't be mad. I *had* to ride Peach. I just had to."

"What are you saying?" I asked.

Nic glanced at Denny, then back at me. "I rode her once already."

"What?" said Denny. "No, you didn't. I would never have let you."

"You weren't here," Nic said, so quietly I almost didn't hear her. "You were at home. It was late at night."

"What?" Denny and I said, in unison. Peach jumped away from us. My heart skittered in my chest, but Nic sat still in the saddle as though the horse hadn't moved an inch. I didn't even see her flinch.

"You need to get off that horse right now," I said.

"I can't. I still need to cool her down." Her words shook with the quiet timbre of desperation.

"Off," Denny said. I could see his jawline tensing. "*Now.* You can walk Peach from the ground."

Nic's shoulders slumped. She swung a leg behind her and slipped off Peach's back. She turned toward Denny and me slowly, as though facing a firing squad.

"How did you get here at night without me knowing? Who drove you?" I asked.

"A friend."

"Who?"

Nic looked down at her feet.

"Who?" I demanded.

"His name is Lucas. He goes to Kirke."

I shook my head angrily. Lucas. He must have been the same kid who helped her take that boy's car off school property. As mad as I was, I could feel Denny's anger looming even larger beside me. "Go," I told Nic, waving her away. "Go walk that horse."

Denny watched her go. "I can't believe she would do this," he said. "What if she'd been hurt?"

I turned to him. "You don't lock the barn at night?"

He bristled. "I lock the gate at the bottom of the drive."

I took a deep breath, reminding myself that Denny wasn't the one I was angry with. "I'm sorry . . . I didn't mean . . ." I sighed.

"This isn't your fault. Nic did this. I can't *believe* she did this." I could hardly bear to think of what could have happened to her. How had she managed to get past the security guard at our house? Who *was* this child? It was as though she had changed overnight, and I had no idea how much the accident was to blame.

Denny stuck his hands into his pockets and rocked back on his heels, squinting out at Nic and Peach as they walked around the far end of the ring. Nic was talking to the horse, and possibly crying. The low hum of her voice carried across the ring to us. The horse seemed to lean toward her slightly as they walked.

"She's fourteen years old," I said. "Maybe I just need to tell her she's not allowed to ride anymore."

Denny's eyes followed Nic and Peach. He didn't answer.

"But it would be like taking away her spirit," I said after a moment. "I couldn't do it."

"No, I don't think you could," Denny said. He rubbed at the stubble on his chin. "Or should."

We both watched Nic and Peach for a few moments in silence.

"I don't quite understand how she's done it," Denny said quietly, "but in all likelihood your daughter has just saved that horse's life."

"Oh," I said. "Wow."

"You know she's going to want to ride her again."

I groaned. "Whatever happened to good old safe and steady Tru?"

Denny shot me a rueful grin. "Remember my mom putting you on those ponies? I think your daughter has officially discovered her inherited need for speed." He adjusted the brim of his hat. "This isn't great timing, G.G., but there was something I wanted to—"

"She's cool now," Nic called, strolling toward us with Peach trailing behind.

"Keep walking!" I barked. When I turned back to Denny, he was studying me, amused. "What were you saying?" I prompted.

"Oh, just that I noticed that Patti Smith is playing in San Francisco next weekend. Do you want to go with me?"

"You have tickets to the Patti Smith show? At the Fillmore?"

"Well, no. Not yet. I wanted to ask you first."

I smiled at him. "I'm sure it's sold out by now."

Denny looked crestfallen. "Shit."

After checking to make sure Nic wasn't watching, I couldn't resist reaching out to touch his arm. I shouldn't have done it, though; it only made me want more.

"Lucky for us, I already have tickets through work," I said. For the moment, my anger at Nic was displaced by the thought of seeing Denny again soon.

I'D ALWAYS THOUGHT that I would be able to sense if someone had been in my home without me knowing, but it turned out I was wrong. Or maybe I'd been lulled into a false sense of security by the sight of Bodie, the security guard who stood watch outside. Or maybe I was distracted by the fact that Nic and I had spent most of the drive home from the barn arguing. I stepped through the front door, walked to the kitchen to get a drink of water, and stopped. In the middle of the counter was a vase of dead red roses, their limp, blackened petals hanging from broken stems. The water in the vase was murky; the air smelled of rot.

When we left for Corcoran Stables that morning after breakfast, there were no flowers in the kitchen. The counter had been clear. I'd wiped it clean myself.

Nic followed me into the kitchen and wrinkled her nose at the smell. "Yuck," she said. "Where did those come from?"

"I have no idea." The only people who had keys to our home

besides Nic and me were Tyler and Simone. There was no chance that either of them had entered the house while we were at the barn and left those rotten flowers behind. I stepped closer to the counter. There was no note, no explanation, just a vase of dead flowers on broken stems.

"'Roses are the loneliest flowers,'" said Nic, behind me. "'If someone gave me roses, I'd consider it a threat.'"

I turned and stared at her. She was quoting me. I'd said this, or something like this, during a show weeks earlier, in response to a woman who had called and told me that her husband kept treating her like shit and then trying to make up for it with bouquets of roses. I knew Nic listened to the show occasionally, but it was deeply unsettling to hear her quoting me as we stood in our kitchen inhaling the stink of the rotten flowers that had been placed in our home while we were out.

I had the disturbing sense that the house was holding its breath, quietly watching and waiting. Somewhere in the neighborhood, a driver repeatedly pressed his car horn.

"We need to go," I said. With one hand I guided Nic toward the front door, and with the other I pulled my phone from my pocket and dialed 911.

Chapter 18

The silver lining of the creepy flower incident was that it completely distracted Nic's mom from how angry she was about the Peach situation. Two police officers arrived and searched the house and determined that nothing had been stolen. Bodie, the security guard, was sure that no one had entered through the front door. There were no broken door locks or windows. Other than the flowers, the house was just as Nic and her mother had left it.

"Who else has a key to your house?" one of the officers asked Nic's mother. "And knows the alarm code?"

"Just my ex-husband and my best friend. Neither one of them would do this." Her mother kept asking Bodie if he'd seen a woman lingering around the house—an old fan of hers who Nic gathered had given her mother some sort of trouble in the past—but he told her that he hadn't seen anyone who looked suspicious.

The officer asked for Nic's dad's contact information. By then, Simone had arrived and she, too, spoke briefly with the policemen. After that, it became obvious that their only lingering interest in the break-in was that it had happened to Gail Gideon. It seemed to Nic that her mom signed more autographs than police paperwork that night.

Simone kept insisting that they spend the night at her house, but Nic's mom turned down the offer. She said that she refused to be chased out of her own home. Also, she said, Simone was a prime suspect.

Simone had laughed and said something about how they could rule her out because if she'd broken into the house she would have stolen all of Nic's mom's Velvet Underground CDs. This must have been an inside joke between the two of them because Nic's mom rolled her eyes and laughed. It was the first time since they'd left the barn that the twin lines of worry between her eyes smoothed.

Later that night, Nic's mom seemed to finally remember how mad she was at Nic. When she threatened to call Lucas's parents, Nic talked her out of it.

"Please don't get him in trouble," she said. "His mom is in a really weird place right now and, anyway, it was all my idea. He was only trying to help me."

Her mother leaned back into the couch and studied her. "It seems like every time there is some sort of trouble, this Lucas guy is nearby."

"Twice, Mom. Hunter Nolan's car and one time riding Peach at night. That's it." She could see that her answer didn't sit well with her mother, so she hurried to add, "It's not going to happen again. It's over."

"With Lucas?"

"No. The *lying* is over. Not Lucas."

To HER RELIEF, Nic's mom allowed her to continue riding, but only Tru, and only in the ring with Denny or another riding instructor present. Riding Tru was like holding a pair of her own baby shoes in her hands and marveling at their tidy quaintness, the impossible fact that they had once fit. She remembered the depth of her love for him, but she could no longer summon the same feeling—only a sweet, nostalgic affection for the times that they had shared. When she dismounted and her feet hit the ground, it felt like awakening from a pleasant nap.

After she put away her tack and groomed Tru and returned him to his stall, she stood in front of Peach's stall. The horse pressed her face against the bars of the stall and Nic rubbed her forehead. Nic wasn't allowed in her stall. Denny's orders. She could feel Denny watching as she pet the mare. She hated that he was disappointed in her and she desperately wanted to earn back his trust, but she could not bring herself to regret what she had done. She saw the way that Denny peered into Peach's stall now, looking at her almost as though she were a new horse. He would never give up on her now that he'd seen what she could achieve with the right rider. Nic had found a way for Peach to show everyone the horse that she could be . . . the horse that she *was*.

Nic wandered back into the tack room. She sprayed Murphy oil soap on a small sponge and began to wipe down Peach's bridle. If she couldn't ride the mare, she could at least keep her tack clean. Denny appeared in the doorway of the room. He watched her for a few moments, then sighed and said, "Even if your mom agreed to it, I don't know that I could let you ride her again."

Nic didn't say anything. She worked the dried sweat and grime from the underside of the bridle crown, her fingers growing numb with the effort.

"Help me understand, Nic," Denny said. "Start from the beginning." He sat on her tack trunk and put his hands on his knees.

Nic glanced at him, then went back to working on the bridle.

"I went into her stall the first day I came back to the barn after the accident. She seemed so alone. She was angry, but scared and sad, too. She knew everyone had given up on her and it only made her angrier—she thought she had nothing left to lose. I just stood in there with her at first, but then I kept going in every day—sometimes just for a few minutes. When she started to trust me, I began to groom her a little. She accepted me. I'm not afraid of her, Denny. I feel like I . . . understand her." *And she understands me*, Nic almost said, but didn't. She had a feeling Denny would know that she meant this, too.

"Sneaking into her stall is bad enough," he said. "But I really can't believe you came here at night and rode her. If something had happened to you, your mother would have been devastated. *I* would have been devastated." He rubbed at his chin. "You broke my trust, Nic."

At this, Nic felt tears well in her eyes. "I'm sorry. I really am. If I'd thought there was any other way, I wouldn't have done what I did. But I knew you'd never let me ride Peach, and I knew she didn't have much time. I heard Javi talking about how no one would ever want her because she was too dangerous to save. But I knew Peach wasn't . . . isn't . . ." She trailed off. How could she explain this to him?

"I can *feel* what she's going to do, where she's going to move, Denny. It's like I know it even before she does. I know what she's thinking. I can *feel* what she's thinking." Her face was flushed. She didn't want Denny to think this was a game to her. She didn't sneak into the barn and ride Peach as some kind of silly prank. She did it because she *had* to help Peach. She had never felt so sure of anything in her life. She'd seen Denny with horses; if anyone could understand what she was trying to say, it was he.

"I don't know why she chose me, but she did. Or we chose

each other. But I understand her better than any horse I've ever ridden." Nic grew quiet. "Maybe it's because of the accident. Maybe something happened to my brain."

"And gave you special abilities?" Denny shook his head. "Nic, you've always had a gift with horses. Ever since you were a little girl."

This is different, though, Nic thought. She was sure of it. Whatever she had with Peach was something she had never had before. If the accident had done this, she was glad. She loved hearing Peach's thoughts. It was a special gift, and Nic's alone.

She rubbed neat's-foot oil into the leather reins, softening them. She pushed back her shoulders and pressed down into her heels the way she would if she were riding a horse that was beginning to think about trying to lose her. She felt a fire burn in her belly as the muscles at her center engaged.

"I want to sell Tru and buy Peach. You saw us out there. You saw how she acted, how she moved. She trusts me. I believe in her. You saw it, didn't you, Denny?"

He studied her for a moment before replying. "It's not every day that I get to see riding like that."

A compliment from Denny was hard-won. Nic tucked it away in her mind, hoping she would remember it, hoping it would burn brighter than all of the memories that she had of feeling humiliated and embarrassed and invisible.

"Will you talk to my mom?" she asked. "Convince her to let me ride Peach again?"

"I don't think your mom is the kind of person who can be convinced to do something that she doesn't want to do." Denny stood and adjusted the rim of his baseball cap. "But I'll talk to her."

Nic threw her arms around him. "Thank you!"

As Denny was stepping through the tack room door into the aisle, Nic called after him.

"You know," she said, "Peach moves well during flat work, but I have this sense that where she's really going to shine is over jumps."

FRIDAY WAS THE day of their Shakespeare presentations and it turned out that Mr. Hylan's great surprise for the class was that not only would they take the stage one by one in the school's theater, but that Dr. Clay and their senior buddies from their Freshman Connection class would be in the audience. Nic turned in her seat in the front row and watched as the seniors trailed into the theater. Lucas took a seat a couple of rows behind Nic's. He smiled at her and raised one dark eyebrow as though in a mix of sympathy and amusement. They'd hardly spoken in school all week, but every time they passed each other in the halls, they shared a private smile. She would feel his eyes following her as though he didn't want to look away, and she would think of that moment in his car when he had told her that he thought she was amazing, that he believed in her connection with Peach.

Not long ago, she would have made herself sick worrying over the Shakespeare presentation and begged her mother to let her stay home from school that day. But now, other than a slight concern that she might forget a line, Nic felt calm. She knew the kids that were sitting in that theater really well. Over the past couple of weeks she had made it her duty to know them, to observe them and to try to understand the people that they were becoming. There was so much goodness in them.

Nic wrote about their generosity, their humor, their intelligence, their quiet focus, their infectious energy, their unique and subtle strengths on the *KirkeKudos* Instagram account. The outpouring of support for *KirkeKudos* both online and in the halls of Kirke seemed to have beaten the Lurk back into his cave; he hadn't posted in a week. Nic had overheard classmates hypothesizing about who ran the *KirkeKudos* account, but so far no one had guessed that it was her. She hoped they never would. She suspected the strength of the posts' impact depended upon anonymity. A compliment from one person could be ignored; a compliment that seemed to come from the community as a collective settled under your skin in a more permanent way.

Lila nudged her. "Nic, you're up."

Nic walked up the side steps onto the stage. Without hesitation, without even a momentary stutter, she looked out into the audience of her peers and began to recite the lines of the soliloquy she'd been assigned. It was only once she had finished and was walking down the stage steps that she noticed Lila was holding something low in her lap. It was a cell phone, and Nic was fairly certain that her friend had just taken a picture.

AFTER ALL OF the students had recited their monologues and there was a brief but enthusiastic final burst of applause, the seniors were dismissed to return to their regular classes. Lucas, pulled into the wave of students leaving the theater, flashed Nic a smile. Nic waved back.

Dr. Clay caught the exchange and sidled up to her. "Well," she said cheerfully, watching Lucas walk away, "you two seem to get along swimmingly. Your mothers must be pleased."

"Our mothers?"

The teacher's face clouded. "Oh, that's right, I wasn't supposed to mention it. But there's no harm, really, is there? Lucas came to me when he first arrived at school and asked to be your senior buddy. He told me that your mothers are good friends, and that they worked together on your mother's show at one time. I thought it sounded like a fine idea. He'd just moved here and was starting school a few weeks late. I could see how a familiar face would be a comfort to him, and it sounded like something both of your mothers would be happy about."

"Oh," Nic said. A lump had risen in her throat, making even this small response difficult. She thought of Lucas asking if her mother was a diplomat, when all the while he'd known that she was Gail Gideon.

She and Dr. Clay both looked again in the direction that Lucas had walked, but he was already gone.

Chapter 19

In my office, I played Sonic Youth's *Daydream Nation*. All week, I'd been having trouble thinking about anything other than those dead roses in our kitchen. Nothing in the house felt as it had before; that asshole's presence was perceptible everywhere, like a layer of dust coating things once clean. The only times I didn't think about those roses were when I had breakfast with Nic, when I thought about how I was days from seeing Patti Smith with Denny, and when I listened to music. By the time Martin appeared in my office, I'd turned Sonic Youth up so loud that the floor vibrated with each guitar riff.

"I KNOCKED," he yelled, dropping down into one of the chairs on the far side of my desk.

I nodded. "WHAT'S UP?"

Martin raised his eyebrows toward the speakers behind my desk. Without breaking eye contact with him, I pointed the remote over my shoulder and turned down the volume.

"How are you doing?" he asked. Adam from security must have told him about the incident with the roses.

I could tell he was really concerned, and it only made me feel worse. If Martin Jansen was at long last actually worried about one of my stalkers, then I was in even more trouble than I'd realized.

"Shitty," I said. "But the show must go on."

He wasn't about to argue. "You know that I doubled studio security. You're safe here."

"Here, maybe. But this happened in my own home . . ."

"We should have given you a security team years ago."

"You did. I refused it. I didn't want my daughter to have to live like an inmate. Anyway, I have security outside my house now, and someone still managed to get in."

Martin drummed his fingers against his thighs. "Gail, I just want you to know that nobody at Talk960—nobody in *all* of Hawke Media—is going to be able to sleep at night unless you feel safe."

I nodded, thinking about those renewal contracts that Martin was eager for me to sign. Sooner or later I was going to have to break the news to him that *The Gail Gideon Show*'s days were numbered. I just wished I could figure out what I would do instead.

He shifted in his seat, glancing toward the stereo. "Is this Sonic Youth?"

I was surprised. "I didn't peg you as a Kim Gordon fan, Martin."

He wrinkled his nose. "Oh, I'm not. My daughter plays this stuff. It makes my teeth hurt."

I laughed. "I think my listeners would love 'this stuff.' "

Martin gave a wry smile. "Gail, they'd love anything you told them to love. You hold them captive in the palm of your hand for fifteen hours every week. If you told them that eating an otter's tail would help them live happier lives, we'd be a nation of otter hunters by morning. Well, *half* a nation," he added, meaning, of course, the female half.

"Maybe I'll test your theory. Play a little Sonic Youth during tonight's show."

The smile fell from Martin's face. "Very funny."

I didn't respond.

"Gail," he said. "This is a *talk* radio station. You host a *talk* show."

Simone opened my door and poked her head in. "Forty minutes 'til air," she said, glancing back and forth between us. Martin kept his eyes on me.

"I'm ready," I said.

"Gail," Martin said.

I waved him away. "I know. No music."

He held my gaze for a beat longer than necessary and then finally nodded, satisfied, and stood. "Have a great show, ladies."

The door hadn't even clicked shut behind him before Simone began to laugh. "What was that little battle about?" She dropped down into the same chair that Martin had just left.

I shrugged, irritated and feeling chafed by the station's rules. I pointed the stereo remote over my shoulder and turned up Sonic Youth, loud. Really loud. Simone grinned. She pumped her fist in the air a few times and bobbed her head. I pounded my boots against the floor. We sang along with kick-ass Kim Gordon, gleefully ignoring the pained looks of Hawke Media employees scurrying by in the hall.

"How was Nic?" I asked Roy as I slid into the car after the show that night. As usual, the backseat held the subtle, lingering smells of Corcoran Stables.

"Great," he answered. I could tell he was relieved and pleased to be able to provide such an upbeat answer. "She's been keeping me entertained. Very talkative this week. I think it's good for her to be riding again. That kid's smile gets me right here every time." Roy patted the area of tweed blazer that covered his heart. "Like an arrow."

"What has she been talking about? Riding Tru?" I asked hopefully.

Roy's lips screwed into an apologetic grimace. "No. Mostly she's been talking about Peach."

Roy knew the whole story of Peach and Nic; I'd filled him in on the weekend's surprises when he'd picked me up on Monday. He'd grown pale as I'd told him that Nic had made the dangerous horse her pet project, driving more and more slowly until I'd managed to reassure him that Nic was okay.

"She's proud of what she accomplished with that horse," Roy ventured now, surprising me. "She feels really good about herself. She doesn't say it, but I can see it. She's carrying herself differently."

I nodded, watching his face in the mirror. This was more than he usually spoke on our rides home from the station, knowing that I preferred to quietly listen to music after talking so much during the show. I didn't mind, though. I never minded talking about Nic.

"And it *is* really something, isn't it?" he said softly. "She's fourteen years old and she saved that huge animal's life. What an amazing feat. Can you imagine being so brave?" He shook his head in wonder. "Some people go their whole lives without worrying about saving anyone but themselves. But not our Nic." He smiled. "I guess a certain someone cut a pretty good path for her to follow." He glanced at me in the mirror and winked, and my eyes, right on cue, swam with sudden tears.

I swallowed. "Are you saying that you think I should let her ride Peach?"

Roy looked aghast. "Of course not! It's much too dangerous. Let someone else take the risks now. Nic's done her part," he said, just as any grandfather worth his salt would.

Chapter 20

On Saturday night, Nic was watching a movie with her brothers when Lucas texted her. Her heart sped up when his name appeared on her cell phone.

> Can you come out tonight? There's something I want to show you.

Nic studied his words. I'm at my dad's house in Mill Valley, she replied.

There was a brief pause and then Lucas typed, Text me the address. I can be there in thirty minutes.

She thought of the feel of Lucas's lips against hers, and the way that sometimes, when he looked at her, the storm clouds in his eyes evaporated and sweetness and affection took their place, softening his features. Why had he pretended to not know who her mother was? She thought back to the moment on his first day at Kirke when their eyes had met in the cafeteria. Had he searched her out? Was he one of those people her father had once warned her about, the people who might want to be close with her only because she was the daughter of a celebrity? Had everything between them been a lie?

Her trust in Lucas, so tenuously built, was now shaken, and she longed to right it.

Okay, she wrote, and sent him her father's address.

Then she went upstairs to her bedroom, flipped through her school directory, and uploaded two new posts to *KirkeKudos*.

Chapter 21

"You got a haircut," I said, sliding into Denny's truck on Saturday night. He wore dark jeans and a wool peacoat and looked as clean as I'd ever seen him. I was glad that he still had a shadow of scruff around his jawline.

He ran his hand through his hair. "More than one," he answered and grinned. He leaned over and kissed me, holding the side of my face in his hand. The move felt bold, the sensation of kissing him still new and surprising. Patti Smith might have been the only person in the world who could have made me do anything but sit in that car all night, kissing Denny Corcoran.

As we drove to the Fillmore, he asked if there had been any developments on the stalker situation. Earlier that week, I'd told him about the dead roses in the kitchen and the whole history with Jenny Long, and he had seemed preoccupied with the subject ever since.

I told him that I hadn't received any threats since the roses had appeared. "It's been quiet—a little *too* quiet," I said dramatically, and then laughed. I was happy to be riding with Denny in his truck and didn't feel like lingering on the topic of Jenny Long.

But Denny wasn't ready to move on. "I worry about you, G.G."

I reminded myself that I'd had years to get used to the downsides of fame; this was all new to Denny, and probably overwhelming. "I know," I told him. "I worry, too. But this stuff comes hand-in-hand with my job. I have to make peace with that or I'll go crazy. I have to be able to laugh about it every once in a while. But all jobs have drawbacks, right? I bet you have to deal with overinvolved, overprotective parents all the time, don't you? That can't be fun."

"When the parent is hot and single," he said, raising an eyebrow, "it can actually be a *lot* of fun." His smile disappeared quickly. "Seriously though, if you and Nic ever want to get away from everything for a bit, you can always come stay with me. I mean that—regardless of whatever happens with us. I have lots of room."

I put my hand on the back of Denny's neck. "I appreciate that. I really do. But I'm not going to run away. Besides, if we stayed with you, Nic would never want to leave. We'd probably find her sleeping in Peach's stall."

Denny cleared his throat. "Well, yeah. About that. You know Nic wants to buy Peach, right?"

"What?" I said. "Now she wants to *buy* her?" I still didn't understand how Nic had gone from lobbying to get back in the saddle of her own horse, Tru, to being obsessed with this troubled horse, Peach. But obsessed she was. She talked about the horse every chance she had, and now even Denny was making a case for letting Nic ride Peach again.

"Nic isn't making the greatest decisions right now," I said. "What if she wakes up one day and completely regrets having sold Tru? And how can we possibly trust her to ride a horse like Peach?"

"I'll train them myself. Nic won't get on that horse unless I'm in the ring with them." Denny paused. "Listen, you take a small risk when you get on any horse, and a bigger risk when you get on a horse like Peach. Nic's decided the rewards—for both that horse and for her—outweigh the risks, but she's fourteen years old. She doesn't get to make that decision on her own."

I couldn't deny that I'd seen something special between Nic and that horse, something that it felt wrong to forbid.

"Fine," I said. "If you'll train them, Nic can ride Peach. But let's hold off on selling Tru for now. Maybe she'll come to her senses."

THERE IS JUST *something* about live music—the primal call-and-response echo of the beat and your own pulse, the roiling energy of the crowd, the excitement of seeing your idols in person. I watched Patti Smith *own* the stage, her long hair swinging as she sang and growled and moved. She was unpredictable and magnetic. A sense of hunger electrified the room like a challenge. The tone of her voice said that she was still searching, she still had so much more to do and say and create. She was passionate and singular and a beast of an artist—in other words, at sixty-something years old, Patti Smith was a fucking rock god. Her voice spoke right to me, maybe in that moment more than ever before.

I knew what I would do with my show. I literally had goose bumps. Patti Smith, personal hero, poet laureate of punk, gave me that final, loving shove of inspiration, as she always had.

When she played "Because the Night," Denny and I grinned at each other. I'd heard the song so many times before, but the idea of feeding on a banquet of love had never felt as true as it did in that moment, standing beside Denny, hearing Patti's voice and feeling so gloriously full of joy that I could only dance and dance and dance.

In my pocket, my phone buzzed. I felt Denny glance at me as I pulled it out. Tyler's name appeared on the caller ID I slid the phone back in my pocket. A few moments later, it buzzed again. And then again. Irritated, I yanked it from my pocket and read the text that Tyler had sent in lieu of leaving a voicemail.

Nic is missing. Call me.

As Denny and I jogged toward his car, I called Tyler. Nic had had dinner, watched part of a movie, and then told her brothers that she was going to read in her room. When Tyler went upstairs to wish her goodnight, her room was empty, and her cell phone lay on her bed. "Do you think she went to the barn again?" he asked.

I told him that Denny had already sent one of his employees who lived near the stable to check if she was there. "I'll call her friend Lila. Maybe she knows something." I still had Lila's number programmed into my phone from when Nic had had a sleepover at her house during the first couple of weeks of school.

Lila claimed to not know where Nic was. When I asked if they'd spoken that day, she said they hadn't, but there was something in her voice that made me question whether she was telling the truth.

"What about this boy she's been seeing?" I asked. "Lucas. Do you have his phone number?"

"Lucas Holt," she said quickly. "Yeah, hang on, let me check the school directory." The line was silent for a few moments. "There's no phone number . . . maybe because he just moved here? There's an address, though. Do you want that?"

I told Lila that I did, and then repeated it so that Denny could begin driving in the direction of Lucas's house.

"Will you let me know when you find her?" Lila asked. "There's something I really need to tell her."

The caginess had edged its way back into her voice. "Lila," I said, summoning my most stern, adult tone. "Is there anything else I should know? Are you sure you didn't speak with her at all today?"

"No, I—I didn't speak with her. But she posted something online earlier tonight . . . maybe forty minutes ago?"

I felt my chest constrict. "What do you mean 'she posted something online'?" On top of everything else, had Nic broken my rule about avoiding social media? She'd been with me when we'd discovered those dead roses in the kitchen . . . surely she wouldn't think it was safe to put her life on display for a bunch of strangers?

"Well, I'm not positive that it was her." Lila told me about an account called *KirkeKudos* that had been posting on Instagram lately. "No one knows who's running it. Whoever it is posts nice things about our classmates at Kirke. New ones have been showing up on the account every day." I had the sense that Lila was trying not to cry. "There were two posts tonight. One was about Lucas Holt. The other was about me."

"And you think Nic wrote them?"

"She said some really nice things. I think she might be the only one who knows me well enough to write that stuff." Now she did begin to cry.

"And Lucas?" I asked. "What did she write about him?"

"That one was sort of strange, actually. It wasn't the usual *KirkeKudos* thing. Hang on. Let me read it to you." There was a stretch of silence.

"'Lucas Holt: Your anger is a flame that will never rage as boldly as your heart. We see you living valiantly, saying yes when all others would say no. You are an artist, and your fire is a mystery that pulls us close even as it burns.' "

Even as it burns? My throat grew dry. What the hell was going on?

TWENTY MINUTES LATER, we pulled up to a small but neat house in San Bruno. I stared at the silver Mercedes with a New York license plate that was parked in the driveway, then hurried toward the house. A woman around my own age answered the door, her eyes widening in surprise and excitement as she saw me. Her hand flew to her mouth, her dark, Jenny Long–like hair swinging against her shoulders. The woman that I'd seen in front of Kirke had not been Jenny Long—it had been Lucas Holt's mother.

"Oh my God! G.G!" she cried. "What are you . . . ? What is going on?" Her eyes darted beyond me, taking in Denny's presence. Her expression toggled frantically between delight and confusion.

I was sure that I had never met this woman in my life; this was the reaction of someone who had opened her door at ten o'clock on a Saturday night to find a famous person—her idol, perhaps—on her doorstep.

"I'm sorry to bother you so late," I said. "I'm trying to get in touch with Lucas Holt. He goes to school with my daughter, Nic, and she's missing."

The woman's eyes widened. "I'm Lucas's mom, but he isn't home. He went to the movies with some friends. Maybe Nic is with them? Do you want me to call him?"

"Yes, please."

"Come in. Let me just get my phone." The woman stepped back from the door so we could pass inside.

"I'm Gail Gideon," I said, because it felt strange to walk into her home without a proper introduction. "And this is Denny Corcoran."

She barely glanced in Denny's direction. "I know who you are, G.G. I'm one of your biggest fans!" The woman's cheeks flamed red. "Oh, I didn't introduce myself! I'm Evie. Evie Holt." Her hand fluttered to her forehead. "No, *Giambalvo*. Evie *Giambalvo*. I'm getting a divorce. I never guessed it would turn out so hard to remember my own last name—and I had it a lot longer than I had my husband's!"

Ah, I thought. *A woman in the throes of a divorce.* My target audience.

The living room held a couch, an armchair, and a TV, but there was nothing on the walls. There was a mess of Legos on a small table in one corner of the room, and an overflowing bin of kids' toys. "I'll just grab my phone from the kitchen," Evie said. "Please have a seat anywhere you like."

I faltered when I noticed a copy of my book, *Number One Single*, splayed cover-up on the coffee table. Denny noticed it, too, and raised his eyebrows at me.

"See!" Evie said, coming back into the room with her cell phone in her hand. She plopped down close beside me on the couch and pointed at the book. "I told you I'm a fan. It's not even my first time reading it! I was just sitting here alone"—she lowered her voice confidentially here—"feeling a little sorry for myself, when I decided to pull out your book and reread some of my favorite parts. I have all the best bits underlined so they're easy to find when I need them." She beamed at me. "And then the doorbell rang! Who knew you made house calls!" Evie gave my knee a playful shove.

"I'm really worried about my daughter," I said, casting an unsubtle glance at her phone.

"Oh, yes. Yes, of course. Let me call Lucas right now." Evie poked at her phone a couple of times and then held it to her ear. I could hear the phone ringing and ringing, the faint sound of a male voice on an outgoing voice message. Evie held my gaze, her mouth twisting apologetically. "Lucas," she said. "It's me. Mom. You'll never guess who I'm sitting next to right now . . . Gail Gideon! From the radio show? Anyway, she's very upset. Her daughter is missing and she says the two of you are friends. Is that true?! Are you friends with G.G.'s daughter? Have you seen her tonight? Call me when you get this, sweetheart." She looked at me. "It's *important*."

She seemed disappointed as she set down the phone. Then she brightened. "Let me text him, too. He might not listen to the voice message when he's at the movies, but I bet he'll see a text." Her fingers pecked at the phone, her brow furrowed with the effort of concentration. After a few moments she looked up again. "I'm so sorry. I wish he'd picked up. Hopefully he'll text back soon."

"Do you know which theater he went to?" Denny asked. "Maybe we should drive there."

It was hard to imagine Nic sneaking out of her father's house to see a movie, but it was also impossible to imagine her stealing a car, or secretly riding a dangerous horse, or signing up for an anonymous Instagram account and posting things about her classmates.

"I don't know," Evie said slowly, embarrassed. She waved her hand in the direction of the hallway behind her. "Lucas's little sisters are both down with fevers. I've been so distracted with them, I didn't think to ask Lucas which theater he was going to. I'm sorry."

"Would you mind if we waited here with you for a few minutes?" I asked. "In case he texts back right away?"

"Oh, no, not at all! Please, make yourselves at home. It's the least I can do. I should have asked Lucas where he was going. It's just that I've been trying to give him space lately. That's what our family therapist thinks he needs." She looked down at her knees. "He's been so upset about the divorce. I think he holds everything inside too much—he needs to let it out! I wish he'd talk to me. But the therapist says not to worry, he'll talk when he's ready. He has his art, at least. Even when he won't talk to me, I know he's processing some of his emotions through drawing."

I was half-listening to Evie, half-staring at her phone, willing her son to text her back. Where was Nic? What teenager goes out without bringing her phone? *The kind*, I thought, feeling a pang of dread as I mentally answered my own question, *who does not want to be found.*

"Would you like to see them?" Evie asked.

I looked up at her.

"Lucas's drawings," she said. "They're really quite wonderful."

I glanced at Denny. "Sure," he answered, surprising me. "Let's take a look."

As we followed Evie down the hall, he whispered to me, "Thought it might not hurt to have a peek in the kid's room."

I nodded.

It turned out that Lucas's drawings *were* wonderful. The boy was an artist. His work was full of movement, tiny lines that filled pages. The room was papered with hundreds of his drawings. There were a lot of studies of trees moving in the wind, darkly beautiful works that reminded me of that strange electrical storm that had hit the city the night before Nic's accident.

"Your son is very talented," I told Evie.

Her face beamed with pride. "I'm just so happy he has this outlet. Art has been his guiding light through everything that has happened—the separation, moving across the country." She kept talking as Denny and I moved slowly around the room, looking at the drawings. "He has his art, and well, frankly, G.G., I've had *you*. I'm sure you must hear this all the time, but I really don't know where I would be without you. You gave me the courage to face the fact that Max would never really love me. Listening to your show every night, reading your book . . . it gave me the strength to leave him."

"I'm glad I was able to help," I told her. "But I hope you know I didn't *give* you that courage. You had it in you all along. Maybe I helped you find it."

Denny was standing in front of one particular group of drawings. I moved to his side. They all showed a girl riding a horse. The girl was faceless, but there was something both powerful and ethereal about her stance that reminded me of the way Nic looked when she rode.

"Yes," Evie said. "I'm sure you're right. I'm sure that courage was in me all along, buried deep down and neglected for so many years. But you guided me to find it. I don't know where I'd be without you, G.G. Not here, though. I know that. You're my role model." She gave an embarrassed laugh. "I even decided to send Lucas to Kirke because I'd read somewhere that that was where you planned to send your daughter to high school. And now they've become friends!"

Her words were still burrowing their way through my mind when I saw it, the drawing that made me suck in my breath. I felt my knees buckle as fear took me in its grip.

Swirls of tiny angry lines that formed a vase of rotting roses, blackened petals falling from broken stems.

Chapter 22

Lucas drove Nic across the Golden Gate Bridge. On one side, the lights of the city glowed beautifully; on the other, the sea was an invisible expanse of darkness. The Pixies' "Wave of Mutilation" played on the radio. Nic wanted to ask him why he'd requested to be her senior buddy, why he'd lied about knowing who her mother was, but when she looked at him, the soft, steady pulse of her heart overwhelmed her. Warmth spread through her chest. She reached out and traced his cheekbone with her thumb, because she could. She believed that her questions could wait. She believed she had time.

"Where are we going?" she asked. They were driving into the city now, one of a line of cars speeding along the curves of the road as it cut through Golden Gate Park.

"You'll see," Lucas answered. "We're almost there."

They turned onto a street that hugged the edge of the park. After a few minutes, Lucas pulled the car to the side and turned off the ignition. He reached into the backseat and grabbed a flashlight and a backpack.

"Ready?" he asked.

Nic's pulse suddenly thudded. There was so much that she didn't know about this boy, and yet—he'd helped her blindly, when there was no one else she could ask for help. "Yes," she said.

They walked deeper into Golden Gate Park. Nic reminded herself that they were still in the city. Hundreds of thousands of people lived within a few miles of where they were now walking. Lucas held her hand tightly, interlacing his fingers with hers. She wondered if the sudden quiet made him feel a bit spooked, too. He turned on the flashlight and they followed its bobbing light into a cave-like tunnel that ran below an overpass. Wind caught in the tunnel sounded like a low moan. Nic's teeth began to chatter.

Lucas stopped in the center of the tunnel. "We're here," he said. "It's time."

Before she could ask what he meant, he leaned down and unzipped the backpack he'd placed on the ground. Then he turned off the flashlight and the tunnel fell into thick blackness. Nic felt a cry forming in her throat—

She heard a click.

Suddenly on the dark walls and the ceiling of the tunnel, a painting emerged, its tiny strokes glowing fluorescent, pulled from darkness by an ultraviolet lantern that Lucas had taken out of his backpack. Nic's portrait was on one side of the tunnel, her hair whipping the air above her as though blown by storm winds, but her hair also seemed to be the storm itself, swirling through the tunnel in spirals big and small, a sheet of rain and dancing winds that were as intricately patterned as embroidered cloth, as mysterious as the lines and dots of some ancient alphabet, a letter written from another time.

Nic turned in the center of the tunnel, her head thrown back as she tried to see everything at once. She lowered her eyes, finally, to meet Lucas's. His face glowed in the strange light of what he had created.

"I've been working on it all week," he said quietly.

"I don't know what to say," she whispered, walking toward him. "It's amazing."

"Of course it is," he said. "It's you."

When Nic wrapped her arms around him, she realized that he was trembling.

On the drive back to her father's house, Lucas told her that the painting was his way of apologizing.

"For lying to me?" Nic asked. "You acted like you didn't know who my mother was, but Dr. Clay said you *did* know. She said you asked to be my senior buddy."

Lucas glanced at her, then back at the road. She could not read his face. "I knew who your mother is," he said. "I've known for years."

Nic listened, frozen, as Lucas told her that a couple of years earlier, his mother had become obsessed with listening to *The Gail Gideon Show*. When Lucas's mother told him that she was leaving his father, Lucas had felt sure that it wouldn't have been happening if it weren't for Gail Gideon. Yes, he'd known all along that Nic was Gail Gideon's daughter. He'd wanted to get close to Nic so that he could get close to her mother, and find ways to make her mother's life as difficult as his own had been for the past year. He told her that he'd called her mother's show and sent her messages and even broken Roy's car's headlights one night.

"I thought I was going to hate you, too," he told Nic. "I wanted to hate you. But I couldn't." He glanced at her and then quickly away again, as though he couldn't bear the look on her face.

"You weren't at all who I expected you to be, Nic. You changed everything. You're so beautiful, inside and out. I started to see myself, what I was doing, through your eyes, and I felt ashamed." When he blinked, a tear rolled down his cheek. Nic squeezed her hands in her lap. She didn't want to believe what he was telling her.

"The night I saw you ride Peach, I knew I couldn't hate your mother anymore. I did one last thing, just to . . . prove to myself that I could, I guess. To mark that the whole thing was done."

"You left the roses in our kitchen," Nic said slowly. He'd seen where she hid the house key. He'd been at her side when she entered the alarm code.

Lucas nodded, his expression pained. "I would never have done anything that physically hurt her," he said quietly. "She didn't do anything to physically hurt me."

Nic felt her temper leap to life. "She didn't mean to hurt you at all, Lucas! She doesn't even know who you are!"

"But that's exactly what made me so mad. She doesn't have any idea about the real lives of the real people who listen to her show."

"She helps a lot of people, Lucas. *Millions* of people. Do you really think that your mother should have stayed with your father? That they were happy together?"

Lucas shook his head.

"My mom can't *make* people get divorced," Nic insisted. She felt angry and confused, her loyalty to her mother flaring bright. He had threatened the person that Nic loved most in the world.

"No, I know she can't," he said. "I just kept hearing her voice on the radio every night, over and over again, and it sank into me. And then I couldn't let it go. But I have now—I've let it go. I promise that I have. I know I was wrong, and I'm so sorry for what I did. I thought that moving here meant that my life was over . . . I thought it was the worst thing that could happen to me." He looked away from the road and into Nic's eyes. "But now I know it's the best thing that could have happened to me."

Quiet fell over the car. Lucas's confession had left Nic feeling sucker-punched. Her whole body ached. But there was a part of her, she was surprised to discover, that felt moved by the ferocity of Lucas's anger, his compulsion to act, finally, and take control of a part of his life that had felt out of his control for so long. It was confusing to still care for him, but she did.

"Can I ask you something?" Lucas said. "You write the *KirkeKudos* posts, don't you?"

Nic hesitated for a moment, wondering if she was ready to give up this secret, before answering. "Yes."

"No one has ever said anything like that about me before." When Lucas glanced at her again, his face was full of anguish. "Can you ever forgive me, Nic?" he asked.

She thought of the picture he had drawn for her in Angel Bully's car, how it had helped her remember the way that the earth had cradled her when she fell from Tru, protecting her, teaching her, sending her back.

She was about to answer Lucas when she saw the headlights that should not have been moving toward them. It was too late to warn him, or to answer him—or to say anything at all. The jolt slammed her backwards against the seat and forward again. The car was spinning, screeching.

When Nic tried to find Lucas, she saw only stars.

Chapter 23

When Evie received the call from the hospital alerting her that Lucas and "a female passenger" had been in a car accident, she ran to ask her neighbor to watch her sleeping daughters and then we piled into Denny's truck and sped toward the city. In what felt like a moment of déjà vu, I called Tyler on the way and he said that he would meet us at the hospital. Denny drove so fast that it was a miracle we didn't get into an accident of our own. My stomach was in my throat the entire ride, my knuckles gripped tight as though preparing to hurt the boy who had put my daughter in danger yet again. I kept hearing Dr. Feldman's voice telling me that a second head injury would be more serious than the first. Every once in a while Denny glanced over at me, his expression a mix of worry, empathy, and stoicism. He didn't say a word, though. Didn't offer one syllable of verbal comfort. Even in the midst of a crisis, he was a straight shooter. I found more consolation in his quiet than in any number of empty words.

Still, I would have traded everything—every paycheck, every

fan, even the unexpected happiness that took hold of me in this man's company—for my daughter's safety.

Denny let us out at the doors to the emergency room, and Evie and I ran inside. Nurses led us straight back to our children. Evie was taken in one direction and I was taken in another. We exchanged one final glance before she turned out of view, and in that look I saw all the worry of a mother in my same shoes.

"Mom!" Nic said as I ran to her bedside. She was sitting up, smiling, and looking ludicrously healthy despite her hospital gown.

"Oh, Nic!" I cried. I hesitated, running my eyes over her body for signs of broken bones, and then threw my arms around her.

She released a sound that was half-laugh, half-moan. "They told you I was okay, didn't they? You weren't worried, were you?"

"Nicola Clement. You ran off somewhere and didn't tell anyone where you were going and the next thing I know, you're in the emergency room. *Again.* Of course I was worried! What the hell happened? How's your head? Has someone called Dr. Feldman?"

"I'm fine. Yes, someone called him. They already did a CT scan and said everything looks okay. I didn't ever lose consciousness or anything. I remember the whole thing. A car ran a red light and hit us."

"You and Lucas Holt."

She nodded. "One of the nurses told me that he broke his arm in three places. But he's okay."

"He won't be when I'm through with him."

Nic's face fell. "This isn't Lucas's fault."

I sighed. "Nic," I said gently. "I'm pretty sure that Lucas is the person who has been threatening me for weeks. He smashed Roy's car headlights. He broke into our house." I was still having trouble wrapping my mind around the fact that it was highly unlikely that Jenny Long had anything to do with the recent string of threats that I'd received, but my daughter looked suspiciously unsurprised by the news that her friend was involved. *Had she known?*

"He didn't really *break in*. He knew where I kept the key. He knew the alarm code."

"What?"

"I'm just saying he didn't technically break in to anything."

"You're defending him? And, wait—what do you mean he knew where you kept the key? You had this guy over to our house?"

Nic ignored this last question. "You just need to get to know the *real* Lucas, Mom. He's an amazing person. He made a mistake. One big one."

"More than one. So many more than one! Nic, he has been *threatening* me. I don't think you understand how serious this is."

"I do . . . but he has reasons for what he did. And he's sorry. And he would never have hurt you. He's an *artist*, Mom. He's passionate and talented and intense . . ." Nic trailed off. She looked beyond me, her eyes brightening. "Denny!" she cried. "What are you doing here?"

Denny walked up beside me, shoved his hands into the pockets of his jeans, and grinned at the sight of Nic, healthy and chatting away. "I wouldn't miss one of your hospital stays, Nic. It's a tradition at this point."

She looked back and forth between the two of us. Understanding dawned in her expression, as well as, I was relieved to see, a smile. "Oh, okay, you two. Riiiight."

There was a faint knock on the door and then Evie was peering tentatively into the room. "Could we . . . would you mind . . . is it okay if Lucas and I come in?"

I was about to say that actually yes, I did in fact mind very much if she brought a dangerous stalker into my daughter's hospital room, but Nic spoke first. "Lucas!" she cried. And there he was, behind his mother: the infamous Lucas Holt. I could see immediately that he was a teenage girl's dream: brooding eyes, a dark flop of hair, chiseled cheekbones. I saw, too, how very young he looked. It was hard to picture this boy smashing Roy's car headlights in the dark of night.

"Oh, Nic, are you okay?" he asked, hurrying to my daughter's other side. "Is your head hurt again? I am so, so sorry." His head was buried into her shoulder. One cast-covered arm poked out from his side.

"I'm fine. Really, I am. How is your arm?" Nic asked softly. She kept her hand on his cheek as she spoke to him. Their faces were inches apart. Her green eyes searched his face.

Evie and I glanced at each other, shifting uncomfortably.

Denny cleared his throat.

Evie spoke first. "Lucas," she said firmly. "I brought you in here because you said there was something important that you needed to tell Nic's mother. Something you needed to set right?"

Lucas faced me, straightening. The color seemed to have drained from his face. He glanced at Nic and she nodded encouragingly. "She knows," I heard my daughter whisper. "It's okay."

"It is definitely *not* okay," I said loudly.

Lucas swallowed. "I owe you an apology, Ms. Gideon. I was looking for someone to blame for what happened to my family, and I found you."

"Lucas," his mother said. "What are you talking about?"

"I called in to her radio show, Mom. I threatened to ruin her life."

"WHAT?"

"That's not all he did," I said.

"No, that's not all," Lucas said. He looked down at his feet. "I emailed Ms. Gideon, too. And I texted her. And I broke her headlights. And left dead roses in her kitchen."

"Oh my God," Evie breathed. She sank down into a chair in a corner of the room. "I cannot believe this. What are you saying? How could you do this to a woman who has been my . . . my *rock* for so many years?" She looked up at me. "G.G. Ms. Gideon. I—I don't even know what to say. I had no idea. I can't believe that I had no idea this was happening."

"He was so angry," Nic said from the bed. She'd reached out her hand to hold Lucas's. "He was going to go to a special art program in New York and then all of a sudden he had to leave his home and . . . his life wasn't his anymore. Anger can make you do things you wouldn't expect of yourself in a million years," she said, sounding so much older suddenly than her fourteen years. The pleading look in her eyes was so fierce that I had to look away.

"I am so sorry, Ms. Gideon," Lucas said. "I'm so sorry, Mom. I know what I did was wrong. Words can't really express how I'm feeling right now." He looked right at me. "But I'm going to find a way to show you how sorry I am."

Oh, boy, I thought, watching his dark eyelashes tremble over his reddening eyes. I glanced at my daughter, and then back at Lucas. In my mind, I kept running through the things that he had done, the calls and email and headlights and roses, trying to reframe them as the acts of a troubled kid. Did I actually have it in me to forgive him? I pictured myself at his age. Had I ever felt so angry that I could have smashed someone's headlights? I realized that I had. I felt so grateful to have shed the worst of my childhood rage and sadness, to have created a life for myself that allowed me to grow and heal.

But weren't girls supposed to be attracted to boys that reminded them of their *fathers*, not their mothers? A young Tyler 2.0 would have been so much easier to handle.

The door to the room opened and a nurse walked in, smiling and whistling as though she were strolling onto the set of *Singing in the Rain*. The smile slid right off her face as she glanced around the room. "Hi, everyone. We just need to run a few quick cognitive tests on Nicola." She shot me an apologetic smile. "Mom can wait here and work her way through a boatload of paperwork."

Nic swung her legs off the bed and stood. Her legs were so long and thin that whenever she stood I half-expected her to stagger off to the side like a newborn giraffe, but there she was, strong and solid and full of grace. She hugged Lucas and then me. Lucas received the longer hug, and yes I was counting.

"I love you," she whispered in my ear. And then, the dynamite: "And I think maybe him, too."

At the door she turned and gave a cheerful wave, and then was gone.

Unlike Nic, Evie rose unsteadily to her feet. "Let's go, Lucas," she said. "You have a lot of explaining to do and I, for one, am not getting any younger." As she steered Lucas from the room, Evie paused and turned to me. "He's a good kid. Beneath all of this mess, believe it or not, there's a really good kid."

"Nic certainly agrees with you, Evie."

She released a grateful smile, then gave her son a much-deserved shove into the hall.

When I turned to him, Denny was waiting with open arms. I pressed my face against his chest and breathed in his deeply soothing scent. "Holy hell," he said in a low voice. Inexplicably, we both began to laugh. Once we started, we couldn't seem to stop. We were still shaking and wiping at our eyes when Tyler rushed into the room. He skidded to a stop at the sight of us. Denny and I stepped away, but not that far away, from each other.

"Hey—hello—I—" Tyler stammered, looking back and forth between us. "Where's Nic?" He took in the empty hospital bed. "Is she okay?"

"Oh, Tyler, I should have called you right away. She's fine. She was here a minute ago. She's just gone for a few last tests."

His shoulders slumped with relief. "Thank God." He looked at Denny, blinking.

"Do you remember Denny Corcoran?" I asked. "He owns the barn where Nic rides."

"Also," Denny added, taking my hand and a little piece of my heart at the same time, "he's dating your ex-wife."

Chapter 24

Later that night, when Nic was discharged with a clean bill of health from the hospital, she asked her parents if she could go home with her mother instead of returning to her father's house.

"You don't mind, do you, Dad? I'd just really love to sleep in my own bed tonight." She also had a feeling that her mother would be sleeping on her bedroom floor that night, and after the crazy night that she'd had she didn't mind the thought of this one bit.

Her father hugged her tight and let her go.

THE NEXT MORNING, Lila came to visit. She sat on the edge of Nic's bed and seemed uncharacteristically at a loss for words.

"It's been a while since *TheKirkeLurk7* posted," Nic ventured finally.

Lila immediately burst into tears. "Oh, Nic! It was me! I've been the Lurk this year!"

"I had a feeling." Nic leaned back and crossed her arms.

Lila blinked. "You did? But you wrote such nice things about me on *KirkeKudos*. That's you, isn't it? It has to be you."

Nic nodded. "It was easy to write nice things about you—you *are* nice, Lila. You're such a good person. Why would you write things that made people feel so bad about themselves?" She gave a little shudder. "I spent *weeks* feeling scared that I would be humiliated by the Lurk."

"I would never have written about you, Nic."

"But I saw you take a picture of me when I was finished with my Shakespeare presentation!"

Lila's brow furrowed and then cleared as she wiped at her tears. "Oh, I was taking a picture of Malin Jones! She was going up to the stage as you were coming down."

"You were going to post about Malin? She's so nice!" Nic had always liked Malin, a dreamy girl with a soft voice and a penchant for long, flowing skirts.

"It wasn't going to be that harsh. Just something about those new purple glasses she's been wearing."

Nic shook her head angrily. Even though she'd suspected Lila was the Lurk, it was painful to hear her friend actually admit these things. "Why do you care what color glasses she has?"

"You're missing the point, Nic. As long as I'm the Lurk, neither of us will ever appear in a post. *I* control who shows up on there. I can make sure it's never you . . . or me." She lowered her eyes. "I don't think I ever told you, but I wasn't always the most popular kid in middle school. People said things that . . ." She trailed off, shaking away fresh tears. "I didn't want that to happen again. So when I started at Kirke and heard rumors about the Lurk, I just decided to do it myself before anyone else could. No one passed it down to me, I just signed into Instagram and created a new account. *TheKirkeLurk7*."

"So you made fun of a bunch of other people to save yourself?"

Lila waved away this thought. "I mostly threw softballs. And I picked targets that could handle them."

"Like that swimmer, Bridget? She was devastated, Lila. I saw her crying in the bathroom."

"Bridget is a swimming goddess and cute as a freaking button. Bridget is *beloved.* No stupid comment from the Lurk could make an impact on how people feel about that girl."

Nic could see that Lila really believed this. Lila, too, in her own way, had thought of herself as a version of Robin Hood, stealing bits here and there from the rich to spare the poor. Nic thought of Hunter Nolan's crumpled Spanish essay in the back of his car, the one with the trail of bright red circles so thick you could barely see what he had written. She thought of Lucas, all confident intensity on the outside, the sensitive core easily hidden below.

"Bridget isn't as strong as she seems," she said. "No one is."

Lila thought about this and slowly nodded. "I guess you're right." She straightened. "I won't do it anymore, Nic. I promise. Just say we're okay. I don't know if I can handle Kirke without you by my side."

"We're okay, Lila. We're always going to be okay. Maybe now that you have a little more time on your hands, you could help me run the *KirkeKudos* account."

Lila brightened. "That sounds like excellent college-essay material."

Nic shook her head, laughing.

The girls pressed their hands together, bowed their heads, and with one final, giggling "om shalom," the Lurk was gone.

SUNDAY NIGHT WAS always Nic's night with her mother. She could not imagine that there would ever be a time in her life when this would not be the case. On Sundays, they ate dinner together. They listened to music. Sometimes they talked until they were yawning more than talking. Other times, they didn't speak much at all—they curled into the couch and watched a movie, or read books.

That night, though, they reclined at either end of the couch and they talked. Patti Smith's *Horses* album played in the background. Her mom told her that she had gone to the Patti Smith concert with Denny.

"Would it be weird for you if I saw him more?" her mom asked. "If we were dating?"

"Yes," Nic said. "But good weird . . . unless you two broke up. Then it would be bad weird."

"We'll take things slow," her mom promised.

"Would it be weird for you if I dated Lucas?"

"Yes. *Bad* weird."

Nic poked her mother with her foot.

"The boy threatened to ruin my life," her mother reminded her. "He broke Roy's headlights and entered our house illegally. It's a little hard to bounce back from all of that. Not to mention that he's seventeen and way too old for you."

Something—her mother's expression, or the way her toe kept moving to the beat of the music; or something else, maybe, something perceptible only to Nic—told her that her mother did not feel as strongly as she claimed. Nic and Lucas had spoken on the phone earlier in the day. He'd wanted to visit her, but his mother would not let him out of her sight. Nic had said that she thought her own mother needed some time to process everything, anyway, but that she suspected in the end her mother would forgive Lucas. "What about you?" he'd asked. "Can you forgive me, Nic?" Despair and hope had fought in his voice.

"Yes," she'd answered quickly, relieved that the car that had hit them the previous night had not stolen her chance to assure him of this.

"Lucas painted the most beautiful mural in Golden Gate Park," Nic told her mother. "It's in fluorescent paint so you can only see it with a black light. It's . . . it's of me. And a storm. Or maybe I am the storm." She felt bashful telling her mother this, but seeing that painting had been one of the most special moments of Nic's life, and she could not fully come to grips with the experience until she had shared it with her mother.

"I'd like to see it sometime," her mother said.

Nic could feel her mother studying her, as she so often did. If anyone knew what to make of everything that had happened to Nic over the past few weeks, it was her mother.

"Do I seem different?" Nic asked.

"Yes, in some ways. But people change all the time. It's one of the things that make life interesting. No one should sing the same tune forever." Her mother's right toe was moving to the beat of the music the whole time that she spoke. "Do you feel different?"

Nic thought about this. "The little things that used to frighten me don't anymore."

"But you've always had that strength inside of you. Your father and I saw it. Denny saw it."

"Maybe it was trapped inside of me and the fall broke the container that held it." Nic frowned. "It's kind of sad that it took a brain injury to make me stop feeling so scared all the time."

Her mother shot upright. "The fall didn't break the container, Nic! *You* did. You told me yourself that you were embarrassed in front of Lucas that day and you were fed up with feeling like the person that you were on the outside didn't reflect the person you were on the inside . . . and then you *challenged* yourself to do something terrifying, something that only the person deep *inside* of you thought you could do. You *pushed* yourself to jump that tree. You did it! You broke the container, Nic . . . you broke it *before* you fell. Who knows if the brain injury has lowered some of your inhibitions . . . *you* set this all in motion." Her mother sat back again, thinking. "Maybe there are two kinds of change. One is the kind that involves transitioning toward something new. And the other is more like peeling away your own layers to find what has always been at your core."

Nic leaned forward and kissed her mother's cheek. "You know, you should really have a radio show. You're very wise."

Her mother hugged her and whispered, "Some of us find wisdom earlier than others. You're one of the lucky ones."

Chapter 25

One morning the following week, Denny took me riding. I hadn't been on a horse in more than twenty-five years, but settling into the saddle felt like finding a favorite old coat that I'd thought I'd lost long ago, slipping it on, and discovering that it still fit.

I rode Tru. His steady gait brought to mind an older gentleman gliding with ease across a dance floor. We followed Denny and his huge black horse, Zed, along the sandy trail that cut down through the cliffs to the ocean. Ahead of us, the vast Pacific Ocean sparkled below the morning sun. I breathed in deeply, overwhelmed by a sense of gratitude that my daughter was able to ride this gorgeous piece of land each and every day. Denny turned back and caught my eye.

"You look good on that horse, Gail Gideon," he said. "Who knows, maybe you'll decide to keep him for yourself."

"Who knows," I murmured. All week, I'd been allowing Nic to ride Peach under Denny's supervision. They both reported back to me that everything was going well—so well, in fact, that Nic was desperate to start jumping Peach. The thought of this gave me mild to severe heart palpitations, depending on how much coffee I'd had.

The trail met the beach and then we walked our horses side by side across the sand. They seemed to like the salt air and open expanse; I could feel Tru itching to move on under my leg.

"So what did you really think of the concert?" I asked.

"Patti Smith? She was great." Denny pulled a bit of straw from Zed's mane and let the wind carry it away.

"You don't sound convinced."

He looked over at me, lines spreading around his blue eyes as he smiled. "To tell you the truth, I'm more of a bluegrass guy."

I laughed. "I like bluegrass, too."

When he reached out and touched my hip, I felt a jolt of desire. He felt it, too, I knew. We looked at each other for another long moment before smiling and looking away.

"Today is the big day, isn't it?" he asked.

I nodded. During a meeting that afternoon with Martin Jansen, Simone and I planned to let him know that we would not be signing our renewal contracts. Instead we were going to produce our own show out of a studio space we'd not yet rented, under the auspices of a production company that we'd not yet founded. For three hours every night I would take calls from listeners, chatting with them about their lives and their relationships, their hopes and their fears, in much the same way that I did on *The Gail Gideon Show*. And then, based on whatever had inspired them to call and ask my advice, I'd select a song that I thought fit the circumstances and dedicate it to them. The show would be a uniquely mixed talk and music format, a strange little hybrid that felt true both to what my fans loved and to what I loved. Shayne was already preparing to present our idea for the show to a wide range of media and radio networks with an eye to national syndication. I felt a sense of excitement that I had not felt in years. There were no guarantees that my fans would follow me in this new direction, but I had faith in them, just as they had had faith in me for so long.

"Did you figure out what you'll call it?" Denny asked.

"*Love Songs After Dark*. It was the name of a show that I used to host. That show only played sappy love songs, but this one will be a mix of music. The idea is that, in a way, all songs are love songs—music connects people to each other, the way that love does, helping us all feel less alone. Nic says that I told her that, but I think that she actually told me."

"She's a smart kid," Denny said. He hesitated. "You know, I think she'll be ready to start jumping that horse this weekend."

I looked over at Denny, perfectly at ease in the saddle, telling me that my fourteen-year-old daughter was ready to jump a horse that a couple of weeks earlier he'd told me was too dangerous for *him* to ride. There was so much about this world of horses that he and Nic loved that I simply did not understand. But I'd never backed away from the unknown before, and I had no intention of starting now.

On Saturday, Nic opened the passenger door and ran toward the barn before I'd even fully stopped the car. I followed as quickly as I could, but when I stepped into the office, only Denny was there.

"She went to tack up Peach," he said.

"Should we keep an eye on her? Is she safe?"

Denny put his arms around me. He kissed my neck, just below my ear. Then again, lower down my neck. I breathed out slowly. When we finally pulled ourselves away from each other, I followed him into the aisle.

At the far end of the barn, Nic was a slip of a girl moving around the huge, gleaming mare on the cross ties. The horse's eyes flashed as Denny and I approached. She pinned back her ears and did an angry, clomping dance.

"We're almost ready," Nic said. "Just need to pick her hooves and get her tack on."

The horse appeared to respond to the sound of Nic's voice. She pawed at the floor again, but it seemed conciliatory. She was a beautiful horse—then again I thought that all horses were beautiful, and always had. But this horse had a special kind of power. It was hard not to admire her, and to admire the way that Nic clearly loved her. Nic's fierce devotion impressed me. I shook my head, in awe of my daughter's strength, her compassion, the goodness that had always been at her core and was now shining from her in new and remarkable ways.

Once Peach was tacked up, Nic led her to the outdoor ring. Denny and I watched from outside the ring as Nic climbed the mounting block. The moment she swung a leg over Peach, the horse immediately shot forward, but Nic seemed to have glued her seat right to that horse's center of gravity and she didn't shift from the spot the whole time I watched them. Peach only fought her those first few minutes; soon, Nic had her so distracted with gait and direction changes that Peach hardly had time to squeeze in a buck let alone an ear pin.

Denny looked over at me and grinned. "Not bad, huh?"

"Exceptional," I said. It was the word Denny had used long ago to describe Nic.

"Yes," he agreed.

We fell quiet then, watching. It was the kind of bright fall day that made you want to lift your face to the sky and close your eyes, but I couldn't pull myself from the sight of Nic and Peach moving around the ring. I recognized the flying lead change, the beat of midair suspension and fresh spark of energy as Peach moved from her left lead to her right lead without changing her gait.

"I can't take my eyes off her," I said.

"Me neither," said Denny, but when I glanced at him, he was looking at me.

Nic and Peach walked down the centerline of the ring toward us.

"Wow," I said to her, shaking my head. "Nic."

She grinned. "I'm ready, Mom. Can I do it?"

I wanted to pull her out of the saddle and wrap my arms around her. I wanted to take her home and tuck her into bed and read her a story. At the very least, I wanted to double-check the chinstrap of her helmet and make sure that it was as secure as it appeared.

I didn't do any of that.

"Okay," I told my daughter. "Just take it slow."

She grinned and turned Peach away, walking her out to the rail. She looked back at me over her shoulder. "Where would the fun be in that?"

"I'm serious, Nic!" I called. "Start small," I said to Denny.

"We'll start over cross-rails," he said, loud enough for Nic to hear. "And work our way up to verticals."

"Cross-rails!" Nic repeated, indignant. She shook her head and moved Peach up into a trot, muttering something that sounded a lot like "fucking bullshit." Damned if Peach didn't kick out and smack the rail with her back hoof.

"There goes my teenager." I only made a halfhearted attempt to sound apologetic—the truth was that part of me loved hearing Nic's defiance. I could feel that angry fire still in my own belly. Everyone should feel it. It might mellow over time, but it should never be lost. Where would the fun be in that?

Denny chuckled. We watched Nic move Peach into a canter as

they cut through the center of the ring. Denny ducked through the outside rails and into the ring. Before he moved to set up the jumps, he turned to me one last time.

"You're sure?" he asked. "You're ready?"

The way he held my gaze, his blue eyes suddenly serious, gave me the sense that we were talking about more than Nic jumping Peach.

Because he was right there and therefore that magnetic pull thing was happening between us, I reached out and drew him toward me. His lips tasted like chocolate. "I'm ready."

Beyond him, Nic moved Peach up into a canter.

"Here we go," he said.

Here we go.

Chapter 26

Peach hardly glanced at the cross-rails as they sailed over them. Nic hardly shifted her position. Those jumps were hardly jumps at all. When her mom finally agreed that Denny could raise the rails, Nic pumped her fist in the air and blew her mom a kiss.

But once Nic caught sight of the proper vertical rail Denny had set up, her heart began to race. Peach took notice, too, blowing air excitedly out of her nostrils, twisting and arching her neck to get a better look at the jump as they circled it.

"Nice and easy," Denny called.

A pit formed in Nic's belly. She was scared. A cold shiver of doubt ran through her.

You can do this, she told herself.

Peach heard her. The horse's power gathered into Nic's hands. They turned off the outside rail of the ring and cantered toward the jump. Nic counted Peach's strides, each one a thundering beat.

One.

Two.

Three.

And then they were pushing off the ground, lifting up, soaring, suspended high above the jump for one exhilarating, shimmering sliver of life.

They reconnected with the earth and pounded forward, the exact beat picked up again. Peach's stride was proud; Nic stroked her horse's neck, sharing the feeling.

The doubt within Nic was gone now, its tremble replaced by a sensation that was quietly familiar: a delicious, irrepressible yearning for *more*.

Acknowledgments

I adore my editor, Emily Krump, and my agent, Elisabeth Weed. They are perceptive, generous, and upbeat book experts and I am so thankful for their hard work and guidance.

It is an honor and a joy to work with the talented team at William Morrow. I continue to be incredibly grateful for the support of Liate Stehlik and Jen Hart. Many thanks also to Kaitlyn Kennedy, Molly Waxman, Carolyn Bodkin, Serena Wang, Madeline Jaffe, Diahann Sturge, and Jena Karmali. Thank you to Mumtaz Mustafa for creating the perfect cover. Thank you also to Dana Murphy at The Book Group.

As ever, thank you to my parents, Carol Mager and James Donohue, and to the entire Donohue, Mager, Preuss, and Hudner families for their love and encouragement. Thank you also to the dear friends who fill my life with love, laughter, and the occasional cocktail: Jeannine Vender, Anna Lesovitz, Nancy Fazzinga, Leah Albright, Christina Greer, Cathie and Ryan Kaiser, Jeanette Perez and James Kim, Issabella Shields Grantham and Ted Grantham, and Liza Zassenhaus and Dave Lieberman. Jeanette Perez deserves a second shout-out and so much more for being an early reader of each of my books and, as my first editor, for guiding me along this incredible path.

Thank you to the delightful Charly Kayle for giving me a tour of the offices and studios of KOIT radio station in San Francisco and for answering my questions about life as a radio host. Any misrepresentations in this novel are my own.

I am grateful to the real people who inspired two of the plotlines in this book. In 2015, a remarkable high school senior named Konner Sauve launched a yearlong anonymous campaign to strengthen his school community. His story warmed my heart and helped me create Nic, who shares Konner's compassionate spirit and borrows his creative use of Instagram. And I feel certain the seeds for G.G. were planted long ago when, alone in my room as a kid in Philadelphia, I sometimes found myself listening to *Delilah After Dark*, a radio show hosted by Delilah Rene Luke. The show was (and continues to be) part soap opera, part therapy session, and part corny music extravaganza. I can't help but think my memory of it must have led me to G.G.'s story. While I'm on a roll here, I'll confess that I brazenly borrowed the show name *Love Songs After Dark* from a radio show that aired years ago in San Francisco.

An enormous thank you to my husband, Phil Preuss, whose love is a gift.

Finally, a special thank you to my mother and to my three daughters, Finley, Avelyn, and Hayden, to whom this book is dedicated. I'm with G.G. on this one: there is magic in the mother-daughter bond. Thank you for making my life sparkle.

About the author

About the book

Read on . . .

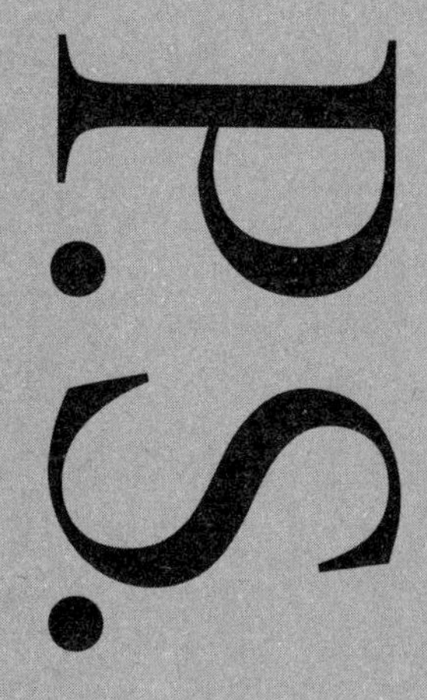

Insights,
Interviews
& More . . .

Meet Meg Donohue

Courtesy of the Author

Meg Donohue is the *USA Today* bestselling author of *How to Eat a Cupcake*, *All the Summer Girls*, and *Dog Crazy*. She has an MFA in creative writing from Columbia University and a BA in comparative literature from Dartmouth College. Born and raised in Philadelphia, she now lives in San Francisco with her husband, three children, and dog.

Gail Gideon Interviews Meg Donohue

G.G.: ***Hi, Meg. Thanks for calling in. I know we're on the radio, but I can tell you're looking great today.***

Meg: Thank you.

G.G.: ***Now let's talk about me. Where did I come from?***

Meg: As I mentioned in the acknowledgments of this book, I think the seed for your character was probably first planted when I was a kid living in Philadelphia and listening on occasion to *Delilah After Dark*, a call-in radio show. Delilah had—still has—a very different shtick than you do, G.G.—

G.G.: ***I'm one of a kind.***

Meg: Yes. But I suppose the stories of her callers, and the way they really seemed to *need* to hear Delilah's advice, stuck with me all these years.

G.G.: ***So you made me a famous radio personality, and then you started the story right at a crossroads in my career. Why?***

Meg: When I set out to write this book, I was thinking about how difficult it can be to understand the many aspects of ▸

Gail Gideon Interviews Meg Donohue
(continued)

who we are, and who we aspire to become, as individuals. This seems like it should be easy, but it's not. Becoming ourselves is a journey.

When I was creating your character, G.G., I was thinking about the particular bumps along this journey for public figures dealing with the expectations and desires of fans. There is, for example, the inevitable backlash that a movie star receives if she dares to have interests and ambitions outside of acting (I'm looking at you, Gwyneth Paltrow). We prefer our entertainers to stay in their lane, as though we can only consume one slice of their personalities at a time.

I was thinking about the subject on a personal level as well. After each book I've written, I've received lovely emails from readers asking if I'm planning to write a sequel. And the truth is that after I wrote one "baking" book (*How to Eat a Cupcake*), I wasn't all that interested in writing another "baking" book, sequel or not. Instead, I wrote a "summer" book (*All the Summer Girls*), and then I wasn't interested in writing another "summer" book. Instead, I wrote a "dog" book (*Dog Crazy*), and then I wasn't really interested in writing another dog book. At each pivot, I wondered if I was making the right decision. I'm so grateful to my readers for their support, and I hate the thought of letting them down. We are in this novel-publishing business together, the readers and I, and with each new book, I felt that I risked turning my back on a potentially growing audience for my work.

That said, the books I've written have a lot in common. They are all uplifting. They all have an element of humor.

G.G.: ***Do they, Meg? Are you sure about that?***

Meg: Well, they might not be HA-HA funny, but . . . you know what, G.G., never mind. My point is that I like the stories I write to have a feel-good tone. But I like to think that if the day comes when I'm excited to explore another type of story, I will feel brave enough to try something new.

G.G.: ***And all of this relates to me because when the book opens I am in the midst of a very successful career, but I am ready for a change.***

Meg: Yes. I was curious to see how these thoughts played out for someone with a really big level of fame and success. I wanted to make you hungry for adventure, but also truly devoted to your fans. And then of course I gave you a teenage daughter to think about, too.

G.G.: ***Let's talk about Nic. She's perfect, obviously.***

Meg: I am also in the Nic Fan Club. I loved the idea of Nic as an unlikely hero. She's a shy kid trapped in her own ▸

Gail Gideon Interviews Meg Donohue
(continued)

head. When she is suddenly able to shed her anxiety and share herself with the world, she wreaks havoc in the most bighearted way.

G.G.: ***Did you always envision her as a horseback rider?***

Meg: Yes. I rode horses from elementary school through college, and taught riding lessons to kids for a time, so I was excited to pour some of my love for horses into a novel. I think my favorite scenes to write were the ones with Nic at the barn. I haven't ridden in a long time, but that horse crazy girl is alive and kicking within me.

G.G.: ***What are some things that I, as your character, might not know about you, my creator?***

Meg: I am a very forgiving driver and rarely experience road rage. The noises made by loud eaters torment me; I've learned that this sensitivity to certain sounds is called misophonia. I always set my alarm to an odd number, such as 6:31 AM. I believe that gratitude is the gateway to happiness. When that doesn't work, I rely on dirty martinis. The earnestness of musicals makes me weep. I can't stand it when—

G.G. (clearing throat loudly): ***Thanks, Meg. That's . . . fascinating stuff. I'm really glad we could end this interview on such a high note.***

Meg: You're welcome.

G.G.'s Playlist for Readers of *Every Wild Heart*

1. Patti Smith, "Because the Night"
2. Velvet Underground, "Pale Blue Eyes"
3. Janis Joplin, "Piece of My Heart"
4. The Rolling Stones, "Sympathy for the Devil"
5. Pixies, "Wave of Mutilation"
6. Sonic Youth, "Kool Thing"
7. The Pretenders, "Middle of the Road"
8. Siouxsie and the Banshees, "Peek-A-Boo"
9. Blondie, "X Offender"
10. Garbage, "Special"
11. Liz Phair, "My Bionic Eyes"
12. Hole, "Celebrity Skin"
13. Luscious Jackson, "You and Me"
14. Sleater-Kinney, "Oh!"
15. PJ Harvey, "Good Fortune"
16. David Bowie, "Heroes"
17. Taylor Swift, "Welcome to New York"

Meg Donohue's Favorite Mother-Daughter Novels

LITTLE WOMEN BY LOUISA MAY ALCOTT

The affectionate relationship between the four March sisters and their wise, beloved mother, Marmee, holds a special place in my heart.

MAINE BY J. COURTNEY SULLIVAN

A sweeping, compassionate saga of three generations of women sharing the family cottage on the coast of Maine.

MY NAME IS LUCY BARTON BY ELIZABETH STROUT

I count not put down this poignant, mysterious, and sneakily uplifting story of a complex mother-daughter relationship.

WHERE'D YOU GO, BERNADETTE BY MARIA SEMPLE

A fast-paced and funny tale of a quirky young girl's quest to find her missing mother.

THE MOTHERS BY BRIT BENNETT

A moving and beautifully written debut novel exploring themes of motherhood, mothering, and the mother-less.

YOU WILL KNOW ME BY MEGAN ABBOTT

The darkest and most suspenseful entry to this list reveals just how far one woman's love for her daughter will push her.

Have You Read? More from Meg Donohue

DOG CRAZY

As a pet bereavement counselor, Maggie Brennan uses a combination of empathy, insight, and humor to help patients cope with the anguish of losing their beloved four-legged friends. Though she has a gift for guiding others through difficult situations, Maggie has major troubles of her own that threaten the success of her counseling practice and her volunteer work with a dog rescue organization.

Everything changes when a distraught woman shows up at Maggie's office and claims that her dog has been stolen. Searching the streets of San Francisco for the missing pooch, Maggie finds herself entangled in a mystery that forces her to finally face her biggest fear—and to open her heart to new love.

"Wonderful! Anyone who has ever loved and lost a dog will find wisdom and comfort in this sweet, smart story."
—Allie Larkin, author of *Stay*

ALL THE SUMMER GIRLS

In Philadelphia, good girl Kate is dumped by her fiancé the day she learns she is pregnant with his child. In New York City, beautiful stay-at-home mom Vanessa finds herself obsessively searching the Internet for news of an old flame. And in San Francisco, Dani, an aspiring writer who can't seem to put down a book—or a cocktail—long enough to open her laptop, has just been fired . . . again.

In an effort to regroup, Kate, Vanessa, and Dani retreat to the New Jersey beach town where they once spent their summers. Emboldened by the seductive cadences of the shore, the women begin to realize just how much their lives, and friendships, have been shaped by the choices they made one fateful night on the beach eight years earlier—and the secrets that now threaten to surface.

"*All the Summer Girls* is an honest and engaging look at the complicated and powerful bonds of female friendship. Donohue takes us on a weekend reunion full of secrets, resentment, and regret—in other words, once you start this book, you won't be able to put it down!"

—Jennifer Close, bestselling author of *Girls in White Dresses*

Have You Read? More from Meg Donohue *(continued)*

HOW TO EAT A CUPCAKE

Free-spirited Annie Quintana and sophisticated Julia St. Clair come from two different worlds. Yet, as the daughter of the St. Clairs' housekeeper, Annie grew up in Julia's San Francisco mansion and they forged a bond that only two little girls oblivious to class differences could—until a life-altering betrayal destroyed their friendship.

A decade later, Annie bakes to fill the void left in her heart by her mother's death, and a painful secret jeopardizes Julia's engagement to the man she loves. A chance reunion prompts the unlikely duo to open a cupcakery, but when a mysterious saboteur opens up old wounds, they must finally face the truth about their past or risk losing everything.

"A sparkling, witty story about an unlikely, yet redemptive, friendship. . . . Grab one of these for your best friend and read it together—preferably with a plate of Meyer Lemon cupcakes nearby."

—Katie Crouch, bestselling author of *Girls in Trucks* and *Men and Dogs*